UNDERCURRENT

PAUL BLACKWELL

JRRENT

Doubleday
Canada

Doubleday Canada and colophon are registered trademarks of Random House of Canada Limited

Library and Archives Canada Cataloguing in Publication

Blackwell, Paul E.
      Undercurrent / Paul Blackwell.

Issued also in electronic format.
ISBN 978-0-385-67698-4

      I. Title.

PS8603.R3246U53 2013   jC813'.6   C2012-906587-0

This book is a work of fiction. Names, characters, places and incidents are products of the author's imagination or are used fictitiously. Any resemblance to actual events or locales or persons, living or dead, is entirely coincidental.

Cover design by Cara Petrus
Cover photo © 2013 by Arman Zhenikeyev/Getty Images
Typography by Lissi Erwin
Printed and bound in the USA

Published in Canada by Doubleday Canada,
a division of Random House of Canada Limited

www.randomhouse.ca

10 9 8 7 6 5 4 3 2 1

For my parents, D & L

A hundred and twenty thousand gallons of water roar over Crystal Falls every second, it says on all the plaques and in all the pamphlets around town.

Which is almost two million glasses—or two thousand bathtubs or six full swimming pools—spilling every second, plunging eighty feet to boom against rocks and turn into mist, foaming and churning and swirling in a giant bowl before raging madly away downriver.

I would've never guessed I'd go along for the ride. But still, I didn't scream. I didn't scream or struggle or do anything like that. I just crossed my arms and went over like I was already in a coffin.

CHAPTER 1

It's black where I am. All night sky and no stars.

And silent. Or at least it was. Because sounds are starting to reach me now: footsteps. Hushed voices. A little beep that never stops. And things are becoming less black, more of a dark red, like a pool of blood. For a moment I even see something—a room, whiter than white—before a light blinds me. Then it's back to the red again.

I still don't know where I am.

"Cal, can you hear us? Make a noise if you can hear us...."

My father's voice startles me, but I can't move a muscle to show it. I feel a hand drawn over my forehead. It's heavy and warm. Fingers brush back my hair. I can hear my mother nearby, crying.

"Just make a noise, Cal," my father begs. "Anything..."

Okay, sure. I'll grunt or something, to let them know I'm alive and listening. How hard can that be?

But it's impossible. Because nothing happens. My throat, my tongue, my lips—they're all frozen.

I try moving an arm and, failing that, waggling a finger.

But my body feels like it's made of stone. The deepest breath I can take is barely enough to make my lungs inflate.

No—no—this is not good. . . .

My panic explodes as I feel hands caress my limbs, my cheek, my head. Christ, I'm paralyzed. I must have broken my back or smashed my head or something—and now I'm trapped in here, a vegetable. I want to scream now—I really want to scream.

Touches and kisses only make it worse. My head rings with shrieks. I pound imaginary little fists against the inside of my skull. I scream, I swear, I cry—but it's all swallowed up by this horrible black hole inside me.

I know where I am now.

I am in hell.

....

Eventually I must pass out and start dreaming. First about our family's life before Crystal Falls, of the fields and forests where my brother, Cole, and I used to run wild and the quiet river where we used to canoe. I miss those places a lot and dream about them often.

But then things change.

Suddenly the day turns dark, and I'm hanging from the swaying footbridge over the roaring falls. Clamped on the icy railing, my fingers are killing me. I can't hold on much longer.

Losing my grip, I cry out:

"No!"

I wake up with what feels like a violent start, but my body still doesn't respond. I can hear the beeps again. They must be coming from a machine monitoring my life signs. Which must mean I'm in the hospital.

Yeah, I'm sure of it now. The reek of disinfectant, the bleached sheets, and the weird odor that reminds me of thunderstorms. I can't mistake them all.

I've always had a powerful sense of smell. It's in the family genes, my father says. And he should know, having built a whole career out of his, sniffing beers and spirits for breweries and distilleries. The Harris nose is a gift, he once told me, like an ear for music or a photographer's eye.

Well, it seems more like a curse to me. For starters, if it weren't for this supposed gift, we would never have come to this stupid town. And because of my own superior sense, I can't stand hospitals—and now it looks like I'm stuck in one forever.

"You can get through this, Cal," my dad whispers from somewhere nearby. "You're such a tough kid—this is nothing to you."

Huh? Okay, now he's confusing his sons. Because I'm not the tough one, that's for sure. It's Cole's favorite excuse for whaling on me, in fact—that I'm such a whiny little wimp:

That's why God made big brothers, he'd explain, while flicking my ear or punching me in the biceps, *to toughen up pansies like you. . . .*

My heart sinks as my mother starts crying. I know this particular sound very well. And I know, if there's anything she can't bear, it's false hope.

"Oh, Cal," she sobs. "Oh, sweetie . . ."

I wish I could answer my parents and somehow let them know I'm still in here. Then a terrifying possibility hits me: What if they're thinking of calling it quits? What if they're thinking of pulling the plug on me?

But wait. There are probably tests that show I'm still in here. Brain scans. I wonder what my life looks like now— some red, an area of green, a few bright blue blobs on some computer monitor?

Yeah, I'm sure they must be able to see me thinking, dreaming. They must know that my brain is not completely dead.

What I don't get is why they keep calling me Cal. It's something they stopped doing years ago, in order to clear up any confusion when shouting across the house. Even before Crystal Falls, my parents had switched to calling me Callum—as had everyone else except Cole, who'd only use my full name to show he thinks I'm being a tool.

Speaking of Cole, I haven't heard him so far. Where is he? Having broken enough bones in his life, he hates hospitals, too, I know; but I would've expected him to come visit his comatose brother. What the hell?

To the sound of my mother softly crying, I must fall

asleep. Because the next thing I know, I'm awakened by a stab of pain in my hand. Surfacing to the red again, I finally figure it out: I'm seeing the insides of my eyelids.

The beeps are back, but the sobbing has stopped.

For a moment everything else is quiet. But then I hear the sound of tape being torn off a roll. There is more pain on the back of my hand as the tape is then stuck on me. It's holding a needle down, I assume—I must be on some sort of IV drip. I can smell the perfume coming off the mysterious person, who must be a nurse. Who else would stab people with needles? Her perfume is really strong, though, and reminds me of toilet cleaner.

There's a bang—something thrown in the garbage, I think. Then the squeak of little wheels. A tray?

There is no more noise for a moment. Nothing but the beeps. I cling to their sound, not wanting to slip back into the blackness. I'm so tired, though.

I suddenly feel hot breath in my ear.

"I hope you never wake up," a voice whispers.

The woman's words horrify me—my body feels like it's been shot through with an electric current. Then the breath is gone, the sickly perfume wafting after it.

I hear soft-soled shoes walking away.

....

My eyes open. The room seems painfully bright, though there's only a single lamp on.

Who cares? At least I can see now. Which means I'm back—I'm back!

But can I move? I'm not sure at first. When I finally become used to the light, I try turning my head.

My head feels as heavy as a sack of bowling balls. But it's moving, my neck creaking with the effort.

Two worn old armchairs come into sight. Orange ones. My mother's cardigan is draped across the back of one, so she must be around. Maybe she went for a coffee or to the washroom or something. I just have to wait for her. And keep my eyes open.

As the room comes into better focus, I can see a window above the chairs. The curtains are open a little, and it's nighttime, with parked cars gleaming in the streetlights. A minivan pulls in. Maybe it's Dad—he has a van. But no. His van is blue, and this one is silver.

I'm getting frustrated. It's becoming harder and harder to keep my eyes open. My blood feels like maple syrup. But I'm able to move my fingers now, and my arms a little. I can even see my toes wiggling under the sheets.

Everything feels like it's working. I'm definitely not paralyzed. If I wasn't so tired, I would be smiling from ear to ear now. This must be a good sign, I tell myself, before my entire head is swallowed up by a yawn.

Man, I wish someone would come into the room! Wait, there must be a button somewhere I can push to get somebody's attention. They always have them by hospital beds.

But then I remember the nurse with the perfume, and I'm afraid she's the one who will come running.

No. I just have to wait for Mom. But I can't hold out any longer—I fall asleep.

When I open my eyes again, I feel very groggy. I don't know how long I've been out. I can still move, but it takes an incredible effort just to turn my head toward the orange chairs.

My mother is still not back.

That's when I notice someone standing there, outside the window. It's a guy in a green jacket with white leather sleeves, a sprinting crocodile embroidered on the chest. With the hood of a sweatshirt pulled up, most of the person's face is in shadow. But still, there's no mistaking the Harris nose, as distinctive as it is sensitive.

It has to be Cole.

What's he doing standing out there? I want to call out, signal to him somehow, but I can't. Instead I stare back blankly at him.

Behind me I hear the door swing open. The figure in the window slips from view like a ghost.

Someone's coming into the room. I try to turn my head back, but I'm only able to move it halfway. Am I sedated or something? I can't keep my eyes open a second longer. But I don't go completely under, because I hear someone speak:

"Hello, Cal. Remember me?"

It's not Mom, or even Dad, but it's still a great voice to hear. It's Bryce. I knew he would come to see me. Despite my exhaustion I feel a fluttering in my eyelids. They're opening. I'm going to wake up for him, I know it.

Just then the pillow is pulled out from under my head. There's a spark of pain as my head bounces off the mattress.

Ow! What's he doing?

"This is for Neil. . . ."

I suddenly feel something press down over my face. And just then I remember how all that water felt, pouring over the falls onto me. It was like a mountain, pounding down, driving me under.

The pillow is nowhere near as heavy. But it doesn't matter. I'm no more able to breathe than when I was at the bottom of the river, slammed against the rocks.

And I'm no more able to stop my best friend, Bryce, who is now grunting with the effort of smothering me.

CHAPTER 2

Everything began going wrong when our family first pulled into town. WELCOME TO CRYSTAL FALLS—POPULATION 12,634, the sign read.

The thing is, the number has never changed since. So unless they'd already added the four of us just before we arrived, the welcome is a lie. Or maybe it's done on purpose, to let people know that if they weren't born in Crystal Falls, they don't really count.

Having lived here four years now, I find this makes a lot of sense.

Cole and I never wanted to move here. We liked where we lived already, at the edge of a city where we chased friends on bikes and waged war in the woods. There was even a river nearby that we canoed up and down, any-where we wanted except the bulrushes, where we once got attacked by some swans we'd scared.

Then my father got a job offer. It was from Holden's, an old family-owned whiskey distillery. Holden's Own was one of the best products in the country, according to Dad.

The problem was, we'd have to move. Cole and I went

nuts. There was no way—no way—we were going anywhere!

"Listen, guys, try to understand," Dad told us. "Positions for master distillers don't come up every day." It was a huge opportunity, he explained, working for a company where art and craftsmanship still mattered. Was he supposed to just pass up the chance and keep slaving away at a big automated brewery?

Yes, we told him before the speech had finished coming out of his mouth.

Mom wasn't happy either. "Crystal Falls?" she exclaimed. "I've never heard of the place." Finding the town on a map, she saw how far east it was. "What about the holidays, Don? How will we see my sister and her family?"

"They can fly out and stay with us," Dad said. "They have the money. Why are we always the ones driving out to see them, anyway? It's their turn to make an effort."

It all meant my father had already made up his mind. Despite our objections, he went and bought somewhere to live out in Crystal Falls. He then put a FOR SALE sign on the front lawn of the only home Cole and I had ever known, in the grass we'd played on since we were babies.

A couple weeks later, the SOLD sign went up. We moved shortly after that, once school was finished.

The new place was an old clapboard house set among some trees just off the road into town. The story was that a pastor used to live in it, until seventy years ago, when his church next door burned down. I would soon discover the grimy outline of a cross on my bedroom wall. Even three coats of paint couldn't cover it up—which, even with a mirror hung over it, remains seriously creepy.

But that wasn't the worst of it. Pulling up in the car, everyone could tell that Mom absolutely hated the house on sight.

"It's really shady, Don," she complained as we waited on the porch for the moving van to show up. "And old. I thought we decided on something nice and bright—a nice, new bungalow or something . . ."

Dad sighed, a dark look crossing his face. He assured us there wasn't anything like that available. Plus this house was close to his work, which made a nice change from his old commute, which had kept him on the road two hours each day. That meant ten hours a week, five hundred hours a year, or so he loved reminding everyone.

"And as far as the shade goes, Liza, I'll just cut down a few trees," my father promised. "It's no big deal," he insisted.

Big deal or not, Dad never got around to it, and the trees have pushed farther in, scraping at the house in the wind. But then, Dad didn't get around to a lot of things since coming to the house in Crystal Falls, which led to arguments with Mom. Even after he hired a guy to fix up a few things, the arguing didn't stop. Not until Dad moved out.

Which was great. They moved the whole family across the country just to split up.

As far as Cole and I are concerned, the problem has never been the house—it's the location. Most people live on the north side of the bridge by the falls, where the stores, the restaurants, and everything else of interest is located.

Meanwhile, down on the south side, where our house is, there's pretty much nothing going on except for the campground and the old quarry. Oh, and the road out of town—which eventually leads back to where we used to live.

The joke of it all is that when Dad moved out, he ended up living on the north side. Okay, so that's where the apartments are, but still, somehow it figures. He lives above a diner though, so his place always stinks like a fryer. Personally I don't know how his supposedly refined sense of smell can stand it.

And if that isn't bad enough, the apartment is tiny, with only a lumpy foldout couch for guests to sleep on. After just one sleepover, I knew that was enough. I don't care how far I have to walk or if it's raining butcher's knives—I'm going home. I need my sleep.

It sucks, though, because Dad lives close to Bryce. And sometimes I get caught up in video games and end up staying late at Bryce's house, so it would be handy to have somewhere to crash nearby instead of walking all the way back home in the dark.

Bryce—I don't even know where to begin. I didn't want anything to do with him at first, to be honest. It wasn't personal. I just didn't want to get chummy with someone who was a punching bag for Hunter Holden and Ricky Cho, who are now two of the school's biggest football stars.

Wait, did I say *stars*? That's a joke. The Crocodiles are what, second to last in the league now? Like I give a damn, ever since my brother was thrown off the team.

I still feel guilty about that, because it was kind of my fault. What happened was this: Since I was the new kid in Crystal Falls, people weren't exactly lining up to be my friend. So rather than die of boredom, I started hanging out with Bryce anyway. He was a little weird, sure, but funny. And spoiled, which meant he had his own TV and a stack of video games.

But as expected, Hunter and Ricky soon started hassling me as well. Which was a little surprising, because they must have known I was Cole's little brother, since we look enough alike. Cole, on the other hand, had wasted no time establishing his reputation at Crystal Falls. Before long he made quarterback and was tearing it up on the field. The Crocodiles became the best team in the league.

But who knows what was going on—maybe they were jealous of him. Some stranger shows up and takes the top slot on their football team? That's gotta ruffle a few feathers.

Anyway, it's not like I cared much about getting picked on. At least I had the guts to stick by a friend instead of running off like a coward. I might not be that tough, but I'm not a total wimp.

And so it went for a few years, with Bryce and me hanging out and taking crap. It was annoying but nothing I couldn't handle—and definitely not something worth getting Cole involved in.

Then one day after getting shoved in the hall, Bryce went and lipped off to Hunter and Ricky. I can't remember what he said—something about what steroids had done to their dicks, I think. But whatever it was must have hit close to home, because they went for him—hard. And of course nobody did anything to stop them. So I ended up jumping in and getting popped a couple of times, including one square in the eye.

Which sucked but was really no big deal. So long as you can still see, a black eye is cool, isn't it?

Less cool was how impossible it was to hide the injury from Cole, though. Because besides him, no one is allowed to pound his brother—not even fellow Crocodiles.

That afternoon things got ugly. Even two on one, the juniors were no match for my brother, the bigger, tougher senior. It was a thing of beauty, I have to say, the way Cole laid them out in the parking lot. He flattened Ricky with one punch—*bam*, down—before throwing Hunter over his shoulder using a judo move he learned when he was ten.

Then Cole dropped on Hunter's chest with both knees and began hammering his face in. That was scary. If he hadn't been pulled off by teachers, I don't know when he would have stopped—when his fists were broken, probably. I'd never seen him that mad—and I'd seen him really lose it before.

Everything was a big mess afterward. Because you just don't screw around with the Holdens, not in Crystal Falls. Not only does their whiskey distillery provide a ton of jobs—our own father's included—but they own like half the town. The best they could do with Hunter's nose was make it stick back out again, with my parents footing the bill.

Cole got thrown off the football team just like that. I bet all it took was one phone call from Dad's boss, Blake Holden—that rich prick probably wasted no time in reminding Coach Keller how he was building the brand-new bleacher seating and paying for the field's upgraded PA system. Instead of getting cut the usual slack as an MVP, Cole suddenly got a lot of zeros on overdue assignments, which meant repeating his senior year.

Hunter was let off with a warning about playing rough with the younger kids. And then he waltzed straight into the vacant position of QB.

None of it was particularly surprising, because that's how things are done around here. At least when the Holdens are involved.

Cole went totally ballistic again. After he trashed Coach Keller's office, it was a miracle he was only suspended. Maybe the school was secretly ashamed about the raw deal he was getting and decided to give him a tiny break. There was no point in fighting it; we were worried enough that Dad might lose his job.

So Cole had no choice. He had to let it go.

Luckily, Dad and his bionic Harris nose aren't easily replaced. And neither was Cole, for that matter. The Crocodiles began tanking in the standings big-time.

Heh-heh-heh.

Still, I felt awful. Cole loved playing football more than anything—and I had screwed it up for him. I should have known better—I should have covered things up somehow. But people saw what Hunter and Ricky did. Cole would have found out eventually.

Then again, I could have just stayed out of things in the first place. I could have let Bryce take the beating he'd pretty much asked for, being a smartass to a couple of gorillas. But I don't know. Bryce is a friend—a good friend.

Or at least I thought he was. Until now.

CHAPTER 3

Just as everything starts going black again, I'm suddenly able to breathe. The relief is incredible. I wheeze horribly, but it feels so good.

Wait—where's Bryce? He tried to kill me! Terrified, I look around the room for him. He's gone—scared off, I think, by the muffled pounding I could hear through the pillow wrapped around my head.

Turning toward the window, I see a few fading palm prints on the glass. But no one is there. No hooded figure in a Crocodiles jacket—just the quiet parking lot. I lie still, staring out, my eyes wide and my heart beating fast. Was that really Cole? It looked like him. Except he never wears that jacket anymore.

I'm really awake now and able to move a little more.

"Callum!" someone cries out from the doorway.

"Mom!"

Tears start pouring down my cheeks. My mother rushes to my bedside, covering my face with kisses as she sobs. A nurse shouts for a doctor.

"Bryce!" I try shouting, but my voice is weak and

hoarse. "Did you see Bryce?"

"What?" My mother lifts her head from my chest, her makeup a total mess. "Lie still, Cal," she says. "Please lie still. . . ."

I'm confused. Was I dreaming? I couldn't have been. It felt too real.

My mother notices the pillow lying on the floor. She picks it up and starts tucking it behind my head.

"Bryce," I croak again. "Bryce . . ."

A doctor rushes in. Mom takes a step back to let him examine me. Before long the room fills with uniformed people. They surround my bed, gawking at me.

Shortly after the room empties, Dad arrives. He hugs me like I'm made of glass. I'm happy to see him.

"Where's Cole?" I ask after he finally lets go.

"He's at home," Dad says.

"At home?" I repeat.

"Don't worry—Edwina's with him."

"Edwina?" I repeat. "What?"

This makes no sense. Edwina is our neighbor, an old woman who insists we call her Ed and has two huskies she calls her children. We used to laugh, because she'd shout for us just like we were her dogs, to give us treats: muffins and cookies and slices of pie that she'd drop still warm into our open hands.

Cole would chomp down the treat, then woof at her in approval.

But besides mowing her lawn—an easy job she over-pays for—we don't have much to do with Ed. So why Cole would be with her I have no idea.

To be honest, I don't even care. Because I'm really mad at him. His only brother almost dies, and he can't even come see him in the hospital?

Another doctor comes in, a neurologist, to examine me. He asks me questions, which I answer as best I can. But I'm finding everything tiring. I could already use a nap.

I look over toward Mom and Dad, who are watching from the orange chairs. They're holding hands. The sight startles me.

"Are you feeling all right, young man?" the doctor asks, seeing my reaction.

"Yeah," I tell him.

"Are you feeling dizzy?"

"No, I'm fine."

I glance again at my parents. They're still holding hands. Huh? After everything that's happened between them? I guess they've been through a lot these past three days, which is how long I've been in a coma, the doctor tells me. Mom and Dad probably thought I was never coming out of it.

I'm really feeling sleepy now. My parents express some concern about this, but the doctor tells them not to worry. I'm out of danger, he says, but I need to rest.

My mother brings her chair forward and holds my hand as I try to fall asleep. Despite my exhaustion it's hard to relax, because I can't stop thinking about Bryce. I can't shake the feeling he's about to come bursting in with a chain saw or something to finish the job. When I tell my mother what happened, she tells me it was just something I must have imagined while unconscious.

When I do finally nod off, I have bad dreams. Dreams where I'm walking, angry, being followed by someone. And then suddenly I'm back, hanging from the footbridge over the falls.

This time I see a shadowy figure rushing up to help or to hurt me I never find out, because again my fingers slip. The figure calls out as I plunge into the river.

Whether it's the fear or the frigid water that robs me of my breath I have no idea. I gasp, trying to get it back. But I can't.

Which means I can't scream, even though I want to. Like every kid in town, I've thrown enough sticks and bottles off that bridge to know what's coming next.

I'm going over.

Body rigid, I turn onto my back and cross my arms just before what feels like a huge ocean wave tosses me into the air. The drop is sickening and never seems to end. But when it finally does, somehow I miss the rocks and plunge underwater, the intense roar instantly muffled.

I'm tossed around by unbelievable forces—tearing

my arms from my chest, yanking my legs apart, and even peeling back my eyelids. All I can see are bubbles. All I can feel is a weight crushing down on me.

The pressure forces out what little air remains in my lungs. It drives me deeper, hammering me over and over like a nail into a board. Then I'm caught in some kind of undercurrent, a powerful one.

Pain flares as the back of my head slams against something hard. How much will it hurt, I wonder, when I inhale this strange, fizzing liquid? Maybe I should do it, get it over and done with.

But then I feel something—a sudden rush upward. I just have to hang on a bit longer, I tell myself, and try not to inhale.

But I can't help it—my body forces me to breathe. Except it doesn't hurt. It almost feels good, even. . . .

When I finally awaken, it's morning. Someone's pulled the curtains wide, and the room is full of sunlight. I look out into the parking lot, where the chrome on the cars sears my eyes.

Seeing that I'm alone, I decide to check my body. I'm feeling pretty sore all over, like a whole football team was beating on me. From the shapes under the blanket, I can see that I haven't lost a leg or anything, but I'm still nervous as I pull back the covers.

I've heard these amazing stories about people coming out of crazy things, like plane crashes or gas explosions, without a scratch. Well, surviving the falls turns out to be nothing like that. I'm completely covered in scratches, not to mention some pretty ugly cuts. There are scrapes and gouges and bruises everywhere except for my upper body, which for some strange reason looks pretty much unmarked.

The door opens. I throw the covers over myself to hide my gaping gown.

A doctor comes in—the first one on the scene when I awoke. "How are we feeling?" he asks, helping me to sit up. Everything really hurts now.

"Pretty crappy," I admit. "My whole body is killing me."

He laughs. "Well, that's not very surprising," he says. "How about your head? Any serious pain?"

I tell him the back of it feels pretty sore, and that's when I learn about the gash there. It's the worst of my injuries, it turns out, and had to get closed up. The doctor decides to have a look at how it's coming along. He peels back the bandage and makes a tutting noise.

"I should fix this a bit," he says.

The doctor pulls my scalp so hard, my ears move. I almost puke.

"Hanging in there?" he asks as I shudder.

"Yeah."

"You know, you're lucky whatever rock you hit didn't crack open your head," he remarks. "But hey, not even a fracture—how lucky is that? And most important, no bleeding on the brain, according to the CAT scan, which is great news."

"Then how come I was out for so long?" I ask.

"Yes, that was odd," the doctor admits. "My best guess is that the coma was brought on by hypothermia rather than head trauma."

Thanks, I think. I really appreciate best guesses when it comes to my health. . . .

"There's probably nothing to worry about," the doctor assures me, as if sensing my unease. "From what we can tell, you haven't sustained any injuries that should affect your mobility or faculties. So you should be able to get back to school in no time and be completely up and running."

"Great," I answer, wondering what's the rush.

"Speaking of which," the doctor continues, "you wouldn't know it from looking at me now, but I used to play wide receiver for the Crocs back in the day."

"Really." I assume he's talking about the Crystal Falls Crocodiles, even though no one calls them the Crocs now, probably because it's the name of an ugly plastic shoe. "Cool," I reply.

"But I still watch the games when I can," he adds. "And I must say, you've sure got some moves."

Okay, now I understand. He's confusing me with my brother. It's not the first time it's happened. There's something about the hair, the nose—we look similar, all right. Especially since the doc probably only ever saw Cole from the stands.

I don't correct him. At least someone thinks I'm a hero for a change. Besides, I might have to explain why Cole is no longer on the team, and that would be uncomfortable.

"Okay, just keep sitting up for a minute," the doctor says. "I'll get someone to replace this bandage."

He leaves, and a few minutes later a nurse named Barbara comes in to finish the job. With her, the silence is heavy. I make a joke, but she doesn't laugh. In fact, she doesn't even answer me except with grunts. *Hello? I'm the kid who just went over the falls?* I want to remind her.

Nurse Barbara doesn't seem to care. If anything, she acts like she's angry at me or something or like I'm being a pain in the ass. Hey, why bother becoming a nurse if you hate people so much? It makes no sense to me. I guess some people don't start out as jerks but just end up that way. Sometimes they get worn down and become a person they never thought they'd be.

Maybe Nurse Barbara is one of those people. Maybe she's dealt with too many drunk teenagers who've treated her like crap, who swore at her or threw up on her. Maybe she assumes I was drunk or on drugs when I went over the falls. Well, I'm not like that.

But I can understand her feelings and decide to give her the benefit of the doubt. I just have to show I appreciate the job she is doing.

"Hey, thanks for patching me up," I say when it seems like she's done.

In response, she smacks the bandage to make sure it's stuck on.

"Ow!" I shout. "That hurt!"

Nurse Barbara leaves the room without a word. No, she is definitely a bitch, I decide.

Throughout the day I watch a little TV and wait for visitors. My parents arrive, but Cole still doesn't show. Well, screw him. I pretend he doesn't even exist.

Surely the word is getting out that I'm awake now. But Bryce doesn't return. I still don't know what to make of what he did. I keep feeling like I must have imagined the whole thing. But there's just no getting around the fact—it happened. I know it did.

I should tell someone. But I'm scared. As crazy as it sounds, I don't want Bryce to get in trouble.

And now that I'm conscious again, Bryce is no match for me. Okay, I'm not that strong, but I'm stronger than Bryce.

No other friends visit either. By other friends, I guess I just mean Willow, a girl I've been hanging out with. We were partnered up in a class last year and hung out over the summer. We like the same music. I play some guitar, and she plays ukulele, and we're talking about maybe writing and recording some songs together. I don't know if we'll ever actually do it, but it's fun to talk about.

It's been bothering me that she hasn't visited either. I've been feeling weird around her lately, probably because this whole "friends" thing isn't really working for me anymore. Sure, she's an oddball, as my mother calls her; but she's pretty and doesn't seem to know it, with her dark curls and clear, blue-green eyes that sometimes scare me when they flash unexpectedly in my direction.

The problem is I'm not that great with girls. Not like my brother, anyway. His latest girlfriend is Monica; they've been going out the past couple of years. But the way they've been fighting lately, I don't know if that's going to last much longer.

As for me, it's not like I can't talk to girls. It's just that I have no idea how to get any further with one. I mean, I've fooled around a little bit, getting up under somebody's shirt once. But I didn't like her that much, and she didn't like me that much, and it was all kind of awful.

I do like Willow, though, and I get the feeling she likes me back. At least I thought she liked me enough to come visit me in the hospital after I nearly died. So I'm pretty hopeful when I finally hear a knock on the door.

"Come on in," I call out.

The door opens. But instead of Cole or Willow or my parents, in walks one of the last people on earth I would expect to see.

It's Coach Keller, my gym teacher.

For a second I wonder if I've passed out and am dreaming. Because other than during phys-ed class, I have nothing to do with Keller whatsoever. If it weren't for my brother having been on the Crocodiles, I doubt he would know my name. Actually I'm still not sure he does.

But something's changed. Because now Keller's acting like we're lifelong friends.

"Cal!" he shouts as he enters, grinning widely. He then snaps his head toward the door. "Well, don't stand out there like a pair of nitwits!" he snarls. "Get in here!'

If Coach Keller took me off guard, this knocks me square on my ass: It's Hunter Holden and Ricky Cho. Shuffling past like they're part of a police lineup, the two football players stop by the window. Combined, they almost block out the daylight.

Glaring, Keller gives them a nod. It's Hunter who speaks.

"Hey, man," he says. "How are you feeling?"

I don't respond. I just stare through him.

"The falls, huh?" Hunter continues, when the silence becomes unbearably awkward. "Pretty smooth."

"Yeah, smooth," Ricky agrees.

"Thanks," I manage to answer. I notice Hunter's nose is looking a lot straighter than Cole left it. I wonder if he's had some more work done on it. If so, it was a waste of money; at least the crooked nose gave his fat face some edge.

With the conversation stalled, Keller revs up. "Listen, we know you've been through a lot," he says, again all smiles. "So we won't stay. But we wanted you to know that the team is pulling for you."

"Thanks, Mr. Keller," I answer flatly.

"Coach," he says. "Please. And I hear that nothing's broken?"

"No," I tell him.

"It's a miracle. We were all pretty worried, weren't we, boys? Worried you wouldn't make it back."

I'm not understanding any of this: why my stupid gym teacher is in my hospital room and why he's brought his two pets along with him.

"I'm fine—Coach," I tell him.

"Good," he answers. "We really need you back on your feet. The school needs you. Now rest up, and we'll talk more in a few days. Now c'mon, guys," Keller says. "Let Cal get some rest!"

With that the coach leaves. Hunter and Ricky follow behind like a pair of trained dogs. They probably like sniffing each other's asses, I think. But as the door closes, I'm feeling blown away. What the hell was that about? I have absolutely no idea.

The truth is everything seems off. But then again I did just have a seriously whacked experience, as sketchy as the details remain. I've been trying hard to remember what happened before I went over the falls, but I can't recall much. The entire last week is fuzzy to me. Was I mad at Cole? Did we have a fight? I feel a strange anger toward him, something I can't explain. Is that why he hasn't visited me?

There's another knock on the door. I hope it's not a nurse or a doctor but someone I actually want to see— someone who might finally fill me in on what's been going on.

The door opens before I get a word out. The person who enters is even more unexpected, and more frightening, than Coach Keller.

It's the sheriff of the Crystal County Police Department.

CHAPTER 4

The big man doesn't even bother introducing himself, he's so certain that every teenager in Crystal Falls knows who the Law is around here. If not, the gold star on his chest gets the message across, and the bushy brown mustache underlines it.

Lowering himself into one of the armchairs, the sheriff makes himself comfortable, something that looks to be impossible as the buttons on his beige shirt strain against his gut. What's with sheriffs, anyway? Always with the big bellies and chicken legs. Still, one look at his forearms and I know the guy could have me in handcuffs and in the back of a cop car without even breaking a sweat.

Even though I haven't done anything, I can feel myself squirming under the sheets.

"Good morning, son," he says when he finally gets around to speaking. "So you're back among the living, I see."

"Yeah," I reply.

"You sure gave people a pretty good scare," he says, shaking his head disapprovingly.

The remark sort of annoys me. People were scared? Well, imagine how I felt, going over the falls. I'm careful to keep the reaction off my face. I can already tell that the sheriff thinks I did something stupid or reckless, and that's probably what he's here to find out.

The sheriff relays how fortunate it was that a woman taking a walk by the river happened to spot me on the rocks. Without her I would have probably frozen to death, he explains cheerfully. Her name is Olive Patterson, he adds, telling me I should make sure to thank her sometime.

I've never heard the name before. Should I send her a gift or something? Flowers? Chocolates? I should probably mow *her* lawn for free until eternity, I guess.

"So what's the damage?" the sheriff asks, leaning over to examine me. "What did the doc say?"

"I'm okay," I answer. "A cut on the back of my head, bruises, scratches . . ."

"Well, dang, if that ain't a miracle, I don't know what is."

"Me neither."

The sheriff stops speaking and peers at me instead. He sits back. "So what was it like?"

"What was what like?"

The sheriff laughs. "Going over Crystal Falls," he says. "Landing in the river. You know, all that fun stuff."

"I don't really remember," I answer, suddenly wishing

I had a better story to tell. Because I suppose I'll be answering the question for the rest of my life.

"Now that's a shame," the sheriff says, shaking his head. "Because of all the other people who've ever gone over them falls, you're the first one I've had the opportunity to ask. . . ."

"What? There were others?"

"Sure. I'm surprised this is news to you."

Well, it is. Though the possibility had occurred to me before, I'd never heard of an actual instance.

"How many?" I ask.

"Well, three." The sheriff starts fidgeting, feeling around in his pockets. He wants a smoke, I know— I remember seeing the same squirming with my chain-smoking late uncle Bud. "Since I've been in the department, at least."

"Three?"

"Yup. The first was about a month after I joined on as deputy. Agnes Thompson, a nice young woman, I remember, and pretty. Reported missing after not turning up for her shift at the diner for a few days. We never found her body, but we found some tracks down by the river. Her parents out west got a suicide note in the mail a couple days later."

I think about my uncle Bud again, who not only lit fresh cigarettes with spent ones but also finally put a shotgun in his mouth and lit that up too. Luckily, I didn't see that, though. And he wasn't the first relative either, at least on my mother's side, where offing yourself has been a bit of a tradition among the males in the family.

I'm suddenly wondering if the sheriff already knows this.

"Anyway, who was next?" the man continues breezily. "A kid. Franklin something."

"A kid?" I feel sick to my stomach. "What happened?"

"Not sure—he either jumped on purpose or fell in by accident. Unfortunately we had no tracks and no note in his case. Found his shoes, though, and some shreds of his clothing, in the river. Best guess is that he jumped too. He was a troubled little guy, it turned out. Picked on at school and all that . . ."

Yeah, I'm really seeing a theme developing here. Well, you've got it wrong, Sheriff, because I haven't had a suicidal thought in my life. Plus I'm too afraid of heights. It took all my nerve to go out on the footbridge over the falls when we first moved to town, and then I only did it because Cole went first.

"If so, what a shame," the sheriff tells me. "Throwing your life away like that. Sure, kids can be cruel, but they don't usually mean much by it. Things just happen sometimes. Am I right?"

The sheriff stares at me intently. Is he expecting me to break down? To start crying about how Hunter punched me in the eye? C'mon. No one is bothering me now, not after what Cole did. And he should already know that, having dragged my brother down to the station over the incident.

Come to think of it, maybe that's what this is about. Maybe the sheriff thinks I'm a hothead like my brother. Maybe he thinks the Harris boys are bad news.

"Now, the third guy," says the sheriff, "well, he was just asking for it." He laughs. "You know, come to think of it, he probably should have won one of those Darwin Awards." Seeing my blank expression, the sheriff explains: "It's a joke award, black humor—when somebody does something so dumb that they remove themselves from the gene pool, they win a Darwin. The idea is that the whole human species benefits by becoming a little bit less stupid."

That's black, all right, but I'm not seeing the humor, considering I just nearly died myself and have come nowhere near reproducing. "Sounds really funny," I say, without smiling.

"Yeah," the sheriff agrees. "The fellow was an old drunk by the name of Dutch Carter," he begins.

Wait a second—that name is familiar. I can even picture its owner: a gray-haired guy with a red face and white stubble. As the sheriff explains how he used to work over at the distillery, I figure that's where I must have met him.

"Dutch and a few of his buddies were drinking down at the river's edge as usual, just above the falls," the sheriff recounts. "They're hammered, the lot of them, when one of them geniuses decides it'd be funny to toss Dutch's smokes out onto a rock in the water.

"So rather than lose a few bucks, Dutch jumps out to get them back. And he makes it—onto the rock, that is. But then he tries to make it back. And I guess that pack of Luckies added a little too much extra weight, because he misses the bank by an inch and lands in the drink. And *wham*: He's swept off downriver."

A sickening feeling is triggered in my guts thinking about that unstoppable force carrying the man off. I know it. I've felt it.

"Then somehow Dutch gets hold of a tree branch dragging in the water. He's holding on for dear life, screaming at his buddies as they go running, trying to grab him. But no such luck. Just as they reach him, he's had enough and lets go.

"And that was that. Old Dutch went over, screaming his fool head off, no doubt. The surviving gang of morons comes running down to the station, all frantic, shouting about how we should go save him or something. I mean really. C'mon.

"But hell, we gave it the old college try. We dragged the river as best we could and had a poke around the rocks. But there was no sign of him, just like the other two . . ."

The sheriff hasn't finished his story though. And I can tell that he really likes this part, because he's feeling around for his smokes again. Judging by his face, he's told it a few times and perfected his delivery.

"Anyway, weeks go by," he says. "And everybody gets on with their lives, including the same bunch of boozers who I heard poured a bottle of whiskey off the bridge in their brainless friend's honor.

"But then one evening, a couple of kids head down to the river along to the observation area, to play a bit of grabby-grab in the mist under the falls.

"Then just as they're getting it on, up he pops—old Dutch, straight out of the water like a cork, all purple and bloated like a big old wine grape."

The image makes me want to gag. I think of how close I came to ending up like that—a swollen, bashed corpse.

I swallow a few times and try to forget about it. I'm alive, and that's all there is to it. But something occurs to me: Why haven't I heard this story before? Somebody working at Holden's gets killed going over the falls? My father would have mentioned it at least.

"When did it happen?" I ask.

"Lemme see," the sheriff answers. His eyes go to the ceiling, and he waggles a stubby, stained finger. "It was six years ago this past summer."

Which is a couple of years before we even came to town. But something is bothering me: Why can I see the man's face so clearly? I'm sure Cole and I met a guy named Dutch once, down at the distillery shortly after we first moved here. And how many Dutches can there be?

"Six years ago—you're sure?"

But the sheriff doesn't answer, having already moved on. Instead he leans in toward me. "So that makes you number four," he says. "Except, unlike the others, somehow you come out with barely a scratch. Kind of hard to believe . . ."

"I know," I answer. But the sheriff doesn't sound amazed or happy for me. "I guess I have a guardian angel or something," I add, shifting uncomfortably around in the bed.

"Actually you had more than an angel," he informs me. "You had something the others didn't."

"Huh?" I have no clue what he's talking about. "What?"

The sheriff leans forward even more. And it's then I realize it's not cigarettes he smokes but cigars. The cloying smell hits me, coming off his clothes and making me feel even more nauseated.

"You," he says, "were wearing a life jacket."

"I was wearing what?"

"Don't make me repeat myself, son," the sheriff says. "Because I hate repeating myself."

"A life jacket? I'm sorry. I don't remember."

And it's true: I don't. But I think about it. I know for a fact that our family owns four life jackets: two orange and two kid-size yellow ones that are no use to anybody anymore. They're in the garage, stored inside the canoe, which has sat up in the rafters for years now. To get at them, I would have had to climb a ladder.

"So what was going on with that?" the sheriff wants to know.

I shrug. "Like I said, I really don't remember."

The man makes a face; he's not buying it, and he's not hiding the fact.

"I'm serious," I insist. "Like, I have no clue why."

"Come on now, think," the sheriff asks me, still leaning in, still stinking. "Were you going for a swim maybe? Or just being careful, in case you slipped and fell?"

I have no idea what he is getting at. No one in his right mind would even dip a toe in the river in late September. But that kind of answer isn't going to get me anywhere with this guy. So I just explain again how I don't remember anything leading up to the accident.

But I'm shaking now. I'm starting to get really scared. The sheriff is holding out on me, hiding something he thinks I know. Sighing, he sits back in the chair. He fiddles with his pockets again, staring at me, before finally speaking again.

"Tell me about Neil Parson."

This takes me by complete surprise. "Neil Parson? From school?"

"The very same."

"What do you want to know about him?"

He shrugs. "I'm not fussy. Anything."

This seems like a weird direction for the conversation to go, if that's what you can call what we're having. I suppose *interrogation* is the better word, which probably explains why I am feeling so defensive.

"Neil's just a guy," I answer. "In my grade."

"Sure, I know. But what's he like?"

"What's he like?"

"Yeah. Would you say he's a good guy? A friend of yours?"

"No. I don't know." I'm stumped. I don't know much about Neil Parson. He's quiet, a brainiac. And he lives on Orchard Street, something I know only because my friend Willow lives across from him. I tell the sheriff as much.

"So you're saying you really don't know Neil?" he responds, jerking his head in surprise.

"Not really. No."

"You don't hang out away from school? Spend time together for any other reason?"

"No," I say, frustrated.

"All right," the sheriff answers, scribbling something down. "If you say so."

"You don't believe me?" I ask, alarmed.

The sheriff opens his mouth to say something but stops as the door opens and a nurse walks in. Instantly I smell the perfume again, like toilet cleaner. Seeing the officer in the room, she stops dead, the color draining from her face like someone pulled a plug on it.

"Rose!" barks the sheriff. The name is pinned to her nurse's uniform. "What are you doing in here?"

The woman looks like a cornered animal. "Working," she blurts out.

"I don't think you should come in here."

"No one told me not to."

"Well, I'm telling you. And I'm going to make sure everybody knows before I go. Do you understand me?"

The nurse turns and shoots me a glare.

"Do you understand me, Rose?" the sheriff repeats.

"Yes," the woman answers before slinking out of the room.

"Son of a bitch," the sheriff swears softly to himself when the door closes.

Okay, I've had enough of this—I'm getting really freaked out. "That nurse . . . ," I say.

The sheriff looks at me with sudden intensity. "What about her?"

"She said something."

"To you? When?" he demands to know.

"Back when everybody thought I was still unconscious."

"What did she say?"

It's hard to say out loud; I get a shiver even thinking about it. But I manage: "She said she hoped I'd never wake up."

The sheriff doesn't look the least bit surprised. "Did

she touch you or anything?" he wants to know. "Did she hurt you at all?"

Well, the needle in the hand didn't exactly tickle, but I don't think that counts. "No," I tell him. "She just did nurse stuff."

"Good," he says, relieved. "Still, I don't want her coming in here in the future. Press your button if she does. I'll tell her supervisor."

"Why?" I ask. "Who is she?"

"She's Neil Parson's aunt," the sheriff says. "His legal guardian."

It's clearly no coincidence, but it doesn't explain anything to me. "And?" I ask.

"Neil Parson is missing," he answers. "And you were the last person seen with him."

CHAPTER 5

I'm alone, sitting up in my hospital bed. I look to the side table, where there is a little card with a gold star embossed on it:

CRYSTAL COUNTY SHERIFF'S DEPARTMENT

MARLON PIKE, SHERIFF

It strikes me that I never knew the sheriff's name until now. Why should I have? I don't get into trouble. But there are plenty of other kids around town who do.

I read the address of the police station, 608 Clark Street. Below that is the station's telephone number. The sheriff told me to call if I remember anything more about either my accident or, more importantly, the whereabouts of Neil Parson.

Well, he'll be waiting a long time. I've already told him everything I know. But he doesn't believe me. It was written all over his cigar-sucking face.

And now I'm getting paranoid. I keep thinking about

all the weird things that have happened. First the business with Bryce and then with that nurse, Neil's aunt. That was news to me—I don't remember ever seeing her before in my life. And she hates me. Why? Because she thinks I did something to Neil? That's ridiculous.

And then there's Coach Keller, coming by with Hunter and Ricky. Another thing I can't explain.

I get out of bed to go to the toilet. On the way I stop at the door and listen. I feel a jolt of fear as I hear Rose talking to her colleagues at the nearby nurses' station. She is speaking in a low voice, but it's clear she's crying. The other staff members are telling her that everything will turn out all right.

I hear my name mentioned. The voices become angry. At one point a man calls me a little bastard and says I should be strung up and left to rot.

This is getting seriously out of hand.

I take a quick pee and climb back in bed before any-one catches me. Wait—*catches* me? This is ridiculous. I'm thinking like a criminal, and I didn't even do anything!

A little while later, another nurse comes in with my lunch. I decide to play up my friendliness. I'll show her what a nice guy I am, and what a great patient.

"Hey, this looks good," I declare of the meal she lays out on a tray in front of me—a sad-looking ham sandwich with some neon fruit salad and a juice box alongside.

The woman stiffens, avoiding eye contact. She stabs

the juice box with a straw and leaves without acknowledging my presence.

Okay, now paranoia completely takes over. I give my lunch a sniff, just to be sure no one has done anything to it. The smell is gross but a familiar gross, like something you'd smell coming from a kid's locker. Not convinced, I begin conducting an autopsy on the sandwich, lifting up the limp lettuce and the sad piece of ham, making absolutely sure no one has messed with it.

It looks normal. Still, I can't eat it. I wrap the dissected parts in a napkin and stick with the sealed fruit salad. I then suck the juice box dry.

I'm starting to wonder if I made the right choice by not mentioning what happened with Bryce to the sheriff. The guy did try to kill me, after all—an action police tend to find interesting. But as stupid as it sounds, Bryce is still my friend. I don't want to get him in trouble, that's for sure. I just need to talk to him—to find out what the heck is in his head. There has to be a rational explanation for what he did. It must be some sort of weird misunderstanding.

But first I have to find a way out of this hospital. And I'm starting to feel like the only way that's going to happen is in a mortician's van. Whatever the word is about me, it's starting to spread. Everyone who comes in either gives me dirty looks or completely ignores me. I can't let my guard down for a second.

It's a relief when my mother finally arrives. She looks

very tired and much older, I catch myself thinking. There is gray in her hair that I don't remember. She is wearing old jeans and a sweatshirt, and she has no makeup on, which is odd.

"Sorry I'm late, dear," she says. "We've just been so exhausted, we overslept. Your father had to go to work though. He took a lot of time off because of your accident, so has quite a bit of catching up to do."

Mom pulls out a magazine she's brought me to read, which is great, because I'm bored. But it's a *Sports Illustrated*—something I couldn't care less about. I don't say anything. I can only guess she picked it up by mistake.

"So what's up with Cole?" I ask, plunking down the magazine on the side table.

"Cole? Oh, he's fine," she reports.

"Good for him," I say.

Mom totally misses my sarcasm. "I know you want to get back to see your brother. And I've got good news: The doctor says you can come home tomorrow."

Good news? This is the worst news I ever heard. "Tomorrow?" I shout. "But Mom, I feel fine! Why can't I go home now?"

"I know you're feeling better, darling. But the doctor wants to keep you in another night for observation and do a scan in the morning. Just to make absolutely sure you're all right. Better safe than sorry, don't you think?"

"I don't know," I answer wearily.

"Just be patient, Cal."

"Mom, the sheriff came to see me today," I say.

"The sheriff?" My mother looks surprised for a moment before sinking her face into her hands. "Cal, what did you do?" she asks, looking up with a steely expression.

"Huh?"

"Tell me," she orders. "Tell me now."

"Nothing, Mom! Nothing!" I protest. "Jeez!"

My mother frowns. She looks totally unconvinced. And now I'm feeling really offended. For a guy who has kept his nose completely clean up until this point, I'm not getting much benefit of the doubt. "What did he want?" she finally asks.

"He was asking about a kid from school," I say. "Neil Parson."

"The missing boy."

"Yeah. How did you know?"

"It was in the newspaper. The whole town is frantic over it. Maybe the sheriff thinks you had something to do with it because he disappeared around the same time as your accident."

It would sure explain why so many people are being funny with me. "The sheriff told me I was the last person seen with him," I admit.

"Well, you should be honest and say what happened."

"Nothing happened!" But even I don't know this for sure, because I still don't remember anything about the day of the accident. "I never hang out with that kid," I tell her.

"Cal," my mother says, "relax."

"How? When everybody thinks I did something I didn't?"

"Well, then it'll all blow over," Mom says. "Maybe he just ran away from home or something. Hopefully he'll turn up soon."

"He'd better," I say under my breath. Mom looks up, alarmed. I suppose it does sound like a threat. But I'm mad. And hurt, to be honest, because I can't shake the feeling that even my own mother doesn't believe me.

We sit quietly for a few minutes.

"You're sure it's just one more night?" I ask. "And then I can go home?"

"One more."

"Okay," I agree, not that I have any choice in the matter. I'll just have to get through it.

Mom says she'll stay and read while I take a nap. And since I'm not planning on sleeping tonight, I want to get as much rest as I can. Despite the awful feeling in my stomach, I nod off quickly.

When I wake up, my father is back, sitting in the other orange chair beside my mother.

"Hi, Dad," I say, yawning.

"How you feeling, champ?"

"Okay, I guess. I just want to get out of here."

"We'll get you home soon, Cal. Look, the nurse just brought you in some dinner. It's probably still hot."

I have a look at the meal—a tiny piece of meat, some peas, and mashed potatoes. But I decide to pass, even though I'm starving. I've resolved to not eat anything that could have been tampered with. So I say I'm feeling a bit queasy and I'm only able to eat the packaged chocolate pudding.

My parents hang out but don't do much talking, to me or each other. I roll over and try to sleep some more, but I can't. I just lie there, staring at the wall. Eventually a nurse pops her head in and tells my parents that visiting hours are over.

They both kiss me on the forehead and say good night. I try to smile, but I'm still in a bad mood. Staring out at the parking lot, I see them get into Dad's van together a few minutes later.

I look up at the large clock on the wall. Man, it's only nine thirty. This is going to be a long night. I turn on the TV with the remote, but there's nothing good on, and soon I turn it back off.

Every noise makes me jump. I begin thinking I should be arming myself, but I can't see anything in the room that would serve as a weapon. The only thing that looks dangerous is the bedpan. I laugh to myself. It would definitely hurt, clanged off someone's head. But even a crummy fighter like me has to have some sort of dignity. I'll just have to stick to my fists. I have sharp knuckles, or so Cole has said the few times I managed to hurt him with them.

Bored, I open the *Sports Illustrated*. Since it isn't the swimsuit issue, it might as well be in German for all the interest I have in it. I drop it into the trash can. But then I start worrying that my mother might notice tomorrow and feel hurt.

So, hanging out of the bed, I try to fish out the magazine. That's when I hear my door creak. I'm up in an instant, but it's too late—the person has the drop on me. I whirl around, arms up in self-defense.

"Hello there, sexy," a dark-haired girl whispers as she climbs under the blankets with me. A mischievous smile full of perfect teeth gleams in the low light. "Miss me much?"

Now there have been some screwed-up things going on, but somehow none of them have been quite as mind-boggling as the moment I realize Ivy Johansen is in bed with me.

Without a doubt, Ivy is one of the hottest girls at school. She has long black hair, an amazing face, and a killer body. Not to mention the fact that she's a full year older than I am, a star athlete, an aspiring actress, and the school's debating champion. I consider myself pretty much on par with insects as far as she's concerned.

But she's right here in the sack.

I swear, trying to claw my way out of bed. But the

sheets seem to have me in a death grip.

"Calm down!" Ivy laughs, pinning my arms. Again she flashes her glowing teeth—it's like they're fluorescent—and then kisses me square on the mouth. "Did I *scare* you? You're such a little chicken. . . ."

Now she's tickling me! What's going on? I have no idea. Ivy's long nails are hurting more than they are amusing me. "Ow!" I cry, struggling so much, it feels like the sutures on my head might pop open again. "Stop it! Please! Stop it!"

Thankfully, Ivy quits, but she clamps a hand over my mouth. "Be quiet!" she whispers into my ear. "Do you want me to get caught?"

Eyes wide, I shake my head.

"I was barely able to sneak in—there are people every-where out there!" She pulls her hand away. Then, prop-ping herself up on an elbow, she stares at me with a pouty expression. "You could have called me, you know," she says, sounding miffed.

"Called you?"

"Or at least texted me. To let me know you were okay."

Ivy leans over my chest and begins nosing around on the side table. Her unbelievably toned body presses down on mine.

"Wait!" she cries, slapping herself on the forehead. She rolls off. "You lost your phone going over the falls, didn't you? Oh, I'm sorry, Cal. I don't know why I didn't think of it sooner. Can you ever forgive me?"

I don't have an answer. As far as I know, my phone is in a drawer, broken, having been dropped in the toilet a few weeks ago. And even when the piece of crap was working, it never contained Ivy Johansen's number. Because I don't know her. Cole does, having dated her just before Monica; but he broke things off pretty quickly, calling her a controlling bitch.

Well, she certainly is in control now, lunging over and pinning my hands under her stomach.

"I waited out there, you know," she whispers, nodding toward the window. "I sat in the parking lot for a full hour, watching from my car until I knew you were alone."

"Really?" I feel even more uncomfortable, if that's possible.

"Yeah. And you know what? I loved it—every second I spent spying on you!" She squeals so loud, my eardrum rings. Then she clamps a hand over her mouth and darts a nervous look at the door. "I actually think I might be some kind of a pervert, you know. . . ."

Whoa, now she's kissing my neck—something I have to admit feels really, really good, especially after the brutal tickling. But it doesn't feel good enough to make me forget for a second that not only is Ivy totally out of my league, she's that psycho Hunter Holden's girlfriend.

"Hey, what's the deal?" I manage to get out as she takes a breath.

Ivy stops kissing me immediately. And I can't help it—I instantly regret saying anything.

"What's the deal?" Ivy repeats. "What do you think? You nearly died!" She presses her mouth against mine and begins full-on making out with me.

Ivy Johansen is making out with me in my hospital bed. I don't have a clue how to begin processing this.

Wait—maybe I've suffered serious brain damage. That would explain a lot. But brain damage or not, I'm thinking I should just go with this.

At that second Nurse Barbara walks in. Ivy shrieks and ducks under the covers. But there's no concealing the five-foot-ten captain of the girls' volleyball team.

"Young lady, come out of there!" Nurse Barbara shouts. "Right this minute!"

Ivy pops her head out. Her shimmering black hair is all in her face. "Tee-hee," she giggles, like a four-year-old.

"What do you think you're doing?" the nurse shouts.

"Duh!" Ivy answers, laughing. "What does it look like?"

"Visiting hours are over," the nurse tells her. "I want you out. Now."

With a groan Ivy flings back the covers. Realizing my gown is riding up at what couldn't be a worse moment, I grab the sheet and pull it around myself as she jumps up.

"Out!" the nurse shouts, ushering the girl through the open door.

But Ivy resists, yanking her arm away. "Get well soon, Cal," she calls to me.

I wave back like an idiot.

The heavy door swings shut. I'm alone with Nurse Barbara, a scene completely drained of any sexiness.

"Sorry," I say, still tasting the lipstick that must be smeared all over my face. "Look, I didn't invite her in. She just showed up—I don't know why." I laugh and shake my head. "To tell you the truth, I don't even know her that well."

I don't know why I'm bothering. Nurse Barbara isn't interested. Upon finishing her duties, she only turns to scowl at me before leaving.

I lie there for a while, holding the covers tight around my neck. I don't think that was a dream—it felt too real. But come on. Things like that don't happen to me. Something is wrong.

Turning toward the window, I see that the curtains are still open. I wonder if Ivy is out there, sitting in a parked car and watching me at this very moment. I can't tell—I don't even know what her car looks like.

But what I do notice with a start is the figure in the Crocodiles jacket strolling down the parking lot. His hood is up, and I can't see his face, but he's definitely looking in at me. It's the same figure I saw just before Bryce came in.

This time I could swear even that walk is Cole's.

Well, I'm pissed. I don't know what he's pulling, but

it's not funny at all. And I'm definitely not playing along.

Legs aching, I get up and pull the curtains shut.

I hear voices out in the hall.

I cross over to the door and listen for a while. It's all just the talk of bored workers over the noises of a working hospital. But then everything goes silent. Silent like a morgue.

On the way back to bed, I pick up the unused bedpan. And though it's not quite as hefty as I'd hoped, it's still made of some sort of metal. A person definitely wouldn't want to get hit in the teeth with it.

I tuck it under my pillow, just in case, and begin waiting out the rest of the night.

CHAPTER 6

More than once, I fall asleep. I awaken each time with a jolt, my hands gripping the cold bedpan. But no one comes anywhere near me—I don't think my door opens even once. Which is strange, I think, because don't the nurses have to check on people?

Apparently not on me.

When morning comes, I begin to wonder if I've been making a big deal out of nothing. Maybe I'm just shaken up from the accident. Who wouldn't be?

Still, it's a happy moment when my mother arrives. Shortly afterward I get taken for some tests. Then there's a wait before the all clear to go home.

"If you're free of symptoms for a couple of weeks—no funny stuff like vision problems or nausea or anything—I see no reason why you can't play sports," the doctor says.

"Great," I answer, as if this is somehow a priority for me.

Whatever—I'll nod and smile at anything if it means getting out of here. And from the looks I get on the way out, I'm not the only one who doesn't want me hanging around any longer.

An orderly pushes me to the exit in a wheelchair like we're in a race. He dumps me outside—no "get well soon," "best wishes," or any of that. He just abandons the chair and heads back in. My mother even notices and glares after him.

"Hey, what a nice day," I say, hoping to distract her from the fact that the whole hospital hates her younger child.

"Yeah, sunny, huh?" she answers, helping me up.

It hurts to walk, and I'm limping as we cross the parking lot to my mother's car. "Oh, you poor thing," she says, looking at me. "You should have waited in reception. I would have driven up."

"I'm fine, Mom." It's probably mostly just stiffness from lying around for so long, I tell her. My joints do feel swollen and sore though. But no wonder—I fell over a waterfall and must have been thrown around like a rag doll.

Mom unlocks her trusty but rusty red hatchback, which she bought for five hundred dollars shortly after we arrived in Crystal Falls. My brother, a self-proclaimed auto expert, poked around its insides and gave the car a year's life, max. But somehow it refuses to die. We used to joke that you could probably drive the car off a cliff, and it would still run.

Well, it turns out that the little rust bucket and I now have something in common. The car doesn't return the fond feeling, however, making me pull four times before giving me enough slack to buckle up. Pain shoots through my shoulder, and again I feel like the stitches on my head are about to pop open.

Safely secured in the cozy little death trap, I try to relax. It really is a nice day, I notice through the grimy window. Crystal Falls is beautiful in the fall, I'll admit. And as the cool nights drive off most of the campers and tourists, you can finally get a parking spot on Main Street and seats in the diner whenever you want. By November the town is ours until the weather turns mild again in May.

Well, maybe not completely ours.

It's funny how you can spend four years in a place like Crystal Falls but still be an outsider. Even Bryce, who moved here when he was five, isn't "OT"—an Original Townie. Meanwhile there are families with streets named after them: the Mayfields, the Daniels, the Wiltons, and the Guises. Those are the names that mean something in Crystal Falls.

And then there are the Holdens, of course, one of whom blows by in a luxury SUV as we exit the parking lot. Their liquor business has been here for 130 years—even operating in secret during Prohibition, I heard, inflating their fortune tenfold. And now they practically own the town.

Which might explain why Mrs. Holden—whose bleach-blond hairdo I glimpse behind the wheel—feels entitled to drive sixty in a thirty-mile-an-hour zone. The road now clear, my mother pulls out. I stare blankly out the window as we head down Main Street.

"Wait!" I suddenly exclaim. "What happened to Electronica Veronica?"

"Pardon?" my mother asks.

"Electronica Veronica," I repeat. It's a store that Bryce and I spend a lot of time in, as it's the only place within a half-hour drive that sells video games. Craning back, I can see the familiar storefront, but the letters of its old seventies sign have been removed. The windows look completely dark.

"Electronic what?" she asks.

But I don't reply. Because I'm noticing other businesses that are gone, like the coffeehouse where some of the older kids go. In its place is a repair shop with a graveyard of vacuum cleaners behind its front window. And there are more that are gone, too, I'm sure of it, either shuttered up or replaced by what look like struggling businesses.

"What the hell happened to Main Street?" I shout. Out of the corner of my eye, I see Mom shoot me a worried look. But I can't help myself. "Okay, this is ridiculous!" I cry. "Where did Burger Delight go?"

"Are you feeling all right, Cal?" Mom demands.

"Sure. Why?"

"Did they give you any sort of medication before we left?"

"No."

"Well, you seem odd," my mother says. She puts on the brakes, stopping to let a group of power-walking seniors cross the street.

"I'm fine, honestly." But I'm lying. Looking around, I don't feel okay. At all. I put my head down and rub my temples as my mother begins driving again. When I look up again, we've left Main and are on the road leading out of town. As we pass the church, I'm stunned: The normally bright white clapboard is dingy and in need of a paint job, and the always well-maintained lawn is wild and weedy.

"You're sure you feel okay?" my mother asks again. "I can turn back, you know. We can get you checked out at the hospital. . . ."

"No!" I shout. "No!"

The outburst only scares my mother even more. She pulls over onto the shoulder, about to turn the car around.

"Seriously, I'm fine," I tell her. "Sorry for yelling. Let's just go home."

"All right," she says. "Put the seat back and try to relax, Cal. We'll be there in a few minutes."

I recline as far as the uncooperative old seat allows. Feeling woozy, I crack the window open a little too. I can see the bridge up ahead. Soon I can even hear the great *whoosh* of the crashing falls themselves.

A few seconds later, we're crossing the dizzying drop over the gorge, the falls visible on the right.

"Don't look at them, Cal," my mother begs me. "You're only traumatizing yourself."

But she has no idea—no idea that my trauma is not coming from morbid thoughts or awful memories but from a much darker place, from the disturbing question hanging over everything:

What the hell is going on?

I turn and look out the passenger window at the gorge and the turbulent river snaking away to the left. I was just hallucinating before, I tell myself. I hit my head, and it messed me up. It's my brain playing tricks on me. None of it is real.

The thought is no more comforting.

When we reach the other side of the bridge, the sign shows the turnoff to the campground along with the large billboard that reads:

HOLDEN DISTILLERY, 8 MILES. VISITORS WELCOME!

I close my eyes and keep them clenched shut until I hear the familiar crunch of the tires on our gravel driveway. Only then do I decide it's safe to open my eyes again.

Unfortunately I'm wrong.

....

I'm too shocked to scream.

Everything is different.

Yes, the number by the front door is still 4275. But the

house is no longer green—it's bright blue. And the whole property has been cleared of trees, except for the magnolia out front. In their place is just grass—a flat expanse of mowed grass.

"How are you feeling?" my mother asks. "Any better?"

"Yeah," I manage to say, though it takes every ounce of my will. "Much better."

"Well, you go on inside, and I'll get the things out of the trunk."

But I don't want to go into the house alone. I'm too nervous.

"Things?" I ask. "What things?" Other than the clothes I'm wearing, I don't remember having anything at the hospital.

"It's just a few groceries, Cal. Don't worry, I can manage them. Here, take my keys. Go on up and see your brother."

My brother's home from school? It figures he doesn't come to visit me at the hospital yet still wrangles a day off when I'm discharged.

Trembling, I get out of the car and head toward the front door. Untangling Mom's keys, I unlock the door and open it, afraid of what I'll find next. But there's nothing particularly unusual inside, other than the absence of Cole's big sneakers, which I usually trip over. I stand in the entranceway, my body tingling all over.

I don't want to see Cole, I decide. Not yet, at least.

Maybe I should lie down for a while. Maybe then things will snap back and start making more sense. I climb the stairs, clinging to the railing as if the whole house is on an angle.

Reaching the landing, I turn right toward my bedroom door, with the peeling sticker that says: Hazardous Zone—Do Not Enter. It might've been funny back when I was twelve, but the warning is getting old these days.

Opening the door, I notice that something is different about my room, but at first glance, I can't tell what. I don't care. I'm getting dizzy and feeling totally nauseated. I just want to lie down. Leaving on the shoes I forgot to take off at the door, I fall forward onto my bed. I bury my face in my pillow for a few seconds, but the sensation immediately reminds me of Bryce's attack, so I turn on my side, breathless. The wound on the back of my head throbs, and my whole body aches.

I'm lying like this for only a minute before I hear my mother come in downstairs. After dumping her bags in the kitchen, she calls for me from the bottom of the stairs.

"Callum?"

At least she has my name right for once. It's only a small return to normality, but I'll take what I can get.

"Cal, are you okay?"

"I'm in my room," I shout back. "Lying down."

"Okay, sweetie. Just let me know if you need anything."

I keep my eyes closed for a while, hoping it will help

my nerves settle. I start thinking again about the possibility that there's a complication to my brain injury and that I might be wasting time just lying here. Maybe I have internal bleeding or something, and it's screwing up my memory.

But the doctor said it himself: My brain looks fine. Everything is completely normal, the scan said. Still, I think of the stories I've heard about people hitting their heads and having all sorts of unexplained symptoms. Like the story my biology teacher read from the newspaper, about a woman in England who woke up speaking with a Chinese accent. If that's true, surely anything is possible.

Forget it—I don't want to think about that sort of thing right now. I just want to get a grip on myself. Keeping my eyes shut, I find myself wondering where Cole is. He must have heard me open the front door. But maybe he's out. Maybe he took Jess for a walk—he's probably been stuck with the job because I haven't been around. And it would explain why she didn't come running when I got home.

No. I hear my mother opening the basement door and the dog bounding out. We can't leave her alone in the house or she'll chew something to pieces. So whining or not, she has to get locked up.

The clicking of Jess's nails on the kitchen floor makes me feel better. She's excited that someone is home and is probably getting a treat for being cooped up for so long. This is the home I remember. This is the home I know.

My breathing slows, and I feel better. I just want my dog.

I open my eyes and sit up.

Something about my room still feels wrong. What is it? Wait—books are missing from my shelves. Half of my collection, maybe more. In their place are weird things: magazines, ugly golden trophies, and a black case. Frowning, I get up out of bed, step over, and open the case. A trumpet? What am I doing with a trumpet? Then I look at the thick stack of magazines lying where the books should be. I pull one out.

I can't believe it. It's another goddamn *Sports Illustrated*!

Just then I begin to feel really uncomfortable. It's like someone is in the room watching me. I spin around.

To my shock, a large, half-naked woman is looming over me. It's a poster of a chick wearing a bikini and crawling on all fours, a tropical surf roaring up behind her. Who the hell put this up in my room?

Okay, it's hardly a difficult mystery to solve. It has to be Cole—who else has such a stupid sense of humor? But it makes me mad all over again. Instead of coming to visit me in the hospital, he stayed home to screw with me, like this is some big, hilarious episode. Does he have any idea how serious things were? How close I came to dying?

Brain-damaged or not, I'm not so out of my mind that I can't figure out what's happened here—Cole has replaced my stuff with his own. Which means he's here somewhere, hiding and cackling to himself. Ha-ha. Well, he is going to pay. He is going to pay dearly at the points of my sharp knuckles.

I check my closet—he's not there. So I storm out into the hall.

"Cole!" I shout. "Cole, you ass-wipe!"

I hear my mother running up the stairs. "What's going on?" she asks, when she meets me at the top.

"Where is Cole?" I want to know. "Where is he?"

My mother goes white. "He's in his room, of course." Her mouth begins quivering. "Where else would he be?"

I thunder past her, down the hall to Cole's bedroom door. I throw it open and see that the room is pitch-black inside.

So he wants to play around, huh? Jump out at me or something? Well, let's see how funny he thinks it is when he gets a punch square in the face. . . .

I flick on the overhead light—and stand there, stunned.

Because his room is all wrong too. The queen-size bed that ate up most of the space is gone. In its place is a twin, made up perfectly. His desk is also gone. There are no more posters on the walls, no babes, no football heroes. And no Cole.

Instead I see the original wallpaper from back when we first moved in.

"Omigod—kittens! Really?" my fourteen-year-old brother shrieked at the time. "You have got to be kidding me!" Meanwhile my parents and I killed ourselves laughing over his shoulder.

"Don't be so hard on the little guys," Dad had told him. "After a few years, you'll learn to love them." But of course it was only a joke; stripping and repainting his room had been the first project they tackled.

Seeing the demented-looking cartoon kittens again, my blood runs cold. I turn to my mother.

"Where is Cole?" I beg her to tell me. I'm no longer angry—I'm scared. "Where is Cole?"

Mom recoils at the question. "What's going on, Cal?" she asks, looking terrified. "What is wrong with you?"

I stare at my mother. I don't understand. She just stands there, wearing an awful expression for a moment, before opening the door to the guest bedroom across the hall. She walks in and waits for me. When I don't follow, she holds out a hand.

"Cal, it's okay," she says. "Come see him."

I'm shaking, head to foot now, as I cross the hall. I take my mother's hand and let her lead me.

The guest room has been repainted, I notice instantly, changed from its cream color to a sky blue. And there are sounds in here. Strange sounds I have never heard before.

I turn my head. At the back of the room is a bed—but not a normal bed. It's like the one I just left in the hospital, except bigger: an electrically powered bed that, from the looks of it, can move into all sorts of positions. There's a machine beside it—a white device that looks like a robot with a hose hanging off it.

The hose leads to a figure that is stretched out on the bed, covered in blankets. His eyes are wide open, but he is not moving.

"Cole," my mother says in the soft singsong voice she uses to wake me up some mornings, when I've fallen into a deep sleep and don't hear my alarm.

The figure makes a noise. A horrible rattling noise.

"Cole, your brother is home," she tells him. "And everything is going to be all right."

CHAPTER 7

I remember the July before we moved to Crystal Falls. I'd just turned twelve; Cole was fourteen. It was a hot, dry summer. Everything felt hazy and dreamlike outside.

My father had said the haze was smoke from a forest fire up north. When we started freaking out, he told us not to worry, that there was no way it could cross the river and make it this far down. Still, the fire must have been huge, because you could even smell the burning wood.

The smell made me uneasy, reminding me of something that happened when I was eight years old. Back then I liked playing with matches and used to steal them from where they were hidden under dish towels in a kitchen drawer. I would light things on fire, like pieces of paper and old toys. But after a while I moved on to trash down at the dump, where I finally set a pretty serious fire—bad enough that they started posting a security guard at the site.

A few weeks after that, I saw that a neighbor had left his garage door open. So I went in to have a look around. There was a pile of rags in the corner. I don't know what was on them, but all it took was the touch of one match to make them burst into flames. I ran back outside.

The whole place went up in a few minutes. To this day I have no idea why I did it—but it felt good, watching the garage burn. They found me sitting in the grass out front, matchbox still in hand.

Luckily, the garage wasn't attached to the house and no one was injured. But still, my poor parents. I ended up getting sent to a psychologist over the incident. Apparently it could be a sign—of what, no one ever told me. The lady kept asking me if I felt bad about what I'd done. And I kept on lying, saying that I did. But I didn't—I knew I didn't. I was just too scared to admit it.

Now I keep away from matches, just in case.

Anyway, the day we could smell that distant forest fire, Cole and I started off in bad moods. We were getting a treat, Dad said—a day out at some big water park. But we didn't care. As far as we were concerned, the treat hadn't been invented that could make up for having to leave everything we ever knew behind.

Still, it was hard to stay mad, at least that day. The park did turn out to be pretty cool. Set up on an off-season ski hill, it had a massive wave pool and tons of slides, including a really long winding one you rode on big inner tubes.

The most insane slide of all went straight down the side of the mountain, dropping off at what looked to be close to a ninety-degree angle.

"Oh, yeah, I'm going on *that*!" Cole declared.

Which meant I was going, too, because there was no way I could let my brother think I was even more of a wuss than he already did. But there was nothing I wanted less than to go on that monster.

I stalled my brother for a while, hoping to work up my nerve on the smaller slides. We even took a chair lift up and rode the big tube ride, which was scary enough for me.

My best hope was that he would just overlook it altogether and only remember later, cursing himself as we pulled out of the parking lot.

But no. It was inevitable.

"There it is, the big one!" he shouted as the baby-blue slide appeared on the steep mountainside. Someone flew out the end of the tube like they'd been fired from a rifle.

I felt my knees buckle.

No, I wasn't doing it, I decided.

"What's the holdup?" Cole asked, jogging back to find me when he realized I wasn't beside him. "You coming or not?"

"I don't know. I think I'll pass."

"Not an option."

"Yes, it is."

"Come on, Callum. Don't be a wimp."

"I'm not a wimp," I told him. "I just don't want to."

My brother made an explosive noise like an angry

bull. But then something came over him. "Cal, seriously," he said. "What's the point in living if you never feel alive? Do this and you'll feel more alive than ever, I swear."

I thought about the garage and how alive I felt watching it burn. "I said I don't want to," I told him again.

Cole shook his head, clearly disgusted with me. "Oh well, your loss," he said, shrugging. "Then make sure to watch me—I need a witness."

"A witness? Why?"

"Wait and see. I'm going to do something extreme."

Something about the gleam in my brother's eye made me even more terrified. He was going to do something reckless, I knew. I had to talk sense into him, I decided, breaking into a run. Glancing back at me, Cole just smiled and picked up his pace.

There was no chair lift, which made it a long climb to the top. Not only did I get winded, but my feet started killing me, because of the stones and pine needles scattered on the pathway up.

Meanwhile my brother looked like he was running up carpeted stairs. Then he slowed down to shout back at me with a grin, "Stop being such a pussy, Callum!" Wheezing, I caught up to Cole at the top. He was standing by a sign that explained the rules for riding. A diagram showed exactly how you had to go down: on your back with your arms crossed over your chest. No exceptions, the sign made clear.

"Hey, look, it's like you're already in your coffin," he pointed out. "That should save Mom and Dad some time when you die. . . ."

"Ha-ha," I answered.

Just beyond the sign an attendant lounged in a lawn chair. Around seventeen or so, he was the most freckled guy I'd ever seen in my life. Apparently his job—other than sneaking looks at the girls in their bathing suits— was to give the signal when it was safe to go.

"Dude, can I go down headfirst?" my brother asked. I knew it—he wanted to do something stupid. I had to stop him.

Fortunately the attendant was already ahead of me. "No way," he answered. "Park regulations."

But as far as Cole was concerned, rules were made for other people. "Oh, c'mon," he said, all smiles. "Please?"

"I said no," the attendant snapped back. "Are you deaf, kid, as well as stupid?"

Cole's eyes narrowed. He was mad. And when he was mad, bad things happened. Punches got thrown. I knew, because I was often on the receiving end.

"Oh yeah?" he snapped back. "Who's going to stop me?"

He was definitely not leaving this alone. I had to say something; otherwise we were getting thrown out of the water park, for sure. And we still hadn't hit the wave pool, the one thing *I* still wanted to try.

"Cole!" I shouted. "Don't screw around!"

My brother turned, looking at me with those same blazing eyes. I was just another one of his enemies.

"Knock it off, or I'll tell Mom and Dad," I threatened.

The threat was a mistake, I thought immediately. Cole would only do something worse. For this was the law that kept the balance of the universe tilted in his favor—never back down. I'd always wished I could do the same, but it's impossible—two such people could never coexist in the same family. Not without utter destruction.

Which meant that I could only stand there, hoping that the water-park employees had a good dental plan. But Cole never threw a punch. I don't know. Maybe it was the summer day or the call of the wave pool or the pretty girl who'd just smiled at my brother before going down ahead of us. Whatever it was, for some reason Cole came up with a more reasonable option.

"Fuck you, Freckles," he said to the attendant. Leaping into the slide, he quickly adopted the proper position shown on the sign and then launched himself.

"Hey!" the attendant shouted after him, whether for the insult or not waiting for the signal, who knows? But it was too late—Cole was gone. Unless the attendant had a radio and had memorized my brother's red-and-yellow-floral surfer trunks, it was game over; Cole would simply vanish into the crowd of half-naked kids.

I could hear Cole laughing as he went into free fall.

Then again the attendant still had me. He turned and looked pretty ready to take out his rage on the abandoned little brother. But instead he just pointed to the slide.

"Get in," he snarled.

That's when things went wrong—again. As the freezing water made me shiver, I suddenly felt scared. Really scared. And when the attendant's signal came, I couldn't do it. I just couldn't.

"Go!" the attendant started shouting at me. "Go!"

Worse still, it turned out that nobody gets pissy faster than people waiting to have a good time. "You're holding up the line!" voices started complaining. "C'mon, kid . . . Either go or get out!"

It didn't make a difference. Embarrassed or not, I couldn't release my white-knuckled death grip. I was going to have to climb out. I was going to have to climb out and walk all the way back down.

But then I pictured Cole. He'd be dripping wet and waiting for me, wondering what the holdup was. What would he think when somebody else came down? And then somebody else? What would he think when I finally came climbing down the hill, a little pussy of a brother who made him look bad?

I wasn't looking forward to finding out. So I let go.

I don't remember much after that. The sudden acceleration, drop-off, and then the free fall. My stomach was in my mouth, and I shut my eyes, terrified.

There was a disgusting squeak as my skin finally regained contact with the slide. When I hit the pool, my feet caught the water, and my body went flying end over end. The landing must have looked bad, because even my brother joined in on the sympathetic groaning as I surfaced.

Cole met me at the top of the pool ladder. "Nice air," he remarked. It was a rare compliment—the last before we moved to Crystal Falls.

....

Fast-forward to four years later. Four years of what my mother describes as ups and downs, but what I call just one steep slide—ever since first setting eyes on that stupid welcome sign.

But I was finally getting used to things. At least I had a friend in Bryce—and something unexpected and exciting with Willow.

Now everything appears to have changed. Could I really have forgotten what actually happened in my life and remember only these dreams? It seems to me there are only two possibilities. Something has either gone very wrong with this place, or something has gone very wrong with me.

I honestly don't know which one it is.

But I've calmed down, at least compared to earlier, when my mother tried to take me back to the hospital.

There was no way I was going. I shook her off and ran straight out of the house. After racing home, my father found me in the driveway pressed up against the red hatchback.

I don't know why I picked there, of all places, to collapse and cry my eyes out. Maybe it's because that stupid old hatchback is the one thing that remains exactly as I remember it, with every dent, scratch, and rust stain— even the same soft tire Cole was nagging Mom about just last week.

But now I'm supposed to believe he hasn't moved a muscle or said a word in four years. Now I'm supposed to believe there was some sort of accident at the water park— the same water park where I don't remember anything except us having the time of our lives.

Mom had been sitting on the porch as she waited for Dad, I guess making sure I didn't hurt myself or something. She was pretty upset, of course, especially when I shouted at her to leave me alone. I don't know why, but I didn't want her coming close to me, touching me. But she rushed over again as soon as my father got out of the van.

Dad also insisted on taking me straight back to the hospital. Hearing him, I became completely hysterical again. They didn't know what to do—they would have literally had to tie me up to get me there.

So instead they just watched helplessly as I cried myself out. Eventually they got me to go inside—back into the wrong color house, where my brother lies paralyzed.

Once we were inside, my parents called the hospital. Sitting on the couch in the living room, I listened in as they talked to the neurologist on the phone in the hallway, occasionally passing the receiver between them. In hushed voices, they described not only my erratic behavior but my sudden inability to accept the tragedy that had struck my brother four years ago: that he suffered a spinal injury that left him paralyzed from the neck down, unable to even breathe on his own.

My parents listened as the neurologist talked, my father having now gone through to the old corded phone in the kitchen. "So Callum is suffering from some kind of posttraumatic shock?" I heard him ask.

"What do we do?" my mother wanted to know. "How is it treated?"

I have no idea what the doctor said next. But whatever it was, it seemed to put a stop to the discussion about taking me back to the hospital.

....

A couple of hours later, I'm having dinner, barely holding down whatever I've put in my mouth and swallowed.

I still can't remember Cole having an accident four years ago. Well, that's not entirely true. After the water park, when we came to Crystal Falls, I watched him crash his bike, smash his sled, and take spills on a skateboard dozens of times. But nothing that caused any worse injuries than scratched knees, big bruises, and a few bloody palms.

"Hey," my father says from the head of the table, a position I haven't seen him occupy in almost a year. "Is there anyone you want to call? A buddy or one of your girlfriends, maybe? Because talking to someone might make you feel better."

Buddies? Girlfriends? He's talking like I've got them growing on trees somewhere.

"Where's your phone?" my mother asks.

"I don't know," I answer. Lying dead under some papers in my room would be my best guess.

"Of course—you lost it," my father says. "Well, don't worry, we'll get you another one. Do you have anybody's number? Do you want to call your buddy?"

"Look, I don't really feel like talking to Bryce right now," I answer. It's an understatement. "But maybe I'll call Willow a little later."

"Bryce?" my father says. "Who's Bryce?"

"And Willow," my mother says, brightening. "That's a lovely name. You've never mentioned her before. Is she a new friend?"

"Wait a second," Dad says. "Why is every girl you hang out with named after a plant?"

I drop my fork on the plate. They are not teasing me, I can tell. They are seriously acting like they've never even heard of Bryce or Willow.

"You know, I'm really not that hungry," I say. "Can I just go up to my room for a while?"

"Sure," Mom says. "But promise to tell us if you feel off or anything."

Off? I almost laugh. Instead I nod.

"Just leave your plate, dear. Go on upstairs."

"Thanks," I say, heading out of the room.

At the top of the stairs, I pause. I look at the half-open door to the guest room. I can hear that machine inside, chugging away, keeping Cole alive.

I can't help myself—I pull the door shut.

I stop for a moment before opening the door directly across the hall. I look into the room that supposedly no one ever moved into.

The feeling of horror is so strong, I actually find myself shuddering. I tear my eyes away and shut the door behind me. I lurch down the hall to my own room.

Sitting on my bed, I try to calm down and convince myself this is normal. I've just suffered a traumatic experience, and it's confusing me. Mom said the doctor suggested sedatives if I'm still feeling anxious.

But no. I don't want any drugs—I don't want to feel any fuzzier than I already do. I need to be ready. For anything.

I look up again at the glossy poster of the sexy girl in her swimsuit. What the hell is that doing there? It still makes no sense to me. If Cole didn't put it there as a joke, then who did?

The woman doesn't care. She just wants to crawl across the sand, straight out of the picture, to tear off my clothes.

My body responds to her desire.

But after a moment, the feeling goes away. Because she doesn't like me. It's all pretend, for the camera.

I surprise myself by suddenly leaping up. With one swipe, I tear down the poster, leaving only a couple of loops of tape behind. The poster falls, torn, to the floor.

I begin thinking about Ivy Johansen now, about her kissing and groping me in my hospital bed. Was she faking it, too, I wonder? I honestly don't think so. Why would she?

And now I can't get her off my mind. The feeling of her long, athletic body stretched out on top of mine, my hands trapped under her taut stomach . . .

I have to feel that again before I die, I decide.

But then I remember Willow. She was here, on my bed, just the other day. Sitting on the edge, listening to me play a new song I wrote—a lame, stupid song I could hardly get through.

She clapped and said it was good, though. And I just sat there, flushed, wondering if she was faking it.

I wonder what would she think about one of the best-looking girls in school climbing all over me. Ivy was touching me and kissing me. Kissing me! I suddenly feel awful about it.

But why should I feel bad? It's not like Willow and I are really going out. And this is Ivy Johansen we're talking about—the entire male student body at Crystal Falls High would probably give me a medal if they knew about it. So why feel guilty?

Because I'm in love with Willow, I realize.

I'm uncomfortable even thinking it. After all, we've only just become friends this last year. I haven't even kissed her yet. But I'm in love with her, I know. Why else would I have a collection of her lost bobby pins in my desk drawer—the ones she uses to keep her bangs out of her eyes and that I always find on my bed and on the sofa?

I can almost hear Cole's voice: *Because you're an effing weirdo.*

Probably, but I don't really care. I reach for the desk drawer but stop myself. Playing with secret keepsakes isn't enough. I really need to talk to Willow now. But I'm scared to phone her. What's wrong? Why didn't she come to visit me?

There's only one way to find out.

I know Willow's telephone number by heart. I pick up the phone in my bedroom and dial. It rings on and on. Just as I'm about to hang up, Elaine answers.

"Hello?" she says, all out of breath.

Elaine is Willow's mother. She hates being called anything else, especially Mrs. Hathaway, I found out the first time I met her.

"Save me the missus, sport—there's no Mr. Hathaway," she told me sternly.

I felt pretty embarrassed. But it didn't last, because Elaine is otherwise fairly easygoing. Yeah, she's got weird fashion sense, wearing pointy boots and patterned dresses that make her look a bit too hippie-witchy for my taste. But I like Elaine. And she likes me, Willow says. Which is the most important thing.

"Hi, it's Callum," I say, feeling nervous. "Is Willow there?"

Fortunately the woman isn't in a chatty mood. "One minute, please," she answers. I can hear her clamp a hand over the receiver and call her daughter.

There's only one phone in their whole house, so usually I have to wait a while. For some reason Elaine doesn't approve of phones, cells especially. To be honest, sometimes I wonder if it's just so she can keep Willow's private business out in the open. Although she's fairly cool, Elaine is still overprotective when it comes to her daughter.

"Who is it?" I finally hear a faint voice say.

"I don't know," Elaine whispers back.

Okay, that's weird. Elaine knows my voice, and I even said my name. Already I'm feeling more unsteady than ever.

"Hello?"

Willow's voice makes me feel better. In fact, it's the best voice of any girl I've met and makes me feel strangely sleepy, sort of the same way lying on a sofa in the sun does. If Cole heard that, he'd call me an even bigger weirdo. Not that he seems to be able to call me anything anymore.

I'm starting to wish my cell phone were working. Then I could have made this call outside, from inside the red hatchback, where something else would at least feel normal to me. But I'm stuck in my strangely unfamiliar room, hovering over the crumpled poster, a single eye staring up at me from the floor.

"Hi, Willow," I say. "It's me, Callum."

There's a pause. "Who?"

"Callum," I repeat. The receiver is now shaking so badly, I'm worried I might drop it. "I just got home. But I'm not feeling too good, to be honest. I don't know. Maybe it was hitting my head or something, but things have gotten really weird. . . ."

As I keep talking, I start to feel hurt again that Willow didn't visit me. But she can be shy sometimes and doesn't like to intrude on family stuff. Maybe it's my fault. I confided a lot of things about my family that weren't that great. She's probably afraid of walking in on some fight, like the ones her own mother and father must have had before he left years ago.

"Wait, is this Cal Harris?" she asks. "From school?"

What kind of question is that? *From school?*

"Yeah, it's me," I say, rocking uncomfortably on the

side of my bed. "What's wrong?"

"Nothing, I guess," she says in a flat tone. "Listen, I'm sorry about your accident and everything, but if this is about homework, I've been off with the flu all week and have no idea what's due. . . ."

I can't believe what I'm hearing. "Willow," I say, my voice cracking, "it's me, Callum. . . ."

"Uh-huh, I heard you," she replies.

"Willow," I plead. Tears fill my eyes. "Please. Why are you acting like this? I'm in trouble. I need your help!"

"My help?" she answers, sounding surprised. "Why *my* help?"

"Because it's me!" I answer, losing my temper. "Don't you want to help me?"

"Oh, help yourself," she says, and then hangs up.

Willow. She hangs up!

I sit there for a while, listening to the dead line. I've never felt so disconnected. Finally I hang up.

This is wrong—too wrong. Maybe I should go to the hospital, but one in another town or in the city even. I wonder if I can convince my parents. If that's the only way I'll agree to go to see someone, they won't have any choice.

I open my door. I can hear the clatter of dishes in the sink and my parents talking. They're using their unhappy voices—the ones I remember from back when Dad still lived here, which I heard long into the night after they thought Cole and I were asleep.

God, I hate those voices.

I get up and walk over to my desk. I pull out an old swivel chair that Cole and I used to have these crazy endurance tests in, spinning each other to the very limits of our stomachs. I sit down and feel its wooden edge poking through the flattened foam into the backs of my legs. This chair hasn't changed. This chair is the same.

I swivel and pull open the middle desk drawer. As always, inside sits a neatly stacked pile of old school notebooks, underneath which should lie my secret shoe box where I keep Willow's bobby pins, among other keepsakes.

I remove the notebooks and put them on the desk. The box, to my relief, is still there. I lift off the lid and place it on top of the notebooks.

Without the overhead light on, the interior of the box is in shadow, so I have to lean over and peer inside.

I quickly discover that nothing familiar is in there. Instead the shoe box now contains two things, neither of which I have ever seen before.

The first is a roll of bills, tightly wrapped in a rubber band.

The other is a gun.

CHAPTER 8

I've never considered blowing my brains out before, but that's what I think about doing when I pick up the heavy automatic pistol. It's real, that much I can tell immediately. Whether or not it has any bullets in it, I have no idea.

I guess I could pull the trigger and find out.

I don't. Like I said, I'm not the type. But I still have no idea what it's doing in my desk. The weapon looks old, not like some gangster's Glock but like a soldier's sidearm. My grandfather's maybe? Actually that makes sense. His uniform, his medals, his helmet; all that stuff is up in the attic somewhere—why not his .45?

If so, I've never seen it before.

And neither have I ever seen this $625 before, which is the exact amount I count out after removing the rubber band. But here it is, in my bedroom, ready to be spent. Sitting on my desk in piles, the bills are practically begging me. And who would stop me?

I hear a noise. I quickly put the pistol and the cash back where I found them in the shoe box, then replace the notebooks and close the drawer. I listen. No one is coming.

I begin to wonder what my mother would say if she found this little stash of mine. As far as I know, she's never gone through my things before. She's never had a reason.

Well, she does now.

I look around my room some more, this time studying every detail for further clues. Who lives here? I confirm again that my favorite books are missing from the shelves, mostly replaced with ridiculous sports trophies.

Wait a second—where is my guitar? And my amp? They're both missing from the room; in their place is a laundry hamper. The skateboard I use to travel into town during the warmer months is also gone from the window-sill where it usually hangs from its trucks.

I look again at the trumpet case sitting on the shelf. You know, I actually wish I could play it, because then I would be in music class with Willow. As it stands, this year we have only two classes together, which is a bummer. But I suppose even in music, we wouldn't get to sit together, because she plays flute in the band, and of course everyone is grouped by instruments.

Then again I shouldn't complain. Last year we had only one class together.

It was biology. That's where we first became friends, after being partnered on an assignment. When I think of the chances of just randomly being handed an excuse to talk to her, to have our heads pressed together over a microscope, I have to consider that maybe there is some force in the universe looking out for me.

Or it's all just chaos and infinite randomness, and I just got really, really lucky.

The class was fun. Our teacher was Mr. Schroeder, a famous character around Crystal Falls High. Normally he taught physics, but he could probably teach any subject—except maybe gym, because of his limp. He looked like a mad scientist and would pace up and down the room, telling strange stories about the mysteries of science.

Mr. Schroeder also has a twin brother, I found out while getting groceries with my mother one time.

"Hey, Mr. Schroeder," I'd called to the person who looked absolutely identical to my biology teacher, even in the way he dressed. When I ran into him, he was crouched, examining the label on an orange-juice carton.

The man looked up at me in surprise. "Do I know you?" he asked irritably.

I immediately turned red. My own teacher didn't remember me? That was a new low. "I'm Callum Harris. From biology class?"

"Ah," the man said, frowning. "You have mistaken me for my brother. He is the one who teaches at the high school, not I."

"Oh, sorry."

But the man had already ended our conversation and returned to reading the orange-juice carton.

Luckily our Mr. Schroeder was a lot friendlier than his brother and could crack up the whole class with his bizarre jokes, sometimes disrupting the lesson for minutes at a time. So it was even more of a blow when the principal came in one day with an announcement:

"I'm afraid that Mr. Schroeder has left the staff indefinitely. Miss Fielding will be here momentarily to fill in for today. But starting Monday you will have a replacement teacher."

The whole room was in shock. "Why?" we demanded to know. "Where did he go?"

"That's none of your concern," the principal told us sternly. But seeing our alarmed faces, he softened a little. "Guys, Mr. Schroeder is fine. He has taken a leave of absence for personal reasons. Hopefully he'll be back at some point. But I can't say that for certain."

He never did come back. And we never found out the story behind his leaving. A rumor started that he'd gone crazy. A few students claimed to have seen him hanging around the bridge above the falls and gazing down for hours.

And then one day Bryce and I spotted him at Electronica Veronica, riffling through the wall of old electrical components and muttering to himself. At least we thought it was him, assuming his twin would have less of an interest in such things.

"Diodes, diodes, diodes," he was saying. "Where are

you hiding, my pesky little friends?"

One glimpse of the wild expression on his face and we got the hell out of there before he saw us.

Meanwhile, back at school, we got a new teacher, and the class became mostly boring again. Which meant I could turn my attention to Willow, who turned her attention to inking pretend tattoos on my hand during class until we were finally yelled at. Then we started passing notes and drawings and managed to never get caught again.

I think more about Willow and about the strange phone call. It was like she didn't know me at all. I decide to look for her messages, which she sends on the computer most days after school. We tried video chatting once, but the PC I inherited from my father is all old and screwed up and useless for anything but homework at this point. Dad promised to buy me a new one, but then I let down my part of the bargain by not coming through with the grades.

I press the Power button and sit back as the machine slowly chugs to life, making its cranky noises and flashing its little lights. When it's finally finished starting up, I type out my password and press Enter.

The password is rejected.

Hmm. Thinking I must have typed it wrong, I try again. Once again it's rejected. I press Caps Lock. No luck. I try an older password. And then another. And another. I try every combination of passwords I can remember using during my entire life. Each time I'm locked out.

I slap the side of the monitor in frustration. How am I going to get into this stupid thing?

I decide to pound out the most disgusting word I can think of on the keyboard, something I call Cole when I'm really mad.

And that's it—I'm in.

I'm still feeling weirded out when the desktop finally appears. There's another picture of a hot girl on it. This time she's posing on a red couch and wearing a ridiculous number of black pearl necklaces and not much else. It's the same girl who is up on the wall, I think, but it's hard to tell from the heavy makeup and wig she's got on.

I think I might recognize her—she's an actress, though I've never seen any of the movies she's in. Chick flicks, mostly, that even Willow won't watch.

I decide to snoop around the computer. I recognize folder names organized the way I've always done it. I look back at the homework and remember some of the topics from last year. But reading them, I don't remember working on any of these assignments.

Most of them seem hurried, which is my style, all right. Only I like using bigger words to help disguise my laziness, while this stuff is sparse and misspelled. A few recent assignments look like they took quite a lot of work, though, something I can't imagine doing.

I launch a web browser. Most of my bookmarks are

missing. But even stranger, there are sites in my history that I'm not interested in at all. There's a bunch of links related to sports, and football in particular—which like the collection of trophies makes no sense to me. I'm just not a sports guy. As far as I know, I stopped pretending to like football when Cole quit playing it.

Even back when I did go to games with Mom and Dad, I never knew much about the rules. Whistles would blow, and flags would get thrown, and I would groan or cheer along with the people around me. When Cole was off the field, I just looked at the cheerleaders, to be honest.

So why would I be visiting sports pages, which my browsing history shows someone compulsively doing on this computer? It scares me to admit: Maybe my memory is really fried.

I log in to check my messages, happy I don't need to enter a password. When they finally load, I can't believe the sheer number of them. The majority are from people at school. Most of them I don't know very well, and some of them I can't stand. But here they are, calling me *bro* and *dude*, writing on my wall and firing off private messages.

The weirdest thing of all is the number from Ivy. Why she would be messaging me is only slightly less mysterious than why she would be making out with me. But whatever the reason, she's messaged me ten times in the past couple of days alone. I quickly check out what she has to say. She's worried about me, is losing sleep, and is hoping I'll call her as soon as possible.

I surprise myself by clicking Reply. I type:

Don't worry about it. I'm home now. :-) Feeling weird still. Callum.

I send the message.

Most of the rest of the posts and messages are boring. Guys making jokes and swearing in all caps. None of what they're saying is funny or makes any sense to me.

A chat message pops up—a reply from Ivy. She's online.

Aww poor baby. Well, let me know if you're up for a house call. <3

The suggestion is exciting. I start replying but stop myself, deleting what I've entered. I'm not ready to start playing games. Dangerous ones. I need to figure out what's going on.

I decide not to answer.

Reading the rest of my messages, I try to make sense of things. Suddenly one sends a jolt through me. It's dated the day before I went over the falls.

And it's from Neil Parson.

Hey, Cal.

Listen, sorry, but I don't think I can help you out anymore. That was really too close with Mr. Phillips & I'm worried we're gonna get caught. I will give you your money back, including what you gave me for last week. OK? I'm really, really sorry. I hope you won't be mad. —Neil

Am I really seeing this? A message from a guy I just told the sheriff I have absolutely nothing to do with, who has since disappeared off the face of the earth?

I'm really, really sorry. I hope you won't be mad.

I scare myself with how fast I delete the message.

Outside my door I hear Jess coming upstairs. With all the weirdness, I completely forgot about her. Normally she stays pretty close beside me at the dinner table, hoping I'll toss her something I don't like. Maybe she was there tonight and I just didn't notice her.

I could use her affection right now—the comfort of an old friend who never asks questions. I open the bedroom door just as she's trotting by, on her way to the foot of my mother's bed, no doubt.

"Hey, Jess," I call.

I'm shocked as the dog bolts away from me, her ears back.

"Jess!" I shout after her angrily. "Come!"

But she ignores me. I can't believe it. I trained that dog myself and can usually stop her dead in her tracks with a single command.

I should give her a whack on the snout for it. Because she can't disobey me like that, living near a busy road where cars blow by at sixty miles per hour. If she runs after one chipmunk, she could be killed. But there is something in her look that stops me from doing it. She seems terrified of me. And that is just wrong.

I close the door again. I've had enough. I shut down the computer and get into bed, still wearing my clothes. At least my flannel sheets are the same. They have moose on them and pine trees. They're so stupid, they're cool. And they feel very cozy.

I pull up the covers around my neck and eventually fall asleep.

....

The next morning I wake up to a knock. My mother pokes her head through the doorway.

"Are you feeling up to eating something?" she asks.

Actually I'm starving. I feel like I haven't eaten in days, and my Harris nose smells bacon frying downstairs.

"Yeah," I say, salivating. "I'll be down in a minute."

Feeling gross and overheated, I throw back the covers. It was a mistake not undressing last night before getting into bed. But at least I don't have to bother putting on any clothes now.

I get up. I feel a bit better, even in my strange bedroom. But then, the brain is an amazing organ. I remember hearing in class once how they did an experiment where people wore these special glasses that turned everything upside down. They walked around completely disoriented. Then, after a few days, their brains simply turned the world right side up again.

The problem was, when the subjects removed the glasses, everything went back to being upside down. I remember at the time thinking that was funny, but now I can really relate to how scared they must have felt. Luckily for them, the effect wasn't permanent.

In my case I have no idea what's going on.

I head to the bathroom. There I find my toothbrush, which is the same color and always the most deformed one in the house, thanks to my hardcore brushing technique. I load up on the toothpaste and work at getting the terrible taste out of my mouth.

While brushing, I notice there are another three toothbrushes instead of the usual two, which is odd.

Finished in the bathroom, I head downstairs. Jess crosses my path at the bottom of the stairs. She stops and backs up to let me go by.

"Good morning, girl," I say cheerfully. "Come here...."

But the dog won't budge. Her ears go back again. This is ridiculous. I want to try to make her come, maybe scratch her neck for a while. But the smell of breakfast pulls me away.

Arriving in the kitchen, I get a surprise. Dad is still here. He's sitting at the table reading the newspaper. Just like old times, only I haven't seen this sight in two years now. And even more unexpected is the fact that he's in pajamas.

He must have slept here. . . .

"Hey, Cal," he says, putting down his coffee mug, a mutant-looking brown one I made him for Christmas when I was little. He's insisted it's his favorite ever since, and he even took it with him when he left. "Feeling better today?"

I stare at him like he's a visitor from another planet.

"Cal?" he says, shaking me out of it.

"Uh, yeah, sure. I had a decent sleep."

"Glad to hear it. Sit down and have something to eat."

As soon as I sit down, I chug my orange juice. I load up my plate with waffles and add four strips of bacon alongside them. Then I drench the whole lot in syrup and start wolfing it all down like someone who's been lost in the woods for a week.

"Well, your appetite is back, at least," my mother tells me. "That's a good sign."

I can't even reply, I have so much food in my mouth. My father offers me some coffee, and I nod. I top it off with milk and dump in three heaping teaspoons of sugar.

"So, about getting back to school," Mom says. "There's no hurry, the doctor says. He'll give you a note for as long as you need."

Actually I'd forgotten all about school. It's, what, Wednesday now? I think so. Considering how behind I was to start with, I'm pretty much screwed at this point. But at least I have a good excuse, for once.

Still, I find myself wanting to get back, if only to see how everybody will act toward me. From my messages it seems as if I'm Mr. Popularity or something. All just because I went over the falls and survived? If so, it's a social-climbing method I wouldn't recommend to others.

"I don't know. I can go back anytime," I tell my mother. "Today even," I add.

My parents look surprised. "Are you sure that's a good idea?" my father asks. "We were thinking you should stay home another week."

"I don't know. I feel like going," I say. And I'm feeling a lot better now that I have some food in my system. "I don't want to miss too many assignments."

"Well, let's consider today a write-off," Dad says. "But if you're still feeling up to it, maybe tomorrow. Deal?"

"Deal," I say, swigging from my coffee cup.

A few minutes go by as we continue eating. "Cal," my mother finally says, "your father and I were wondering if you remembered anything more about your accident."

"Not really. It's still pretty much fuzzy," I tell her.

"Are you sure?" my father asks. "Is there anything you want to tell us?"

"No. Why?"

"Well, you've seemed kind of withdrawn lately, for starters," Dad says. "Before the accident. Like you've been a bit depressed or something."

"Depressed?" I laugh. "No, not at all. What made you think that?"

"Come on, Cal," my mother says. "You've been coming home later and later, going straight up to your room without even saying hello. And when we do see you, we can hardly get a word out of you these days."

I laugh again, but this time uncomfortably, because as far as I'm concerned, I haven't been acting like that at all. If anything, that describes Cole—or at least the Cole I remember. "What are you talking about?"

"We just want to know if you're feeling depressed, Cal," my father says. "If you've had any thoughts about hurting yourself. Because if you have, we're here for you. And it's important to get you help."

Now I'm stunned. And scared. "What? No!" I reply, offended. "Look, just because I fell into the river doesn't mean I was trying to kill myself. Jeez!"

"Calm down. It was simply a question, not an accusation," my mother says.

"But try to kill myself? Why would I do that?" I demand angrily. "Believe me, I'm glad to be alive. Really glad. I'm not Uncle Bud, you know!"

My mother turns white at this remark. Her head drops,

and her mouth quivers.

"Cal!" my father shouts.

"Drop it, Don," she says, still looking down. "Just drop it."

I do feel bad for mentioning Uncle Bud like that, though; it was one of the hardest things my mother ever went through. "I'm sorry," I say. "I just don't like what you're saying. Look, I know I don't remember what happened, but I'm sure it wasn't anything like that. Okay?"

Mom just stares at the table, her eyes bright with tears.

"Okay, Cal," my father finally says.

Mom returns her attention to her breakfast, pushing the remains of a waffle around on her plate. My father breathes heavily and then goes back to reading his newspaper. An uncomfortable silence hangs over the table. I try to eat, but my stomach feels all sour.

I still can't get over Dad sitting here at the breakfast table. In his pajamas! I think back to the four toothbrushes—has he been staying over here or something? No, that couldn't be—Mom wouldn't let him. Would she?

He sips from the stupid-looking mug again. I'm sure I saw it hanging from a hook in the kitchen at his apartment. Did he bring the mug with him?

I look toward the kitchen door, where Jess is now standing. She's eyeing the food on the table but won't enter the room.

"Here, girl," I call to her.

Jess doesn't budge. So I hold out a piece of bacon. Her hungry gaze fixes on it, and her body twitches slightly. But she still won't come into the kitchen. I give the bacon a waggle. She cocks her head as if she's trying to figure out what kind of game I'm playing.

"Jess, come here," I say as sweetly as I can. "Come here."

The dog finally slopes into the room and sniffs the offering. She slowly leans in and takes it, reminding me of how a wild squirrel might snatch a crust of bread from a person's hand. She really is afraid of me now. Which is so unfair. Because except for a few light whacks that hurt me more than her, I've never done anything but love that dog since I was ten. But now she's acting like I've been beating her with a stick for her whole life.

"Good girl," I say as she retreats to the kitchen door-way. Only then does she start chewing, like she's ashamed to accept gifts from me.

I call it quits on breakfast. My stomach is still feeling gross, and the coffee has me buzzing on top of it all. I could use a shower and then a walk outside. I ask my parents if that's all right.

"Okay," my mother agrees, her voice still heavy. "But why not spend some time with your brother first? I'm sure he's missed you."

I look up at her. Missed me? He doesn't even seem to see me. It's horrible, but I can't believe it. I can't make any sort of connection between the wheezing bundle of bones upstairs and my brother. I just can't.

"Uh, sure," I feel obliged say, to make her feel happier. "I'll go up right now."

I head upstairs. But I can already feel myself going back on my promise. Because I don't want to see that guy again. I don't want to sit there, staring at the wavering eyes in that frozen face.

I can't.

So I sit down in the hall, my back pressed against the wall. I listen to the machine making its steady noise, the wheezy rise and fall of artificial breath.

That can't be my brother in there; it just can't be. The jock with attention deficit disorder, who couldn't even sit still until he was fifteen and medicated? But if he isn't Cole, who is he? I'm feeling the fear again, like a giant hand crushing my chest, making it impossible to breathe. Something has happened to me. Maybe I've lost my mind like Mr. Schroeder. Because I don't know what is real or what is a dream.

The dark splotches appearing on my jeans make me realize I'm crying. I try to be quiet. Because I don't want my parents to come looking for me to ask what's wrong. How could I ever explain? I don't know what's happened to me. All I know is that, unlike the experiment with those upside-down glasses, my brain isn't fixing anything, putting the world back to the way it was. Which means I'm here to stay. At least for now.

I just need time to think, to figure this all out. Because I don't want to go back to the hospital. I'm too afraid of what could happen to me there.

Just as I'm wiping the last of my tears on my sleeve, I hear my mother coming up the stairs. I have no choice—I get to my feet and quickly slip inside the guest room.

I stand facing the door. I can feel the presence behind me and imagine piercing eyes boring into my back. But I don't turn around. As soon as Mom hits the landing, I leave the room, closing the door behind me.

"Was he awake?" my mother asks me.

Awake? How can you tell?

"Yeah," I reply. "But he fell asleep," I add, hoping it sounds plausible.

My mother looks at me sadly. "Well, at least he saw you. He was wondering where you were, I'm sure. He knew something was wrong."

I don't know what to say. I shuffle uncomfortably. "I'd better get a shower," I finally say.

"Okay."

We head off to our separate rooms. Once alone, I get undressed and wrap the towel on the back of my door around my waist. Then I pick out some fresh clothes to bring with me. That's when I discover yet more weirdness.

The first thing is my underwear. They're all briefs. And I never wear briefs—I wear boxers.

I have a look at the jeans I just kicked off and am

surprised to see the knotted-up pair of briefs inside. They're skimpy—black with purple stripes. What the hell?

I search through the drawer and find a pair that are at least boxer briefs, like the ones I wore back from the hospital and something I actually remember wearing. Then I open the next drawer down, where I keep all my T-shirts. I don't recognize any of these either. I like plain tees, maybe a band shirt or two, but these are all from name-brand sports companies.

Then there's the next drawer down, where I keep my jeans. What's with all the sweats and track pants? As I remember I had one pair, and those were for gym class. But now they take up the whole drawer. But wait, that's right—now I'm supposed to be some kind of athlete.

I have to dig around to find a pair of jeans. Even these I don't recognize and would never wear—they'd make me look like a douche bag.

But I have no choice. Douche bag or not, I don't want to prance around Crystal Falls with my ass showing. So, along with the boxer briefs, I take the jeans and one of the few unbranded T-shirts I can find and head off to the bathroom.

I take a long, hot shower. I wash my hair, forgetting I've still got a bandage taped to the back of my head. Screw that—I'm done with Band-Aids. I pull it off. A small piece of red-stained tape falls into the bath and starts circling the drain, before—*poof*—it's gone, sucked in to be spat out God knows where. I drop the rest of the gory bandage on the edge of the bathtub.

The water stings a bit on the exposed wound, but otherwise it feels good just to soap up and rinse off. I stand there and let the water bounce off my face for a while, which is nice until the moment when I go to take a breath and inhale some water—and for a horrible second I feel right back there, in the depths of the river under the falls.

Jumping back, I slip and fall inside the tub. It hurts, but luckily I didn't hit my head.

"Cal!" It's my mother, pounding on the door. "Are you okay?"

"I'm all right!" I call back, over the running shower. "I just slipped."

I hear my mother shout something else, but I can't make out the words. I call out that I'm okay and get back up, my hip throbbing.

I finish rinsing and then turn off the water and get out.

After drying myself as best I can in the steamy bathroom, I get dressed. I carefully towel off my head some more and go back to my room to grab some socks and a hooded sweatshirt.

When I'm finally ready, I head downstairs. Dad is on the phone to work, sounding unhappy about something and saying he'll be in shortly. He smiles at me though. I point to the front door, and he gives me the thumbs-up.

I put on a jacket and some running shoes and then head out into this new, uncertain world.

CHAPTER 9

I stand at the bottom of the drive for a while, trying to figure out which way to go. Maybe it doesn't matter. The walk into town is pretty far, and I'm still feeling stiff and sore—a short stroll is what I need.

I pass Edwina's house, setting off her dogs in a barking fit. A few minutes later, I come to a fork in the road ahead, where a sign points the way to the campground and trailer park.

The road up to the campground is where I usually take Jess for walks. There's a big, empty field up there where she can chase balls and sticks without me having to worry about her getting run over. And if she takes a dump, I don't usually have to pick it up, which is a bonus.

Even without the dog, I need to be careful and stick to the shoulder while on the main road. The last thing I need right now is to get hit by a car. But I do begin wondering if such an impact might put the world back, at least.

I turn off toward the campground. Traffic along here is light this time of year, and the road is pretty bumpy, which slows people down.

Since nothing's coming, I walk right down the middle of the road. I'm enjoying the day, which, though colder than expected, is otherwise sunny and bright.

It feels good to be alone.

I draw up alongside the field, where I usually let Jess off the leash. The grass is really tall. Which is strange, because the campground operators usually take pretty good care of it. At the moment the field looks like it hasn't been mowed in months. I doubt Jess could even find a ball if I tossed one out there. Which is funny, because I clearly remember having a big marathon session with her here last week.

I head along to where the park's reception office is supposed to come into view. Here, I'm stopped right in my tracks.

Because it's gone. Vanished. Instead of the big log cabin, there's nothing but a bunch of trees and some tangled brush. It's like the place never existed.

Just beyond the trees, I see an old trailer propped on cinder blocks. On the other side of the road, an old beat-up pickup sits on a square of mud exactly where I remember there was a lame painted replica of Crystal Falls.

The big, wooden gate at the entrance is gone too. There's now just a length of rope blocking the road, strung between what look like two broom handles.

I don't know what to make of this, but it's freaking me out. I feel like I should run away, but curiosity gets the better of me. As I approach, I can now make out the actual campground itself. The whole site looks neglected, with overflowing garbage cans and plastic bags blown into the trees. At least three-quarters of the rental trailers are missing, and I can't see a single tent anywhere. The tennis courts, the miniputt, they're gone!

The transformation is so disturbing that I just want to get out of there. After one last look, I begin heading back.

I'm stopped by a shout: "Hey, where do you think you're going?" I turn around and see a man in a plaid shirt who is climbing down from the trailer.

"Come back here!" he yells after me.

For a second I consider making a break for it. The guy looks old; even feeling stiff and sore, I figure I could probably outrun him. But I'm not a criminal. So why start acting like one? Besides, he could easily catch me in his truck if he really wanted to.

So I start walking back.

On closer inspection I see he's not a stranger. It's Mr. Guise, the park owner. I don't know him personally, but I know his face from around town. With business brisk at the Crystal Falls Campground, he's usually well dressed and driving a flashy new four-by-four.

But now he looks terrible, his clothes filthy and his face red and flecked with broken blood vessels. And he's been drinking, I see, as he staggers up the road.

"Hello," I say when he reaches me. "Nice day, huh?"

But he isn't here for a pleasant exchange. "Well, well, well," he says, spitting in the dirt. "Where do you think you're headed?"

"Home," I tell him, not that it's any of his business.

"Oh, really?" he says, sneering. "You didn't just see my truck and decide to hightail it?"

The man's breath is really bad. "Pardon me?" I say, taking a step back, out of range.

Mr. Guise screws up his ravaged features. *"Pardon me?"* he rasps in what I think is supposed to be a girl's voice. *"Pardon me?"*

This can't be happening—the guy just won Citizen of the Year. "Listen, I'm sorry," I say, trying to remain as polite as possible. "But is there some sort of problem?"

"Pardon? Sorry? You've really found your manners today, haven't you, punk, coming onto my private property?"

All right, now I'm getting fed up. I'm feeling uncomfortable, being alone on the road with this guy. But still, I don't have to take crap from someone so drunk, he's swaying with every breeze.

"It's a public road," I tell him, although, to be honest, I have no idea about this. "I'm allowed to walk on it."

His bleary eyes go wide.

"Oh, you teenagers always know your rights, dontcha?" Mr. Guise cackles, giving me a glimpse of a jumble of stained and broken teeth. "Yeah, you're right—this is a public road. But everything on the other side of that rope is mine," he says, flipping a thumb backward.

"Okay. So?"

"So the only people allowed on the other side are my guests," Mr. Guise informs me. "And like I said, every guest owes me rental fees."

"Huh?" I reply. "Rental fees?"

The man explodes. "Yeah, rental fees!" he shouts at me. "For using my facilities. How many times are we going to go over this?"

Wiping spit from my face, I take a step back. "What are you talking about?" I ask. "I don't owe you anything."

"Oh no?" he says.

"No."

I really don't expect what happens next: Mr. Guise lunges for me. Grabbing me by the front of my sweatshirt, he yanks me toward him.

Eyes stinging from whiskey fumes, I feel totally helpless.

"Are you jerking my chain, son?" he demands, lips tight against those awful teeth. "Because if so, you'll be sorry for it!"

"Let go!" I yell at him, almost retching from the assault of his breath. "Let go of me!"

Surprisingly, he does, but unfortunately he does it with a violent shove. I'm sent sprawling, and I land flat on my back, the impact knocking the wind out of me.

Through stars like I'm a cartoon character, I see the man hover above me, jabbing the air with a finger.

"You spoiled little jerks think you can use my property and get away with it?" he shouts. "That you can sneak in here at night and have parties or whatever you please? Well, you made a deal. And either you pay up or I'm getting the law involved. Do you hear me?"

Still lying on the road, I flinch as the park owner unleashes a kick at my face. But he stops midway, sending up a cloud of dirt and rocks instead. Half blind and sputtering, I can hear him laughing at me. I scramble to my feet and take off.

"Run, little boy!" Mr. Guise calls after me. "Run back to your mama!"

I don't stop until I hit the main road. By then I am completely out of breath. I know I'm not the fittest guy in the world to begin with, but both the accident and the stint in the hospital seem to have really taken it out of me. My lungs are burning, and I can't get enough air. I try and try, but it feels like I've got a plastic bag over my head.

My vision begins darkening, and I know I'm going down.

I'm in the black place again, where I was stuck after I went over the falls. And I've missed being here, I find. Everything is quiet, and there is nothing to worry about. I feel like maybe this time I could happily stay forever.

A loud noise startles me. It's a car horn, blowing hard.

My eyes open, and I look up. Crying out, I roll onto the shoulder of the road. A set of tires whooshes by, no more than a foot from my head.

The driver doesn't stop, though, or even slow down. How long was I lying in the road? Because that was too close a call to even consider.

The memory of my abuse at the hands of Mr. Guise returns, making me feel humiliated. That filthy drunk. I start fantasizing about coming back for him with the gun. I imagine myself jamming the weapon under his chin before knocking him to the ground.

He would deserve it.

I start heading home. I make only about a minute's progress before there's more honking, this time behind me. Jumping in fright, I almost dive into the bushes to get out of the way.

In a cloud of dust, the car—a sporty little silver compact—comes screeching to a halt beside me. A tinted window rolls down. Ivy's grinning face appears. She's leaning over the passenger seat. I can see down her shirt, into a dark recess of cleavage.

"What, did I scare you?" she asks, laughing.

"Actually it's not funny," I tell her irritably. "I almost got run over a few minutes ago."

"That's because you're a total spaz, my friend."

"Ha-ha."

Annoyed as I am, I can remember how those bright

red lips felt the other night, working their soft magic on my face and neck. I'm shocked to realize that they were the first real kisses I've ever had in my whole life—other than the pecks from the uninterested girl during a game of spin the bottle years ago, the girl whose boobs I was also obliged to touch in a closet.

Ivy's mouth felt pretty different, all right.

"Get in, little boy," Ivy orders. "I'll give you a lift."

I don't know why, but I'm scared to get into her car. But standing here by the side of the road just looks stupid. So against my better instincts, I climb in.

Ivy's car is small but muscly—and brand-spanking-new, I can tell just from the way the leather seat squeaks as I sit down. The bass from the sound system plasters my jeans against my legs. From all the girlie trinkets hanging from the rearview mirror, I'm guessing this car is her full-time ride.

Come to think of it, I remember hearing that her parents were pretty rich. Her father is a dentist, if I'm right, and her mother is an interior designer or something like that.

Spinning her wheels in the dirt, Ivy peels out onto the road. Since she doesn't ask for directions, I assume she must know I live just up ahead. And at the speed she's driving, I'll be home in seconds.

"Cig?" she asks, shoving a pack in my face.

"No, thanks," I answer, disgusted, though I feel lame

somehow. "I quit," I tell her, even though the truth is, I never started.

"Cal Harris off cigarettes? Wow—good luck with that," she says. The remark surprises me, but she doesn't notice. She drops the pack back into the yawning purse wedged between the seats. "Actually I shouldn't smoke in the car anyway. Not until I put at least a thousand miles on it."

"Yeah," I reply, relieved. "It'll ruin the new-car smell."

She turns to me, removing her eyes from the hard bend we're now taking at high speed. "You know, you look handsome even with dirt on your face," she says.

Embarrassed, I wipe my face as Ivy turns her attention back to the road. My house is coming up. But Ivy doesn't slow down; instead she floors it.

"Um, that was my house," I tell her as it whips by.

"I know."

"So why didn't you stop?"

Ivy is now steering with an elbow. Flipping down the vanity mirror, she doesn't answer but instead starts reapplying her lipstick. Her front tire misses a chipmunk by inches.

"Hello?" I say.

"Listen, Cal, I know you're cute and all, but I didn't cut class just to drive you half a mile," she lectures.

"You're cutting class?" I ask. "For what?"

"Didn't you get my message asking if we were still on today?" Ivy asks.

"No," I answer. "I didn't even turn on the computer."

"I figured. You're just lucky I assumed you were waiting for me. You really need to get a new phone, like immediately."

Waiting for her? I don't know what Ivy's talking about. "Where are we going?"

"To take care of your little errand," she says. "It was today, wasn't it? Today or tomorrow, I couldn't remember."

"My errand?"

"Don't you remember? You asked for a lift last week."

"Oh," I reply. But I still have no idea what she's talking about. I feel like I'm living in another world, in someone else's body. My skin is tingling. My heart is racing.

But still, I don't want to ruin things. As scary as this ride is, I'm enjoying it. How often do I bomb around in a sports car with an amazing-looking girl?

And I like watching Ivy drive. With her seat way back, the girl's bare legs are completely outstretched, her calf muscles flexing every time she stomps the pedals—which, with her hell-bent driving style, is often.

"So you're coming Friday night?"

"Where?" I manage to get out, throat clenched as we barely make a turn.

"To Becca's house," she says. "Her parents are away, so she's having a party. It should be fun—she has a big house, man."

"I don't know." Having heard neither about this party

nor anyone named Becca, for that matter, I seriously doubt I'm invited.

"Well, you're dumb to miss it," she informs me. "Where else are you going to sell your stuff?"

Again, I'm not following. What stuff? The feeling of enjoyment is quickly evaporating. I feel stressed—I can't keep this up. Why don't I know what she's talking about?

At that moment I notice we're almost out of town. Where is the girl heading—to Waterford?

Holden Distillery comes into view, the old buildings looking brilliant white among the red and yellow leaves. According to my dad, the business has been continually operating from the same premises, making a world-renowned rye whiskey—a beverage of infinitely greater quality than the more popular corn-based bourbons.

Whatever. It just tastes like smoke and fire to me.

Even at this speed, I quickly spot my dad's van already sitting in the parking lot. I slump down in my seat.

Ivy brakes hard, signaling to turn. As I'm thrown forward, my head is almost chopped off by the seat belt.

"Whoa!" I shout. "Why are we stopping?"

Ivy looks at me like I've lost it. "Where else do you do your shopping, dude? Love the jeans, by the way—why don't you wear those more often?"

I don't understand. Okay, Holden Distillery does have a retail shop. But it's a whiskey shop, naturally, run by a horrible woman named Esther, who does not take kindly to underage boys hanging around the store, even a son of the master distiller himself.

"Do my shopping?" I repeat. "Ivy, they won't sell anything to us!"

"Thanks for pointing that out, Captain Obvious," she says, rolling up like she owns the joint. Hiding my face, I look around in horror as Ivy does a circuit of the parking lot before drawing up behind one of the outbuildings—an abandoned bunkhouse Dad says once accommodated migrant workers.

I breathe a sigh of relief. At least no one can see us from here.

"Go do your thing," Ivy says. "I'll stay here and keep your seat warm."

Okay, now she's got to be kidding me. But her smiling face, framed by shiny hair like a pair of black curtains, says otherwise.

"Ivy, I can't steal booze!"

"Ha-ha," she says, shoving me playfully toward the door.

"I'm serious!"

Ivy looks at me, suddenly concerned. "Cal, are you feeling okay? You're really acting weird."

"I'm fine," I tell her.

"I don't know. Are you sure you don't need a doctor or something? You were just in a horrible accident, remember. And you don't seem like yourself."

"I'm fine!" I insist.

"Okay, okay," Ivy replies. "It's just that you're being a little bit of a wimp."

The word feels like a knife in the ribs. "I am not a wimp!"

"Then go see your guy and get it over with!" she shouts back, before unexpectedly kissing me. "Just hurry—I have a math test after lunch."

I have to stop looking at Ivy—I can't think straight. On the one hand, I've never stolen anything in my whole life. But neither have I burned down country roads with a gorgeous girl—a habit I don't want to lose just yet.

It's ridiculous, but I can feel myself bending to the pressure of not wanting to look like a chicken.

"All right," I say. "Wait here."

Getting out of the car, I'm wondering what I can pull off. Maybe lifting a single bottle isn't that hard, after all. I could go visit Dad in his office for a few minutes and, if I'm lucky, see a bottle I could slip into my sweatshirt on the way out.

But come on. I can't steal from my father's work. First, I could get in trouble—a world of it. And who knows, maybe Dad could even get fired over it.

The second possibility makes me surprisingly excited. But what good would that do? It's not like we'd be magically transported back to our life before Crystal Falls, when we were one big happy family.

No, I can't take the risk. But maybe I can make it look like I tried; that should be enough to impress Ivy. I can always tell her they installed new security cameras, and it was impossible.

I make my way across the parking lot. Then I crouch down on the curb at an empty parking spot near the building entrance. I just need to wait a few minutes. Then I can head back and tell her it was a bust.

I hear a low whistle. Looking down the length of cars, I see a figure in overalls standing on the grass. Pinching a cigarette between thumb and forefinger, he whistles again, clearly at me.

I recognize him now. It's Ross Marshall, who works in the warehouse. I know him because he did some renovation work at our house.

I stand up, wave, and smile. Except he doesn't smile back. In fact, he looks downright furious. And he's impatiently motioning for me to come over.

I can't help but cringe, remembering how things went with the park owner. At least I'm pretty sure Ross isn't drunk, despite the thousands of gallons of liquor at his fingertips every moment of the day. But he's still a big dude, and I don't like the idea of being on his bad side.

Just then there's a roar as a shiny black Mercedes comes bombing into the lot and then barreling straight into the space where I'm standing. Perfect—I'm in Blake Holden's personal parking spot! I leap out of the way onto the grass.

The owner of Holden Distillery gets out of his car wearing a suit and tie, along with a face full of suspicion and disgust. At first I wonder if he's mistaking me for Cole, who beat the hell out of his son. But then I remember the fact I'm still trying to swallow: that Cole was paralyzed long before that event could have unfolded.

"Hi, Mr. Holden," I say politely. "I'm Callum, Donald Harris's son."

The introduction doesn't put so much as a chip in the ice. Holden's eyes bore into me before he speaks. "Yes," he replies, looking down his nose at me. "And you play for the Crocodiles—running around catching the ball my son throws."

I have no response, because I have no memory of this. Holden turns away, calling to Ross. "Mr. Marshall," he says, looking at his watch. "You're taking a break already?"

"I was walking back from the offices," Ross says, suddenly looking much less frightening. "I just stopped when I saw the kid loitering around the parking lot."

Ross sounds like the liars at school explaining why they don't have their history projects finished. And like all liars, he's quick to change the subject.

"How was the trip to Asia, Mr. H?"

"Long," Holden replies. "But worthwhile. The Japanese and the Koreans both love our whiskey, so we've got some big orders to fill," he says, holding up his briefcase.

"Booyah, sir. Outstanding."

I forgot about this particular quirk: the movie-like military lingo. When Ross was working at our house, he constantly bragged about having been a marine: "I was there, you know," he announced whenever I walked by him. "Not cooking eggs or washing sacks, but right there on the front line." Feeling obliged to stop and listen, I would then get treated to a detailed story that invariably ended with either a charred bunch of corpses or a detached head as its centerpiece.

He'd then laugh and laugh. None of his disgusting stories seemed funny to me then. But now, watching the self-described insurgent killer squirm in front of his portly civilian boss, I'm pretty amused for once.

"So Marlene tells me you're behind on installing the new shower room," Mr. Holden says unhappily. Marlene is Holden's wife—the mother of three pug-faced boys: Hunter, Gunner, and Chase. I used to wonder if the snobby couple might have a crack at making a Buck or a Moose to complete the set, but from the looks of things, they're done making little Holdens.

And it sounds like Ross hasn't drifted out of the weekend-renovation business. In fact, he's moved up to the boss's mansion. Nice work for someone who reversed the hot and the cold water taps in our kitchen.

"Yeah, sorry about that, Mr. H," he answers. "The tiles are on special order from Italy. So I haven't been around for a couple weeks."

"Oh?" Mr. Holden says, surprised. "Because my house-keeper says she saw you leaving on Sunday. . . ."

"Huh?" Ross says. "W-wait, that's right. I dropped by around thirteen-hundred hours to pick up a few tools—I'm working on another little renovation job in the mean-time."

Now I'm really enjoying this. I've seen better fibbers in the fifth grade.

"Well, let's get it done, Mr. Marshall. With all these overseas orders, the warehouse is going to get very busy shortly. And I want your best work. On both jobs."

Ross stands to attention. "Roger that, sir."

Mr. Holden eyes the man for a moment, then heads inside without so much as a glance at me.

"*Psst,*" I hear Ross hiss when Mr. Holden is finally gone.

I turn. "Hey, Ross," I say. "What's up?"

Instead of answering me, he glowers. His eyes dart back to the building's entrance—I guess to make sure Mr. Holden is inside.

Only then does he finally speak, using a low, angry voice.

"What are you doing here?" he demands.

"Just stopping by to say hi."

"I thought you were still in the hospital."

"I got out. Good behavior," I say, hoping to lighten things up.

"Well, you still should have called first! That was our arrangement. Hell, you can't just change the plan!"

I don't know what the guy is talking about. But that seems to be pretty much the norm lately. So I ask: "What arrangement?"

"What arrangement?" the guy repeats, trying to control his voice. "The arrangement, smart guy, that makes sure I don't get seen with you, copy? Now c'mon, let's move out. . . ."

With no idea of what's going on, I trail behind Ross as he heads around back, to the two warehouses. We stop at the heavy metal door to the first one.

"To be honest, I thought the only way you'd make it out of the hospital was when the funeral people came for you," he says.

"I guess I got lucky," I reply uncomfortably.

"Yeah," Ross mutters. "Or I got unlucky."

It doesn't sound like a joke. Facing yet another person who wishes me dead, I don't know what to say. And I sure don't know what I've done to offend the guy. As far as I know, he gets along well with my dad and was friendly enough to me when he was working on our house. But I do remember Mom saying he was a creep, though I didn't know why exactly.

Ross unlocks the door and enters the building without another word. I stand outside for a second, wondering what he wants me to do. Only when I hear my name hissed from inside do I head in after him.

The fumes are unbelievable in the warehouse, like they're keeping a swimming pool full of whiskey in here. It's spillage, I guess, from years of broken bottles. My nose is instantly on fire, and it feels like my sinuses are filling with molten lava. Tearing up, I can't see anything for a moment. When my eyes finally clear, Ross is nowhere in sight.

I carefully tread down the hall until I come to a break room lit by a dust-encrusted lightbulb dangling from a cord in the ceiling. There's a table covered in coffee-cup rings, with a half-eaten sandwich sitting on some paper in the middle. But no other signs of life.

Just then a memory comes back to me—a really vivid one, set off by the reek of whiskey, I think. Apparently smell is the sense linked most closely to memory, my father once told me. And it must be true, because I am instantly right back there.

I was twelve years old at the time. Dad was bringing Cole and me on a tour of the distillery. I remember the same thing happening to me that time as we entered this building, my nose burning and eyes streaming. I begged to leave, but my father ignored me, keen to show us the stacks of final product ready to be shipped to drinkers around the world.

Before we left, we stopped off here, in this same room. Inside was an old man with a red face; he was sipping from a steaming thermos cup. Across from him a younger guy was busy leafing through a magazine. Before the younger guy slapped it closed, I caught sight of the most enormous breasts I'd ever seen in my life.

"I'd like you to meet my sons, Cole and Callum," my father said to the two men. "Guys, this is Ross," he said, pointing to the embarrassed-looking younger guy. "And this here is Dutch."

Wait a second. Dutch. That's the guy the sheriff said went over the waterfall. I did really meet him. Here, with my dad.

"All right, stop farting around and let's go," Ross says, startling me. Under his burly arm, he's carrying a case of Holden's Own.

But I don't move. "Hey, does that old guy still work here?" I ask.

"What old guy?"

"His name is Dutch or something," I say, as if uncertain. "Yeah, I'm pretty sure it was Dutch."

"Dutch?" he repeats. "Is he a Làtino guy?"

His name is Dutch, dumbass. What do you think?

"No," I answer.

"Well, then he probably doesn't work in the warehouse," he says. "Now where'd you park? Behind the old bunkhouse? Come on."

Ross heads for the door and opens it. Stepping outside, he stops me with a raised hand. As I lurk in the hallway, he pulls a pack of cigarettes and a lighter out of a shirt pocket, then somehow lights up, all with the same hand.

Hearing a raised voice, I freeze.

"Yeah, you first!" Ross shouts back at the person, before wedging the door open with the case. Standing in a cloud of blue smoke, he continues puffing away for a minute. I'm trapped now, choking on two smells I really can't stand.

"All right—it's clear," Ross finally tells me, snatching up the case again. "Gimme a sixty count and then get on my six."

"Okay," I answer. I'm assuming he wants me to wait for minute and then follow him.

But Ross doesn't go. "Wait," he says. "When you said Dutch, did you mean Drunk Dutch?"

"Maybe."

"The guy who went over the falls, just like you?"

"Yeah! So you know who I'm talking about. . . ."

"Sure, who wouldn't? But I never met the guy. Because, unlike you, he drowned. It was before I started working here, while I was still overseas, doing my tour with the Marines. . . ."

Uh-oh. I can tell that Ross is tempted to start relaying some heroic anecdote about himself. But he stops. "Why are you asking about Dutch?"

I'm stumped to come up with an answer; even I'm a worse liar than a fifth grader. "No reason."

"Hold on. I saw you looking in the break room. Did you just see the old bastard's ghost kicking around in there?" he asks, pointing inside.

"What? No!"

"Or wait—did you see him when you fell in the drink maybe?" Ross asks, eyes alight. "Was he down there at the bottom, all bony and gooey, hoping you'd come to rescue him?"

Is he making fun of me now? I can't tell. But I shake my head, feeling light-headed—unsure whether it's from the smoke, the fumes, or the image of a rotting corpse reaching for me.

"Well, that's too bad," Ross says, disappointed. "Because that would've been one helluva story." He looks around again. "All right, wait one minute," he orders. "And don't screw around this time—I want my share by next week." He closes the door in my face.

Great. It's dark in here. It's dark, I'm terrified, and I'm about to pass out. For some reason I start counting off to myself, like we're playing a game of hide-and-seek or something. But by twenty-two-Mississippi, I've had enough. I open the door and go out.

Ross is nowhere to be seen. I head off toward the old bunkhouse, hugging the edge of the parking lot and staying as far out of eyeshot of the main building as possible.

When I reach the car, I find the crate full of Holden's Own sitting by the car's back bumper. Inside, Ivy is stretched out, seat back, looking sound asleep. Her shirt is gaping open, giving me a glimpse of her black, lacy bra. I feel strangely furious, knowing Ross probably had himself a good look.

She jumps when I bang on the window.

"Another whole box?" she cries in disbelief after popping the trunk and letting me back in the car. "Nice one, Cal. Seriously, I don't know how you pull it off. . . ."

"To be honest," I answer, "I don't either."

She kisses me on the lips. She lingers, and I feel electricity course through my body as her tongue flicks around my mouth like a little lizard.

I'm the one who finally pulls away. "Now please drive," I beg her. "I want to get out of here."

CHAPTER 10

While we idle in the driveway outside my house, Ivy lays another kiss on me. But she's in a hurry now, shoving me out the door, worried she's going to be late for her math test.

Wiping off Ivy's greasy lipstick, I get out of the car. And I would have headed right inside were it not for the sound of the popping trunk.

The box of whiskey! I was hoping she'd keep it. But I guess I have no choice.

The effort of lifting the heavy box makes me grunt. Balancing it unsteadily on my knee, I slam the trunk closed. Ivy waves to me before backing out and screeching off, and I'm left standing in front of my house clutching a box that reads Holden's Own in bold, black lettering. There isn't a human being in Crystal Falls who would mistake it.

I look over to Edwina's. I have to get inside my house— quick. I still can't believe what I've done, stealing a dozen bottles of liquor from my father's work. And obviously I've got something going on with Ross, or he wouldn't have helped me. Not that he seemed happy about it.

Turning around, I notice that the red hatchback is

gone. I'm in luck—Mom must have gone out. I head up the path, glancing toward Edwina's place to make sure she doesn't see me with the whiskey.

Balancing the box on my knee again, I try the front door. It's locked. Checking my pockets, I discover I don't have my keys on me. Where are they, anyway? They probably fell out during the accident and ended up in the river.

But what now? I've got to hide this stuff. Not only that, it's cold and looks about to rain. With no cover over our front porch, I'm going to get soaked out here.

Then I remember how our family keeps a spare key hidden under a big, flat rock by the porch. Or at least we used to, at the house I knew.

I put the box down on the porch and have a look for it. I'm relieved to spot the exact same rock—a big, gray one with two white veins down its center. Prying it up, I find the key right where it's supposed to be.

Hallelujah. Within ten seconds I'm inside the house with the whiskey, rubbing my aching hands together.

Like a well-trained boy, I kick off my shoes. But then I notice how someone else didn't bother. Mud is tracked inside, right across the carpet. Mom will go nuts. Well, it wasn't me—it must have been Cole.

Wait—I forgot again. Cole isn't tracking anything in from anywhere.

The house is deathly quiet. "Hello?" I risk calling out as I hang my jacket on a free hook. If anyone is home, I'll have to stuff the box in the closet for now.

But there's no answer.

I head into the kitchen and open the basement door. The light's not on. Jess is not down there.

Heading upstairs, I notice that the mud trail continues to the second floor. I'm starting to feel uneasy, seeing the tracks lead to my room.

I put down the heavy box.

Taking a deep breath, I open the door. But there's nobody in the room, at least that I can see. I check the closet. Empty. I get down on all fours and check under the bed. Nothing but a few lost socks and some dust wads.

I remember the spot under my desk, where I used to hide from Cole when he was on a rampage. I kick out the swivel chair. But there's no one there either.

Maybe I'm imagining things, I think with relief. But there's still mud on my floor. Looking closely, I can even make out a clear sneaker print.

I go back into the hall and have another look around. There are faint mud tracks down the hall, I discover, stopping at the door of Cole's room.

I open it quietly and peek inside.

There's that figure again, the wasted body covered up in blankets. I freeze, watching the slow rise and fall of its birdlike chest. A length of tubing hangs out of its throat, running to the nearby machine that is doing all the breathing.

With the bed jacked like a monster truck, I can see there's no one hiding underneath. I walk in. Fist raised, I check out the closet. There are sheets, a few blankets, and some medical supplies, but otherwise nothing of interest. And definitely no one hiding inside. Checking out the floor, I find no more mud.

No one's here, I'm certain. My shoulders relax.

That's when I hear a strange noise.

It's coming from behind me—a sort of gargling sound. The figure in the bed is calling out to me, I know. I don't want to turn around. I don't want to go over. But I feel like I have no choice.

The noise stops as I approach the bedside. The person wears my brother's face. I stare into familiar green eyes, now regarding me with eerie stillness. And I keep staring, thinking about life with my brother, and all the things that have happened to us since we arrived in Crystal Falls.

The eyes seem to never blink but just look at me.

You're not my brother, I think.

It's a terrible thought. But it's true. I know this because now I remember the last moment I saw him. It wasn't even a week ago. I was dangling above the roaring blackness, and Cole was there, holding on to me by my wrist. He held on with all his might, promising over and over to never let me go.

But I was too slippery. He couldn't help it. He couldn't hold on.

"I'm sorry," I say now, to the unmoving figure. "I'm really sorry."

I watch as tears spill from the staring eyes.

....

I remember the whiskey.

I rush out into the hall, where the box still sits. Grunting with the effort, I hoist it up and bring it into my room.

Where do I hide it?

Looking around, I decide that the only possible option is my closet. Unfortunately this requires some excavation. Once again I uncover strange things—hockey sticks and baseball mitts, balls, bats, and hats of all varieties. None of them interest me.

I dump everything on my bedroom floor until there's a path to slide the box to the very back. Then I pile all the gear on top.

I look again at all the mud on the floor. Having no explanation for it, I don't want to even start discussing the matter with my mother. So I fetch the dustpan and broom and begin sweeping up all the crumbs of mud from the entranceway, the stairs, and finally my room.

I then get the mop and clean up what remains.

My timing couldn't have been closer, because my mother comes home literally a minute after I've gotten rid of the evidence. She catches me just as I'm coming out of the kitchen after returning the mop to the cupboard.

Jess is with her. Instead of greeting me, the dog runs straight into the living room as if being chased.

"Hi, Cal," Mom says. "I just needed to zip into town to pick up a prescription for your brother. I hope you weren't worried when I wasn't here."

I shrug. "I think I lost my key in the river," I mention. "So I had to use the one under the rock to get in."

"Oh, dear. I didn't think about that," she replies. "It was just a quick errand. . . ."

"It's fine."

"You're not mad at me?"

"Mad?" I repeat. "For what?"

"For leaving Cole alone. I know you don't like that."

"Oh."

"It's just that with you being in the hospital, we really relied on Edwina a lot last week, and I felt like I couldn't ask her again. But I made sure his tube was extra secure first, and there's the backup generator in case the power went off." The shame of leaving her paralyzed son alone shows on my mother's face. "I'm sorry, Cal. I know I should have waited until you got home. . . ."

"Mom, it's all right—honestly," I tell her.

Fortunately the phone rings. Mom runs off to answer it. Relieved to escape, I start heading back upstairs.

"Hello?" I hear her say. "Oh, Coach Keller!" she exclaims brightly.

I stop on the stairs. Coach Keller? What does the

guy want this time?

"No, Cal's doing much better. In fact, he's just come back from a walk. Would you like to speak to him?"

No, no, no.

She calls out for me.

Cursing, I head downstairs again. Taking the phone like it's a live hand grenade, I speak: "Hello?"

"Cal!" the voice of my gym teacher buzzes in my ear. "How's it hanging?"

How's it *hanging*? I really can't stand talking to this guy.

"It's Callum, actually," I correct. "Only Cole is allowed to call me Cal," I explain.

Whoops—my mother overhears this. Out of the corner of my eye, I see her shoot me a disturbed look. But then something hits me: If I'm so sure that the Cole upstairs isn't my brother, who is she supposed to be?

Keller interrupts the thought. "Er, all right," he says. "Whatever you say, bud."

The dead air remains between us for easily ten seconds as I turn and watch Mom tidying the kitchen counter. Except for the weird old clothes she wears now, she doesn't seem that different.

"I hear you went for a walk," Coach Keller continues. "That's great. Keep that body moving. So when do you think you're coming back to school?"

"I don't know. Maybe tomorrow," I tell him flatly.

"Tomorrow? Wow, now that's terrific news! Listen, I don't want to pressure you, but the sooner you're back, the better. We need you, son. You know that. The school needs you."

The school needs me? What is he talking about?

"And the team's pulling for you, hoping you'll make the next game. Do you think you will?"

The game? He means football, obviously. Why does he care?

"Um, I don't know," I answer. "Maybe."

I don't know why I say this. The truth is I haven't been to a Crocodiles game since Cole got thrown off the team. Why would I want to freeze my ass off cheering for the second-to-worst team in the league?

"Just maybe?" Keller asks.

"Probably," I lie. "Listen, I need to go. But thanks for calling, Mr. Keller."

"Coach Keller," he corrects.

"Coach Keller—sorry. Good-bye."

"Good-bye, son. Keep that body moving!"

Hanging up the phone, a weird notion hits me. Was Keller asking if I would go to the game or *play* in the game?

"Are you sure that's a good idea?" my mother asks.

"What?"

"Cal, you've just suffered a serious head injury," she reminds me. "I know you made a commitment. But you're not going anywhere near that field until the doctor says it's safe."

"Okay, okay," I answer impatiently. It's not like I want anything to do with the football team anyway. I just want to know: Why is Coach Keller calling me? What does he think I am exactly?

I head upstairs to check if I have any messages. Waiting for the computer to boot, I find myself staring at one of the trophies on the top of my shelves. It's gold painted, and it features a helmeted figure running with a football. I have to climb on the desk to get it down.

I look closely at the plaque beneath. *Callum Harris*, it's been engraved, *Rookie of the Year, 2011. Crystal Falls Crocodiles.*

I think again about what Mom just said: *You're not going anywhere near that field until the doctor says it's safe.*

I get a chill. Is that why the coach is calling? Because I don't play football—that much I am sure about. I can barely catch a ball, and throwing one, well, that's even worse. Even Cole gave up on me, saying I was just pretending to be that uncoordinated to drive him nuts. But I honestly wasn't pretending. I just suck at football, like I suck at most team sports.

A quick poke around the equipment I've tossed back into my closet quickly turns up a pair of football cleats, still filthy with dried mud and grass. On the tongues the initials CH are traced in ballpoint. Weirder still, it looks more like my careful capitals than Cole's messy scrawl.

I try one on—it fits perfectly.

I turn up a worn old football, also with CH on it, this time written in black marker. What I don't find is a Crocodiles helmet or uniform or any sort of football pads. But then I remember how Cole's kit really stank and got kept in the garage.

Putting the shoes and the ball back, I close the closet door. Behind me, one of the ancient computer's drives makes a sound, presumably asking: *Hey, whatever happened to floppy disks? Why don't you use them anymore?*

My messages. I want to look at them again, to see if anything new has arrived.

That's when I notice my desk.

One of the drawers isn't properly closed. And I know for certain I shut this drawer, because it's the one that contains some pretty incriminating items: a roll of money and a gun.

I pull out the notebooks and lift the lid off the shoe box. And for some reason, I'm not even that surprised at what I find in there.

Nothing. Nothing at all.

CHAPTER 11

With twelve hundred students, Crystal Falls High is a big school, with kids coming from a number of towns nearby—the Bus People, as they're called. From the front, the concrete building looks pretty old and outdated, but inside, everything is brand-new thanks to a renovation the year before we arrived in Crystal Falls. Out back is the new library annex along with a large sports field surrounded by a running track and bleacher seating.

The school my mother pulls up in front of is just as depressing as I remember. Most days I would rather be anywhere but here. And as you might expect, this attitude isn't exactly helping my grades. I got away with a lot the first couple of years, but now that I'm a junior, the teachers are wise to my tricks. Suddenly I'm "not applying" myself enough, they're telling my parents. Suddenly I'm "barely skating along" and "on thin ice" and every other winter-related metaphor they can think of.

"Don't forget your lunch," my mother says. She's in a rush, because Dad is waiting at home with Cole, having promised not to leave for work until my mother returns.

She is still reluctant to ask more favors from Edwina and is worried about picking me up later.

"Seriously, I can make my own way back," I tell her again. "I could use some exercise."

"Well, I guess it's fine. But I don't want you lifting weights, all right?"

Lifting weights? That's about as hard for me to believe as being Rookie of the Year. But Mom is serious.

"I promise," I assure her. "No weight lifting. And no trapeze either."

"Very funny. Remind Coach Keller that you're not allowed to do anything strenuous. Doctor's orders."

"Okay," I answer. I'm wishing I had a doctor's note though. Then I could just head straight to the library instead of to gym to be excused. But do I really need a note? It's not like anyone's going to doubt my story.

In fact, I've learned that my miraculous survival made the news all over the country. For the first few days afterward, our home was swamped with phone calls from newspapers and TV stations. My parents declined all interviews. And soon after I woke up, the world moved on from the boy who went over the waterfall.

Yup. The world moved on, all right. It moved on so far from what I would call reality that it made me the star running back at Crystal Falls High. I confirmed the fact on the internet, in a year-old picture in the local paper's online edition of me getting a touchdown, with the caption: *Sophomore Star Callum Harris secures Saturday's victory against the Burnside Hawks.*

I couldn't see my face, which was hidden under a helmet. But the article mentioned my name three times.

Well, I still can't believe it. Heck, I'm a guy who still can't even throw a football properly. And now I know for sure because I proved it to myself yesterday afternoon.

Hoping to get back on better terms, I decided to take Jess out to play fetch. Searching the garage, I'd been hoping for a tennis ball but could instead only find the chewed-up old football that Cole liked to throw for her. He could make that thing hang in the air for what felt like forever. Jess would race off in pursuit, barking and darting looks over her shoulder to be on target when it landed.

It was something I could never do. But I needed something to throw. So I took the football.

At first, Jess was reluctant to follow me, but she soon caught a whiff of all those great roadside scents, and we were off. Not wanting to run into Mr. Guise, I headed us in the opposite direction from the campground, up the road to the intersection where the Starlight Motel is located. This time of year, the motel is pretty quiet, I remembered, which meant there would be a nice open parking lot where we could play.

Unfortunately, when we got to the intersection, the Starlight Motel was gone—completely razed to the ground. Walking around, I could now only barely make out the outline of its foundation and the torn-out parking lot beside it. Even its neon sign, a local landmark, had vanished—along with the words NO VACANCY, which for six months a year were normally lit underneath.

Just standing there gave me an eerie feeling. But there was now plenty of room to throw a ball for Jess, without the worry of breaking a window or denting a car like before. So after letting the dog off the leash, I placed my hand carefully around the football, just like Cole had once shown me, my fingertips lined up behind the laces. Then I wound up.

"Go on, girl!" I shouted to Jess. "Fetch!"

It was pathetic. The football flew end over end as usual. Even Jess, who had so far been warming up to me on our walk, seemed ashamed by the display, trotting after the ball with little interest.

So I'm sure: Article or not, instead of magically turning into a football star, it's more likely I've magically turned out of one.

Now, walking up to the school, I'm still casting some sort of spell, it seems. Because people are sprinting up to me, asking me how I feel and what it was like going over the waterfall and being in a coma. I don't stop and barely answer, except to say I'm okay. But they keep grabbing on to me, asking questions and following like a pod of dolphins in my wake.

It makes me uncomfortable, all the fist bumps and

high fives I get inside on the way to my locker. Most of these people I don't even particularly know. I notice other kids, younger ones, scrambling out of my way like I might smack them or something.

This is not what I was expecting.

By the time I get to my locker, I've managed to shake off everyone, at least for the moment. Thankfully one of the keys I found in my desk opens the lock. Dumping my bag, I look for the copy of my schedule I keep taped inside the door. But in its place is a torn-out magazine page—a picture of that same woman who seems to be plastered on every surface available to me.

Once again I tear her off. The schedule is right underneath.

"Hey, what day is it?" I ask the little freshman staring at the crumpled poster at his feet.

The kid jumps. He turns and stares at me, clutching his books to his chest.

"Hello?" I say. "Do you know what day it is?"

"Thursday?" he answers uncertainly.

"I mean on the schedule," I explain.

The kid now looks like he's having some kind of fit. Is there something wrong with him? "Sorry!" he says, clearly terrified of me. "It's day two. Sorry!" Slamming his locker shut, he runs off down the hall, shooting a frightened look over his shoulder.

What was that about? I was just asking a question.

"Hi, Cal," says a voice behind me.

I turn around.

It's Ivy.

She looks amazing, wearing a leopard-print cardigan and a red scarf, with her hair tied back into a bun and a pair of large sunglasses perched on her nose. Like a Hollywood actress straight out of an old movie.

"Hi there," I answer. Her perfume washes over me. As sensitive as I am to most smells, I find myself wanting to drink whatever it is straight out of the bottle. "How are you?"

She steps in closer. "Me? I'm fine. But I'm not the one who went over Crystal Falls. So the question is: How are you?"

"Okay, I guess." It takes all the effort in the world not to stare—she is so gorgeous. "I'm not supposed to lift any weights," I say, cringing immediately. But instead of laughing in my face, Ivy squeezes my biceps.

"Hmm, you *have* lost a lot of muscle," she says, frowning. "I guess being laid up in a hospital bed will do that to a guy." She leans forward, squeezing me against the locker. I can feel her body, soft and warm, for a few seconds before she pulls away.

"Did you decide about the party on Friday?" she asks. "You can't miss it. It will be great for business."

I don't know how to answer. "I'll try to make it," I say.

"Do better than try, Cal," she answers, sounding

slightly annoyed. She checks her watch. "Look, I have to go," she says hurriedly. "But I'll see you later, right?"

"Yeah," I reply.

"Great." She trots off at high speed.

I can't help myself: I stare at Ivy's swaying rear. That is, before I see Hunter Holden glaring at me from down the hall. I freeze, terrified, while Ivy walks straight into his open arms. He kisses her on the top of her head. They walk off, pressed together.

What the hell? She's still going out with him?

A slender, brown-haired girl dodges around them. It's Willow! And that's it—I forget all about Ivy and Hunter. Smiling, I try to catch Willow's eye, but she doesn't even register my presence as she passes. She continues on with a stack of books tucked under her arm.

"Willow!" I call after her. "Wait up!"

She turns with a confused expression—the way someone might look upon hearing their name announced over a loudspeaker at an airport.

I wave to her and feel a goofy smile stretch across my face. But she just stares back at me. I leave my locker open and jog up to her.

"Hey, how are you?" I ask.

"Um, fine," Willow replies, frozen, holding up her books almost in self-defense. "You?"

"Good, good." Already the conversation feels dead on arrival. "Listen, sorry about the other night," I say.

"Was it too late to call?"

"I guess not," she answers. Her eyes flit around the hallway, avoiding mine.

"It's just you got off the phone really quick. I thought maybe Elaine was pissed or something."

At this Willow's eyes widen. Her expression turns suspicious and angry. "How do you know my mother's name?"

I realize there have been a lot of disturbing things that have happened since my accident. Experiences I can't explain, like my best friend trying to kill me and everything having changed. And worst of all, being expected to believe that my brother hasn't left his bed for four years.

But even after these mind-bending events, the blow that completely breaks me is that Willow no longer even recognizes me as a friend.

Looking into her rigid face, I can feel a sob welling in my chest. But no, I can't cry at school. I have to get ahold of myself.

"What do you mean, how do I know?" I plead. "Willow, I know your mom. I've been over to your house a ton of times." From her startled reaction, I can see it isn't reassuring her and instead it's having the opposite effect: She's getting scared.

"Are you okay?" I ask.

"Just stay away from me," she says. Turning on her heel, she hurries off down the hall.

"Willow!" I call after her. "Wait!"

She doesn't stop.

"Harris!" a husky voice barks from behind, before I'm cracked one between the shoulder blades. The pain is incredible. Doubled over, I crane around, expecting to see someone standing over me with a shovel.

The person's hands are empty but are just as huge as shovels. It's Holt, a linebacker for the Crocodiles—a gigantic teenager who eats four cheeseburgers for lunch and whose tuft of curly hair, lack of neck, and dull animallike eyes always make me think of a buffalo. I normally stay well out of his way—just in case he accidentally crushes me into the lockers or steps on my foot.

"Hey, you really must've nearly died," the massive herd animal says.

"Huh?"

He nods after Willow. "Because you're even sniffing the mutts now."

My eyes blaze. Words fly out of my mouth before I can stop them.

"*What* did you say, fat-ass?"

Holt the Buffalo looks like he's been stuck with a cattle prod. He thrusts his huge face straight up to mine and reveals an unsettling line of tiny teeth.

"Hehehehe," the linebacker laughs, the sound rumbling up from the depths of his massive chest. "Good to have you back, little buddy," he says. "See you at the game. *Go, Crocodiles!*"

I watch in amazement as Holt lumbers off down the hall.

Just then the first bell rings. I'm going to be late for class if I don't get moving. I rush off to check my schedule. I have history—oh no. Grabbing the books I think I'll need, I slam the locker shut.

I arrive at room 106 out of breath.

"Mr. Harris," Mr. Potts announces as I enter. "How delightful to see you!"

The guy is a jerk. I can't tell whether he is being sarcastic or not.

"Sorry I'm late, Mr. Potts," I say, hoping I won't get a detention. Taking a seat, I feel everyone in the classroom staring at me.

"That's all right," Mr. Potts says, waving a hand. "After what you've been through, the fact that you're here at all is remarkable."

So Potts is being sincere, it seems. Usually he makes a personal mission of cutting me down. I don't know why; it's not like I act up in his class. I really think he just can't stand my face.

Today he looks fascinated with me though.

"So what happened exactly?" he asks.

"I'm really not sure. My memory is still kind of foggy."

"Really. It's not uncommon, though, with such traumatic experiences. Do you recall the sensation of actually going over the falls?"

"Yeah. That part I remember."

"Then what did it feel like?" Mr. Potts asks, leaning forward. "Details! Details!"

The teacher and class listen intently as I describe the experience, the horrible drop and the feeling of being helplessly tossed around the depths of the river. But when the discussion moves to what might have happened before, how I actually came to fall into the river, I feel increasingly uncomfortable. With still no concrete memories of the day before, it feels like I'm giving them a blank sheet they can fill in as they like. The sheriff is already convinced I did something to Neil Parson, and so is everyone on the hospital staff apparently. So why not the people in this room?

Some of them must think I'm lying, I decide, that I never even went over the falls. But why would I make up something like that?

To hide something, of course. But what?

I can see it making sense to people, that I hurt Neil and then swam out to the rocks to play dead. It would explain my life jacket, for sure.

But that's crazy. What if I hadn't been spotted? It's freezing in the river this time of year—I would never have made it back alive. Everyone must know that.

Thinking of Neil, I suddenly realize he was in Mr. Potts's class. I look over at his desk, which is now empty. I meet the eyes of another person:

Bryce.

He's across the room, sitting one back from the empty desk. And he hates me. It's written on his face.

But he's afraid, too—I can see from the way he drops my stare. Well, he should be. The more I think about Bryce, the angrier I'm getting. The guy tried to kill me! After all the lumps I took for him? Well, luckily he failed. But it means there's a score to settle between us.

With that thought, my eyes narrow at him, my once friend, my now would-be murderer. But he doesn't look back, glancing instead at the empty desk in front of him.

Mr. Potts looks up at the clock. We've wasted a chunk of the period, he sees. Thankfully the attention is taken off me as he finally begins the lesson. I've missed some reading assignments, but I'm off the hook for them, he informs me. So I just sit back and listen.

It's a nice change. I sure hope all my classes are like this.

I'm relieved when the bell finally rings and I can get out of the same room as Bryce. Fortunately the next class is biology, which we don't have together.

Mr. Gould—Schroeder's replacement from last year— is running late. I sit down in the last open seat, beside the anatomical dummy with its plaster organs out for all to see and only part of a face. The dummy's single eye, perched in its open socket, stares down at me.

I look around the room. That's when I notice Willow.

She's sitting right beside me. But her body is twisted away, and all I can see is the back of her neck and the pink crescent of an ear poking through her wild curls.

Whatever. I'm happy just to sit this close for a little while—close enough to detect the smell of her mother's incense sticks, like black licorice, which always clings to Willow's clothes.

Again I think about how much smell is linked with memory. That must be true. Because right now I'm remembering this past year with Willow: the long walks after school to my house; crossing the bridge to the south side, where we'd sometimes stop to watch the falls. And then later, sitting in my room, working on songs together, my fingers aching by the end of the session.

This all happened, I know it. And yet Willow is acting not only like she doesn't know me, but she can't even sit facing me.

Mr. Gould's monotonous voice washes over me as I steal glances at her for the rest of the lesson.

When the bell rings, I wait in my seat, watching everyone exit. Willow looks back at me. Her face is full of suspicion. I really screwed up somehow. Just by saying her mother's name? I don't understand.

"I would hurry up, Mr. Harris, or you'll miss your next class," Mr. Gould says, looking up.

"Yes, sir."

I hustle to my locker and check my schedule. My next class is gym.

I quickly grab my sneakers, shorts, and T-shirt, just

in case. As everybody knows failure to bring your gym uniform is an automatic detention. Even with such a spectacular medical excuse, I don't want to test Keller on this.

Then I head off, trailing just behind Manuel Rivera. He's a scrappy little dude who never fails to elbow me in the face no matter what the sport—he even got me through a badminton net once. "It's your big nose," he usually tells me as an apology. "It gets in the way."

Today he's a lot chummier though. Spotting me, he slows down. He offers a fist bump as I draw up alongside him, which I return awkwardly.

"Hey, Cal, what's up?" he asks. But before I can answer, he lowers his voice: "Yo, I heard you got your hands on some more stuff. Is that true?"

"Stuff?" I ask. "What stuff?"

"Keep it down," he warns me. "Some Holden's, man," he whispers. "Me and my buddies were hoping you could sell us a bottle."

He wants Holden's—the Holden's hidden in my closet. I don't like this. I don't like this at all.

"Uh-uh," I tell him, shaking my head.

"Really? That sucks—there's a big party this weekend we're gonna crash. Some chick's place."

"Sorry," I say flatly. "I don't have anything."

But the guy just won't leave it alone. "Hey, that's not fair, selling only to seniors. We can pay, man, whatever they're paying. . . ."

"Look, I'm not selling anything!" I tell him.

With my voice still echoing down the hall, Manuel drops the subject. But I'm still feeling uneasy. Does the whole school know I have a closetful of whiskey? Did Ivy tell everyone?

As I approach the gym, I hear the thud of basketballs. And, as usual, it sends a shudder through me. I hate basketball. And not just because of Manuel's elbows, which are a complete nightmare, but because I'm really bad at it. I'm not that tall, I can't jump, I can't dribble, and I sure as hell can't shoot. So except for randomly knocking the ball out of somebody's hands, I contribute pretty much zero to any team I'm put on. And it's a fact I'm always made aware of:

"Christ, Harris, get out of the way!"

"Pass the goddamn ball, Harris!"

"You suck, Harris!"

But hold on—Keller knows I'm supposed to go to the library, I remember. Mom told the school. No sports for me! And certainly no weight lifting, I laugh to myself.

When I don't spot Keller in the gym, I head to his office. He always waits a few minutes before making his big entrance, blowing his whistle like he's been trying to get our attention for the last half hour.

"Come on, you buncha monkeys!" he always yells. "What the hell are you all doing?"

Waiting for you, numb-nuts is the honest answer we can never give.

Keller is in there, all right, reading a magazine before making his appearance. "Harris!" he cheers when he sees me. "You're back already. Great to see you!"

"Thanks, Coach Keller." I still hate calling him "Coach." Because he's not my coach—he's just my phys-ed teacher. And that is already too much for me.

"So how's the head? You ready to get back at it?"

"Well, no, to be honest. I'm under doctor's orders to stay away from contact sports."

"Basketball?" he says, snickering. "Since when does Callum Harris consider basketball a contact sport?"

Since when? Ever since starting at Crystal Falls maybe, when I began spending most of every game skinning myself on the floor?

"Since the accident?" I say instead.

"You need to start working on the cardio, my man," Keller tells me. "Gotta get those lungs back. . . ."

I remind myself that he thinks I'm his star running back—the article I read online even included an interview with him, where he singled me out for securing the win. Well, tough, bucko, because shortly I'm quitting the team. I don't need to get my neck broken on top of everything.

"Well, maybe, but I'm supposed to avoid exerting myself completely," I tell him.

"Okay, okay. I'm not forcing you. The important thing is to get better as soon as possible. Take your time—but hurry up!" The gym teacher cackles, filling the room with his stale breath.

"Can you write me a note so I can go to the library?"

"The library?" he says, surprised. "Sure, sure. Good idea. That's a great place to catch up on some z's." He scribbles on a yellow pad and tears off a sheet with a flourish. "But when you feel up to it, try a few laps around the track at least. Remember, we need those legs!"

"Laps—gotcha." I'll agree to anything to get out of his sweat-stinking office.

The coach gets to his feet. With a slap on the spot where Holt nailed me, I'm sent on my way. Over the basketballs, I can already hear Keller shouting at the class as I head out into the hall.

"Ladies! Ladies! What are you doing? Knock it off and listen up!"

I couldn't be happier to put gym behind me as I escape into the hush of the hallway. And I waste no time heading to the library.

The most recent addition to the school, the library is accessed by means of a covered walkway, just after the office. With its big windows, the walkway always reminded me of something a giant hamster would run through. Here, though, the rodents keep tagging the Plexiglas with markers, so it's now a bit of a mess.

Just at its entrance is the music room. Hoping to catch a glimpse of Willow, I turn my head to peek in—and then walk straight into something really hard. I stagger backward, clutching my head.

The entrance to the walkway—it's gone. There's just a solid wall of cinder blocks where it used to be.

Rubbing the swelling above my eyebrow, I turn to the nearby fire exit. I push open the heavy door and step outside.

I can't believe my eyes. The library. It's gone too.

It's drizzling, but I continue on. Crossing a parking area, I head through the gate and onto the field as if in a dream. Unlike at the motel lot, here there isn't even an outline where the annex once stood. Instead there's a bunch of old trees obviously planted before I was even born.

There's a flash and some thunder. I look around the field, toward the woods that lines the north side. For a moment I see a hooded figure heading along the outside of the fence. It's the same figure, I'm sure, from the hospital parking lot, the same guy wearing the Crocodiles jacket.

"Hey!" I shout as loud as I can. "Hey!"

There's another flash and a really loud bang—a close strike that makes me jump. Looking again, I see the figure slipping into the woods.

Oh no, you don't, I think. Dropping my gym bag, I start running after him.

Sprinting across the damp field, I think of Keller's comment about my lungs. Well, they're back, all right, and burning in my chest like a couple of fireplace logs. But I don't care. I'm going to catch up to that guy, whoever he is. I'm going to pin him down and find out what's going on.

Even winded, I surprise myself at how fast I'm up and over the chain-link fence. Landing on the other side, I feel pretty amazingly agile. I spot fresh footprints and follow them into the woods. Not wanting to lose my quarry, I fall into the same stride, noticing that the prints are about the same size as my own. It becomes too hard to keep up though. I slow down, feeling like I'm going to throw up.

Eventually I have to stop, but it doesn't matter. With the drizzle, the trail is pretty clear in these muddy woods, even though the tracks occasionally get lost across bare rock and fallen leaves. Wherever they end up leading, I'm confident I can follow. And at this point, I'm committed.

Unfortunately I lose the tracks completely down by the river. Cursing, I head to the riverbank, hoping to pick them up there. But there's nothing. I keep walking, following the fast-flowing current. I look at it nervously, imagining falling in and being swept off to the long drop that even now I can still feel in the pit of my stomach.

I have no doubt how it would turn out this time.

Soon comes the steady boom of the falls themselves. Now cold and soaking, I'm suddenly gripped with fear. I want to turn back, to run away. But just then I spot them again: tracks from the same running shoes, this time on what appears to be a familiar-looking hiking trail.

There's no time to be scared. I need to keep going.

The trail ends at the edge of the falls themselves. Through the trees I catch sight of the footbridge. Someone is standing in the middle of it. Below, the water curling over the lip of the falls looks strangely dirty, like a storm has churned up the bottom of the river.

Okay, this is not how I imagined this confrontation: high atop what is now the most terrifying place in the world for me. But I need to find out who that guy is and what he's trying to do. So against every fiber of my being, I clamber up the wooden stairs to the bridge.

And sure enough I still see a figure there—it's just not the one I was expecting. Because it's Mr. Schroeder, my old biology teacher. In a heavy rain jacket like something a seaman might wear, he's making adjustments to some sort of metallic-looking cylinder. As I watch from the stairs, a red light suddenly begins flashing on the top end.

I'm stunned to see Mr. Schroeder drop the cylinder off the bridge into the water. The man produces another device, a little black box with a red light flashing on it, just like the cylinder. After watching it for a minute or so, he suddenly returns the device to his pocket and begins heading my way.

I head back to wait for him on more solid ground.

Mr. Schroeder looks at me quizzically as he thunders down the stairs with surprising speed. He was a teacher, so I'm expecting to catch some crap for skipping class. But I don't. Instead he darts a look over his shoulder and asks:

"How did you do that?"

I don't understand the question, but he doesn't seem particularly interested in my answer, turning to head off. I'm confused. Could this be Mr. Schroeder's twin brother who I met in the supermarket? He seemed the grumpy type.

"Wait—sir!" I call after him. The man stops and turns around.

"Yes. What is it?"

"Were you Mr. Schroeder, the teacher at Crystal Falls High?" This sounds weird, and the man's face shows it. "I mean, are you that Mr. Schroeder?"

"I am," he says.

"Hi. It's me, Callum Harris. You taught me biology."

"Oh, I remember you, Mr. Harris," he says. "I remember you as the most disruptive and uninterested student in the whole class, if not the entire school."

Now wait a second—that isn't fair. "What do you mean I wasn't interested?" I protest. "I got a ninety on almost every test you gave." Although I did flunk one, I'm ashamed to recall.

"Whatever you say, Mr. Harris. My congratulations on your past success." My former teacher turns again to go. This time I notice that his limp is completely gone.

"Wait! Mr. Schroeder!" I call out, stopping him again.

"Yes, Mr. Harris?" he responds, this time with a loud sigh.

"What were you doing?"

"What was I doing where?" he asks impatiently.

"On the bridge," I say, not that it could be any more obvious. "Just now. What did you just drop into the falls?"

Mr. Schroeder looks at me while the rain bounces off his jacket—and I am probably as wet and cold as when they pulled me out of the river. "It was a message," he tells me wearily, "saying I was on my way." He pulls out the little black box again, which now has a solid green light on it. "And according to this, the message was delivered."

CHAPTER 12

I make it back to school about a half hour later. I'm soaking wet, and my teeth are chattering. I really hope I didn't give myself hypothermia again, but I'm not feeling sleepy or weak or anything. And I'm not burning up and wanting to take off my clothes, which I heard is what happens just before you die.

I am feeling totally confused, though, by what I just saw: my old biology teacher dropping some weird device into the falls. And the whole thing about it being a message—if so, who was the message meant for?

I asked that very question at the time but never got an answer. Mr. Schroeder blew me off and headed down the trail.

I stood there for a few minutes, puzzling over what just happened. Mr. Schroeder remembered my name, at least, but he seemed to have me mixed up with some student who acted up in class. To be honest, I can't remember anyone behaving like that; he was a great teacher, and everyone pretty much hung on every word he said. Which, for Crystal Falls High, is amazing.

I also found it strange that he didn't even mention my accident, especially with us standing right there at the scene. Surely everyone in town had heard about my going over the falls.

Once Mr. Schroeder was gone, I remembered the hooded guy. But there was no way I could catch up to him now. I couldn't go out on the bridge, not even crawling on all fours. It was too intense.

So I headed back, this time along the marked trail, which came out on a road that eventually leads to the school. By then Mr. Schroeder was nowhere in sight.

Classes are still in session when I get back. Retrieving my dripping gym bag from behind the school, I hear the bell ring for lunch. This is perfect timing, because it means the front doors will be unlocked in a minute. Which is great, because I wasn't looking forward to having to use the intercom, which would have meant reporting to the office.

Making my way around the building, I look back at the field and the site of the now-vanished library. Once again I get the same awful feeling in the pit of my stomach as a memory returns to me.

It happened a couple of weeks ago. I had gone to the library annex after school, hoping to pick up a few books that I needed to complete a project on a mythological creature of my choice. I'd decided to go with Bigfoot, the reclusive monster Cole and I had spent hours hunting down in the woods near our old house. Assuming he lived off chips and chocolate bars, the litter we'd found suggested we were hot on his trail a number of times.

Of course, the assignment was due the next day, and as usual I had put off the research until the last possible moment. But within minutes I had my hands on two books—*Myths and Mysteries of the Natural World* and *Real-Life Monster Hunters*—which together seemed enough to add a few facts and plump up the bibliography section of my Bigfoot project.

Looking at the evidence, I had to admit to feeling more skeptical about the creature, but whatever—that wasn't as important as finishing my project. As far as I was concerned, Bigfoot existed, period. Heck, I'd even seen him working the kitchen in the local taco shack, if the teacher asked.

Unfortunately the librarian wouldn't let me check out the books until I paid my late fees, which were now closing in on ten bucks. Having blown everything I had at the cafeteria on pizza and two chocolate puddings, I began begging and pleading, promising to bring her the money the next day.

"I'm really sorry, Callum," the librarian said. "But I let you take out books before, when you had a fine, remember? And even those haven't been returned."

She had warned me; it was my own fault.

"Look, you can always work right here in the library," she added.

Glancing up at the clock, I confirmed there was nowhere near enough time to do a decent job. So I either had to make my peace with failure or scribble out some nonsense and hope for a D plus. Bigfoot is still a mystery, after all; I could pretty much make up my own theories.

But then there came a tap on my shoulder. Willow was behind me, fanning herself with a crisp ten-dollar bill:

"Wow, it's hot in here!" she declared. "I think I might need to strip off some layers."

So maybe her phrasing came off a little racier than she'd intended as she slapped the money on the counter. But the image of Willow throwing off clothes along with my gratitude proved too much. I was overcome. It was groveling time.

"What's wrong?" she asked worriedly, seeing my face go so red. "Callum, are you having some sort of allergy attack or something?"

Desperate, I made up some weird explanation. Willow laughed like I was crazy but thankfully didn't ask any more questions. I took out the books and polished off the assignment later at home. The effort got me a B, my best grade of the year—*a B for Bigfoot*, I remember thinking.

Entering the school, I become absolutely certain this happened. It's not a fantasy or something I dreamed up in my coma—it happened. I'm sure of it. Which must mean that, somewhere, the new library annex still exists. And wherever that is, Willow can't be far away—hopefully not looking any deeper into my story about the strange spores that come off library books.

The thought frustrates me. What does it matter? Because I'm not living there anymore, apparently. Now I live in a town where my old friends completely hate me, and the wrong people seem to love me. It feels like a very dangerous combination.

And unlike in the Crystal Falls I remember, I don't have a big brother to protect me anymore. Which means until I can get to the bottom of things, I need to start looking after myself. Whatever that takes. Because I'm getting sick of the way people treat me, the things they think. Sick of it!

"Ha-ha-ha," a kid cackles quietly to his friends as I pass on the way to my locker. They all turn, their eyes lighting up at the sight of my soaked clothes. "Did Harris go over the falls *again*?" the first kid says. "Or just piss himself?"

This is not the first time I've heard crap like this. Usually it's to my face. And each time I just ignore it or maybe say something back if I can think of anything smart, which I usually can't until five minutes later when it's too late.

But this time something snaps in me. I can almost hear it, my patience, breaking like a dried, old twig. And the next thing I know I've got ahold of the kid by his greasy brown hair and am slamming his head as hard as I can not once, not twice, but three times into a nearby locker.

The sound is incredible, stopping everyone in their tracks. Shocked, I let him go—but instantly regret it. The guy is a dangerous little prick, I now recognize, the toughest sophomore in the whole school. And he is surely about to come at me with fists flying. Being a year older and a couple of pounds heavier isn't going to help me much. I should have just kept on hammering.

But instead of retaliating, the kid falls down on the floor. "Come on, man!" he shrieks. "It was just a joke!" He's clutching his head: a picture painted in tears and snot. His friends step away, terrified, leaving the boy lying helpless at my feet. I'm free to abuse him as I please.

But he's not getting up. So I'm done here. I pick up my gym bag and continue down the hallway, kids pressing themselves against the lockers to get out of my way.

That's right: Move. Amped up on adrenaline, I feel ferocious—like a wild animal making little creatures scurry away. It's a strange feeling, both sickening and unsettling, yet somehow pleasurable at the same time.

Stranger still is the certainty that I won't have to pay a penalty for what I've just done. Because no one has shouted or called for a teacher. And no one is going to report me, I know. Because they're afraid of the consequences. Look at what happened to Little Mr. Big Mouth, and that was over a few words. Get me in actual trouble? I'd be scared, if I were them.

One of the frightened faces comes into focus. It's Willow. I don't know exactly what she saw, but she looks horrified.

I turn away and continue on to my locker.

....

If anyone missed me while I was off school property, no one says anything about it. Putting on a stale T-shirt I find at the bottom of my locker, I quickly eat some lunch, sitting soaked from the waist down.

Ivy is in the cafeteria sitting with Hunter, Ricky, and a bunch of other people from the jerk population. From time to time, she looks up at me and flashes a smile. I smile back—until Hunter catches us and gives me a murderous look.

Okay, it's time to stop playing that game in here.

And it's a good thing I'm quitting the football team first chance I get, I think. Other than Holt the Buffalo, it's not looking like I have that many friends on the team. Add that to all the bruisers on the other teams, who are ready to bring me down on the field? Er, no thanks, Coach.

I coast through the rest of the day, trying to avoid any interaction with other students. With my violent outburst in the hallway, it's a lot easier. I'm in a bad mood, everyone appears to have heard, and they don't want to test me.

When the bell rings, I don't linger. Getting my jacket, I slip out of the building, not even bothering to check my homework and bring home the necessary workbooks. This is how my brother used to leave, I remember—he just tossed a couple of random books into his bag and took off. And I have to admit: When it comes to leaving, not caring sure saves time.

Walking home, I'm on my own, feeling relieved to be out of school. My pants are dry, except in the crotch, which is beginning to chafe. No wonder I'm in a bad mood! I can't wait to get home. But it's a long walk, especially alone.

Reaching Main Street, I notice again how changed things are. The street is dirty and dingy, totally unlike the well-kept dining-and-shopping stretch that I remember swelling with tourists in the summer. The souvenir shops that sold Crystal Falls magnets and snow globes are gone, as is Electronica Veronica.

I think again about the time Bryce and I saw Mr. Schroeder shopping for components in the store—and then of the cylinder he dropped in the falls and the box with the lights on it. The two devices looked like they were assembled at home.

Well, I never saw Mr. Schroeder buy anything here, that's for sure. Peering through the dirty window, it looks like the store has been closed for years. The counter and cash register are covered in dust, and there are crumpled bags and empty boxes strewn on the floor. I'm pretty sure I can make out a dead rat in a distant corner, its neck snapped in a trap.

"Something interesting in there?" growls a voice behind me.

I know it's Ross, the warehouseman, before even turning around. He doesn't look like he's mellowed since we last saw each other. If anything, he seems even more pissed off.

"Nothing," I reply, stepping back defensively. "I was just wondering why the store is closed."

"Why is it closed?" Ross scoffs. "Why do you think? Because the whole town is going bankrupt."

"Huh?"

"Wake up, kid. If it weren't for Holden's, there'd be tumbleweeds blowing down the street. Now—"

"What do you mean?" I interrupt. I don't remember things being bad in Crystal Falls. In fact, I remember just the opposite. "What about all the tourism?"

"Tourism?" he says, scoffing. "Why would tourists ever come to this hellhole?"

"Why? I don't know. To go camping," I offer. "And hiking. And to look at the falls."

"To look at the falls?" Ross laughs. "Get real, Cal. No one's driving out to see a bunch of brown water falling over a cliff beside some eyesore of a town."

Brown water? What is he talking about? There's a reason they call it Crystal Falls, after all. But I remember how it looked earlier, when I saw Mr. Schroeder standing on the bridge.

"How long has the water been brown?"

"I don't know, a few years. Someone upriver is stirring up all the silt or dumping stuff or whatever. All I know is it went brown and stayed brown. And the town turned to shit with it."

"Oh."

"Anyway, enough of that." Ross shoves me up against the window. "What's this about you having photos?" he demands.

With my jacket balled up around the fist at my throat, it's hard to even get a word out. "What?" It's the best I can do.

"You texted me a minute ago saying you had 'hot pics' I'll definitely want to purchase." He twists my jacket some more, this time really choking me. "What are you talking about, Harris? What pictures?"

He releases me enough so that I can speak. "Huh? I have no idea!" I protest. "Look, I really don't know what you're talking about!"

"The hell you don't!" Ross shouts. "You just didn't bank on running into me downtown! Now tell me: What pictures are you talking about?"

"Ross, I don't have any pictures. I don't own a camera. And hey, I don't even have a cell phone right now, so whatever text you got wasn't from me!"

"No phone, oh, really?" Ross says. "Mind if I search you then?"

I do mind, actually, but this is not the time to be asserting my rights to privacy. "Whatever, man," I reply. "I don't care."

Ross spins me around and slams me up against the window. He pats me down like he's a cop and I'm some criminal he's nabbed. A couple of people pass by but don't even give us a second glance.

"See?" I say, when he's finished. "Nothing."

"The bag. Open the bag."

I take off my backpack and do exactly as he says, and then I stand there, getting awkward looks from passersby as Ross rifles through my stuff. I cringe, knowing I wouldn't want to feel around the crumb-filled depths of my schoolbag. But he doesn't stop until he's certain the phone isn't in there.

"All right, smart guy, who has your phone?" he demands.

"Nobody has my phone. Because I don't have one. I lost it going over the falls."

"You don't say?"

"Yes. And why do you think the text was from me anyway? Did someone write my name on it?"

"Of course not, moron. You know you never put your name on your messages."

I never put my name because I've never texted you, I think. "Then how do you know it was from me?"

"Because you're the only guy who calls me that,"

he says, glaring at me.

"Calls you what?" I ask.

"That name."

"What name?"

I wait. The man looks pretty unhappy before finally saying it out loud: "Floss."

Hearing this, I almost laugh—because I immediately think of "butt floss," something Cole and I used to call thongs and really small bikini bottoms. The day at the water park, one of us was constantly yelling: "Butt-floss alert! Butt-floss alert!"

But I don't laugh. Because laughing is only going to get me murdered. So I come up with something else: "That sounds like autocorrect for 'Ross,' dude." From his blank expression, I can tell he doesn't know what I'm talking about. "You know, when your phone changes the word it thinks you're spelling wrong? I'm sure it happens a lot. Honestly, I didn't text you."

It's a good excuse, I think, and very possibly the actual case. But Ross doesn't look like he's buying it. However, just at that moment, the sheriff starts walking up the street, eyeing us both intently.

"Yeah, so, good to see you're okay," Ross says, way too loud for a normal conversation. "But I gotta go. I'm still on shift at the distillery—just had to come into town for some supplies. All right, see ya, kid. Great you're up and around."

Ross heads off in the opposite direction from the sheriff, who has come to a complete halt and is watching us suspiciously from about twenty feet away. I decide to play things the only way I know how: with complete innocence. Nodding politely to the mustached cop, I continue on down Main Street. And even though I don't look back, I can feel his eyes on me.

I'm glad when the road bends, and I'm off Main and out of sight. Being on foot gives me a lot more time to see just how much the town has changed from my memory. It's true what Ross said—this is an ugly town now, with porches that badly need paint jobs, rusty cars on blocks, strewn garbage by the side of the road, and a pitted and cracked roadway that I follow all the way to the bridge.

When I get there, I see it again—the falls are brown, a curtain of falling sludge. I have to agree with Ross: Who on earth would go out of their way to see this disgusting view?

I stop on the bridge and stare out at what looks like the overflow from a giant sewer pipe. What happened to the crystal water that almost seemed to reflect the world back at you? I look for the lower observation deck. It's still there, but it appears uncared for, swallowed up by tree branches.

High above, the footbridge glints in the light. That's where it happened—where I fell and everything changed. Where everything was lost. Maybe I should head up there again and jump this time.

I stare at the water churning over the black rocks. I shudder, picturing my broken body among them. Just then I see something down there, bobbing up in the froth. It's blue and looks kind of like a piece of a sleeping bag. Tossed around for a moment, the unknown object disappears back into the foam.

I blink a few times. Did I really see that? Up ahead I notice a person standing at the river's edge, holding out a long pole and trying to hook something in the water.

It's Mr. Schroeder, I'm almost sure. Yes, there's the rain jacket and a flash of the same gray shoulder-length hair. Shivering in the breeze, I watch him for a while, but he doesn't seem to be having much luck. So I head across the bridge, back to the south side. Here the sidewalk soon runs out, and I'm hugging the shoulder, air sucked around me as each car passes.

I look back and see a pickup heading toward me. All of a sudden, I hear it accelerate. The truck is barreling down on me.

"Hey!" I shout. "Hey!"

I jump out of the way, but there's very little room against the wall of sheared rock by the side of the road. As I press up against it, the side mirror barely misses my head.

"Idiot!" I swear after the speeding vehicle. "Are you trying to kill me?"

That's when I glimpse the bumper sticker:

KEEP HONKING, I'M RELOADING!

Actually, I know that idiot. It's Ross. And I think he did just try to kill me.

....

"Cal, are you okay?" my mother asks as I come through the door. "You look as white as a sheet."

I can imagine. "I'm fine," I tell her. "I had a close call on the road."

"Oh no," she says. "Somebody speeding?"

"Yeah."

"I wish the sheriff would do something about it. Someone's going to get killed on that road someday."

Not likely, I think. He's too busy watching me.

I follow Mom into the kitchen. My heart is still pounding as I sit down at the table. But at least I'm warming up.

We're having dinner late, I find out, because Dad is catching up on some work. I bet he is. With Mr. Holden back from overseas, the whip will be getting cracked again. I've seen the way my father behaves around his boss a couple of times. It's embarrassing and nothing like the way he acts at home. Master distiller or not, he's just another employee, like that psycho Ross.

Mom's reading a magazine. There are frosted cupcakes on the cover. "Can I ask you a question?" I say. "Do you remember that guy from the distillery? The one who worked on our house for a while?"

"Sure, I remember. What about him?" she asks. But she doesn't use his name either. And I can tell by the clench of her jaw that she doesn't like talking about him.

I go on anyway. "Why did you say he was a creep that time at the supermarket?"

It was actually on the very same day I had mistaken Mr. Schroeder for his twin brother. She made the remark under her breath, when she spotted Ross in the parking lot. Mom didn't think I heard—and I didn't feel comfortable enough to ask. But I knew she'd already talked Dad out of hiring him again, and that it was an uncomfortable subject.

"Do we really have to talk about this?"

"I want to know what happened. What he did."

She sighs. "He made a pass at me, that's all," she says.

Whoa. Now I'm pissed. It's one thing to try to run me over—but that big oaf harassed my mother? I picture his face and imagine kicking it in.

"Calm down," she says, seeing my expression. "It happened only once, when you and your father were out of the house."

"What did you do?" I demand.

"Well, when he wouldn't take no for an answer, I just got in the car and left. What else could I do?"

"Call the police?"

"Cal, really."

"Christ," I mutter. "I'll kill him!"

"Don't even *think* of doing anything about it," she orders. "This stuff happens sometimes. And it was a while ago. So drop it. I don't want to make things at your father's workplace any harder."

Any harder? For a second I wonder what she's talking about. "Why? Because of Cole punching out Mr. Holden's son?" I ask.

My mother looks like I've thrown my plate at her. "Cal, is that supposed to be some kind of weird joke?"

What am I thinking? "Sorry," I say, feeling terrible. "I don't know why I said that. It was a dream I had last night. Never mind."

Mom goes quiet and begins poking around the fridge. Uncomfortable, I sit there for a moment, but when she still doesn't speak to me, I finally head upstairs. Passing by the door of the guest room, I stop and listen to the machine humming for a while—and to the awful breathing.

I retreat into the bathroom, locking the door. I stand there, looking at myself in the mirror before counting the same four toothbrushes over the sink. Which one is Cole's? I wonder. How often do they brush his teeth?

I look at my father's bathrobe, hanging from the back of the door. Maybe he never even left. Maybe he stayed to help care for Cole.

If so, are my parents even the same people? The question makes me uneasy. Because I don't know anymore. But then again I don't even know who I am.

I look at myself in the mirror. My face is the same. My eyes are still green, and my bottom teeth are still scrunched together. I still have the same Harris nose.

That's how I look, but that's not me.

I remember my father lecturing me that people are defined by the choices they make. At the time, I made a face, wondering if he'd pulled it line for line out of one of his cheesy self-help books. But after choosing to slam a kid's head into a locker over a few stupid words, I have to ask myself: Who am I?

I don't really know. As far as I remember, the only other choices I've made were unimportant. What to have for breakfast. What to have for lunch. Should I wear shorts or bring a jacket? Should I pick science or music or art?

But maybe that choice tells me something. For instance, I know I'm the guy too afraid to take a few lessons and switch to music, even though I wanted to and it would have meant seeing more of Willow. Why? Because I'm too scared to make mistakes out loud.

So instead I took art, where I can hide all my efforts under a blank piece of paper if I have to.

Because I'm a coward. That's what that choice meant.

Callum Harris is a coward.

I take a leak and head back to my room. Closing the door, I notice all the trophies stacked up on the shelves again. I stand there looking at them. They're mine, I need to start telling myself. They're all mine.

And why wouldn't they be? I went over the falls and survived. That's right, bitches. I went over Crystal Falls.

....

A little while later, there's a knock on my door.

"Are you hungry?" my mother asks, holding a grilled-cheese sandwich. "Dinner is going to be late."

"Yeah," I say. "Thanks."

She puts the plate on my bed and then turns to leave.

"Wait," I say, stopping her. "Look, I'm sorry about what I said before. It wasn't a joke. I don't know what it was. It just came out of my mouth."

"It's all right," my mother says. "You've been through a lot. I'm just worried about you."

"I'm fine," I assure her.

"Okay," she answers, then moves toward the door again. But I don't want her to go.

"Wait," I say. "I want to ask you something."

"What's up?"

It's harder than I expect. She's standing there looking at me.

"What's up, Cal?"

"What's going on with you and Dad?"

"What's going on with us?" she repeats, surprised. "What do you mean?"

"I mean, are you guys okay? That's all."

"Cal, you gave us a really big scare," she answers. "It was awful. We never imagined going through anything like that ever again. But everything turned out fine. We're relieved."

"No," I say. "I mean are the two of you okay—with each other?" I don't know how to ask this question, to find out if my father is sleeping here, living here. "With Dad here, in the house?"

Mom looks puzzled for a second. "Well, you know it's been hard these past few years as a family, caring for Cole, coping with what happened. But we're all right, I guess—the best we can be, under the circumstances. Why? Does it seem like something's wrong?"

"No," I say, although something is clearly wrong here, just not what I remember.

"Then why are you asking?"

"Are you still mad at Dad?" I ask. "For bringing us here?"

"Mad? Over what?"

"Well, everything was fine before he took that job. And then everything went bad."

Mom sits down on the bed, careful not to disturb the plate. She brushes strands of gray hair away from her cheeks; in the lamplight I suddenly see the creases of exhaustion that have taken over her face.

"Yeah, I was unhappy when I first found out. This town is so far away from the people I care about—my friends, my family. But what could I do? Tell your father he couldn't follow his dreams? I just hoped things would work out and that we would be all right.

"But after your brother's accident happened, none of it seemed to matter anymore. We'd already bought this house, and we really needed the extra money and benefits to properly care for your brother. So there was no choice anyway. We had to move."

"But you don't want to be here. In Crystal Falls."

"No," she admits. "No, I guess I don't. I just don't really think about it anymore."

"And you don't want to be with Dad anymore."

"Cal!" she says, shocked. "Why would you say something like that? I love your father."

I know she means it. I know she never stopped loving him. But I can't forget what Cole and I both lived through: the two years of bickering that broke them down. Once they started pulling apart, there was nothing that could bridge the gap. So when my father moved to the other side of town, finally putting a real-life gorge between them instead of an imaginary one, it wasn't much of a surprise to me.

But for my brother, it was a different story. He became even more moody and sullen. And then there was the whole football fiasco. Both events took a big toll on him— he never seemed the same after.

But none of that happened in this world, I remind

myself. What happened here was much, much worse. A tragedy that can't be undone.

"What if nothing had ever happened to Cole?" I ask. "Would you and Dad still be together?"

Mom sighs. "Oh, I don't know, Cal," she says. "All I know is that it happened, and that your father and I are partners. It's that simple. We can't afford to think about anything else now."

It all makes perfect sense. But I don't know what else to say. Because as hard as I try, I don't feel a part of it, this painful family history. Everything still feels like a dream to me, something I hope to wake up from at any moment. So even though I feel like I should be reaching out, hugging my mother or holding her hand, I just sit there.

Suddenly she turns, her eyes full of tears. "Is that why you did it?" she asks.

"Did what?" I ask.

She chokes up. She's having trouble speaking. "Tried to hurt yourself," she finally says.

So that's it. She still thinks I threw myself over the falls on purpose. That's why she's so upset—she thinks I'm just like her brother, Uncle Bud. "Listen, Mom," I say slowly. "I didn't jump, I swear. I would never . . ."

My mother won't let me continue.

"Your father and I know things have been hard these past few years, dear. We know you're angry and depressed. And that's why we tried to get you help. But instead of making an honest effort to help yourself, you were only ever interested in being disruptive and playing games."

This is ridiculous. "What did you expect?" I protest. "I was only eight years old when I lit that fire—I didn't even understand what was going on!"

"I'm not talking about the incident with the garage, Cal, and you know it. I'm talking about these past two years and your sessions with Dr. Morrison."

"Doctor who?"

Instantly my mother is furious. "See what I mean? You've been seeing the woman for two years, and you still treat it like a big joke. Well, she's very concerned about you. She thinks you blame yourself for what happened to Cole, and that you have been trying to be just like your brother ever since, to make up for what happened. And your father and I agree."

I want to explain how I haven't the slightest idea who this Dr. Morrison is—and that if there's one person I have no interest in acting like, it's Cole. Heck, where would I even start? But something tells me that interrupting my mother again is only going to bring on a complete melt-down.

"Do you even remember how much you used to hate sports?" she asks. "As a little boy, you hated them. You couldn't catch a ball, wouldn't even try. All that time you were so secretly talented. And we're so proud of everything you've accomplished in the last few years. So proud.

"But you're doing it for the wrong reasons, Cal. You should be doing it for yourself, not because you feel guilty about what happened to Cole. There was nothing you could do. Nothing. You know what your brother was like. He was fearless, a daredevil. He would have never listened to you.

"But all this other stuff—the violence, the drinking, the recklessness—it's not making you more like your brother. It's only hurting this family. And it has to stop. Otherwise you're going to end up in jail." My mother shudders. "Or worse . . ."

"Mom, seriously."

"Because I can't lose you, too, Cal!" she blurts out. "I just can't!" Tears pour down her cheeks. Strangely they remind me of the falls, seemingly unstoppable, until she finally retrieves a tissue from her sweater sleeve and wipes them away.

"Mom, I didn't try to kill myself," I tell her in a low voice. "I swear I didn't. I would never do that to you."

But the rest of what she said hangs in the air between us—that I'm causing our family to suffer even more than we already have. Except I can't remember this Dr. Morrison or anything else I did that was so bad. My mom's worried I'll end up in jail—or worse? It's insane!

But then again there was a gun in my desk and a roll of money. Where they are now I have no idea. But there's a crate of stolen whiskey in the closet, which I hid myself.

And today I even hurt someone, possibly badly, just because he had a big mouth. And the truth is, it felt good.

Who am I?

"Eat your sandwich," Mom reminds me. "It's going cold." She gets up and leaves the room without another word, closing the door behind her.

Soon after, I can hear her crying in her room.

CHAPTER 13

Dad has a meeting first thing Friday, so I get up early and offer to make my own way to school. My parents agree. I'm glad, because I don't think I could make small talk with Mom this morning or, worse, suffer a silent ride into town. Luckily it's a sunny day but cool outside. As I cross the bridge, a sharp wind makes my ears ache. I keep my eyes focused ahead.

It's a relief to reach the north side, to put the chasm behind me. Just then a flock of geese passes directly overhead, honking with delight as the geese continue their epic journey south.

If I had wings, I'd seriously consider joining them.

I should talk to Bryce today, I decide once the geese finally disappear behind the trees. As a normally gentle guy, he would need a pretty good reason to attack anyone, never mind his once best friend. And whatever that reason was, it would probably go a long way toward explaining what's been going on around here lately.

So, bad blood or not, I should at least try to get a few answers from him. I start thinking about an opener that might break the ice between a would-be victim and his almost-killer:

"Hey, buddy, whatcha been up to?"

Wrong.

"Hi, Bryce. I get the feeling you're mad at me."

Wrong.

"Yo, bro, about the whole pillow thing . . ."

Wrong, wrong, wrong.

I have yet to come up with anything better when the school comes into sight. Hearing the first bell, I realize I'm running late and have to jog the last block. My legs are feeling better, at least. The human body is an amazing machine, I have to admit, automatically repairing itself without any instructions or assistance. Unless it's really broken, that is. Unless things are really hopeless.

On that topic I've come to the conclusion that my brain is either permanently busted or totally fine. Either way, the world is not going back to how it was. So there's no point in worrying my parents or, worse, getting doctors involved. No, definitely no doctors. I keep getting horrible flashes of what brain surgery would be like: having my scalp peeled back and the top of my skull sawn off like a jack-o'-lantern; then a surgeon poking around the mess inside with sharp instruments. *Did you feel that? What do you see? What do you smell?* Er, no thank you. Until I start seeing fairies and unicorns, I'm going to pass.

Arriving at school, I don't run into Bryce, but it's not

like we'd have time to talk anyway. I quickly get my books for my first class and hurry to beat the second bell. I make it just in time. As I collapse into my seat, Ms. Lewis is already taking attendance.

"Bryce?"

There's no response. I look around for him; he's not in the room.

"Bryce Trimble," Ms. Lewis calls again, without looking up.

"He's probably home sick," a student chimes in.

"Yeah, he threw up in history class yesterday."

"Ewww . . ."

There's some snickering before Ms. Lewis orders the class to settle down. I understand now: Bryce must have gone home with a migraine. He gets a lot of them, and they're brutal and come on suddenly. But that's the first time he's spewed in class, as far as I know.

Anyway, after a night of excruciating pain and nausea, Bryce will be wrecked, so his mother usually keeps him home the next day. Which means I'm screwed until Monday—unless I want to call him tonight. But something tells me that's a bad idea and that he'll just hang up on me. Then he'll have a whole weekend to work himself into a panic over it. No, it's better to talk to Bryce face-to-face—let him see in person that I mean him no harm.

I don't want to speak to anyone at break, so I duck into the boys' washroom and hide out in a stall. It's not the most dignified thing I've ever done in my life, perching on a toilet seat, but at least no one will bother me here.

As usual, half of the lights are out. Sitting in the gloomy cubicle, I start yawning uncontrollably. With no friends and a bunch of people to avoid, it's going to be another long day, I know. And there's no gym today, which means no nap in the library.

I decide I'd better get moving. I exit the stall and splash cold water in my face to wake up. Then I dry myself with a scratchy brown paper towel.

Heading out of the boys' room, I walk into a fleshy wall with a whistle in the middle. It's Coach Keller, the only teacher who takes a leak alongside his students.

"Harris!" he says.

"Coach," I answer, trying to squeeze past.

"What's up, my man?"

"Not much," I tell him.

"I was hoping to run into you. How are the legs doing?"

"Good, actually," I admit, thinking about my run for the bell earlier.

Which was a stupid answer, because Keller is instantly all over me. "That's great news!" he says, hands on his hips while he blocks the exit. "Really great news!"

"Thanks," I answer, itching to get out of the dingy restroom.

"So—I suppose you heard," he says.

From the look on his face, I'm half expecting to hear

that someone died. "Heard what?" I ask.

"About us getting stomped last week," he tells me gravely. "By Colchester. Colchester!"

Oh, brother, I think. "Oh well. Better luck next time."

"We need more than luck, my friend," he says. "We're really slipping in the standings fast."

"That sucks."

"I know. But a win against Middlefield and we're back on track. Or close, at least."

"Middlefield?" I say, faking disgust for a high school I've never even heard of. "Don't worry, Coach. We'll cream them."

I move to go. But no. Keller stops me with a hand so hot, I can feel it through my shirt.

"So wait—you'll do it?"

"Do what?"

The coach looks at me and laughs. "Play some football! You must be dying to get back in. . . ."

"I don't know, Coach," I tell him. "I'm not sure if I'm ready."

It's an understatement. I can't even throw a football to my own dog's satisfaction, much less catch one.

"Look, I know what's bothering you," Keller says, sidling up to a urinal and unzipping himself. "You want to be QB. But look, let's face it: it's never gonna happen. You're small and tough. That's God's own secret recipe for the perfect running back."

I try to ignore the sound of the coach's whizzing—man, how much does the guy drink? "Look, Coach, I'll think about it," I say. "But I'm not promising anything."

"Okay, okay. But we need you, Cal. We need you."

The bell rings. "I don't know. Look, I gotta go, sir."

Finally I'm able to get out of the washroom. I'm offended at the coach's remark though. Small? That's an overstatement. I don't know. I suppose, compared to most football players, he's right. Even Cole looked on the smaller side out there, come to think of it. Even while wearing pads and a helmet, I personally wouldn't want to tangle with any of those other guys.

I should have just quit, then and there. But then the coach would have tried to change my mind, I'm sure, right there in the john. And that was a scene I wanted to avoid. No, I'll quit later. I'll quit when I'm good and ready.

I keep to myself for the rest of the day, blowing off anyone who tries to talk to me. For the most part, I'm successful. But at one point between fifth and sixth periods, Ivy Johansen sneaks up in the hall and sticks a finger down the waist of my jeans.

"Having a good day, sexy pants? Can't wait for tonight."

I turn red and jump away. She laughs and continues on with her friends.

After the last bell, I get out of the building as fast as I can. Head down, I race home, the pavement a blur under my feet. Crossing the bridge, I refuse to even look at the falls and try to ignore its thunderous drone.

When I come into the house, I'm pretty tired. But Jess is there in the entranceway, waiting.

"Hey there," I say, looking into her wide brown eyes.

She whines: the signal she needs to pee. I feel glad she's at least feeling comfortable enough to approach me now.

"Wanna go walkies?" I ask, hoping I'm wrong.

She starts wagging her tail in response. Tired or not, I can't refuse her. I want my old dog back—the fun and affectionate one, not this timid creature that runs away from me.

"Okay, just let me get some water first."

After guzzling down some liquid, I'm ready to go. Jess stands obediently as I put the leash on her. I open the front door, and she heads out urgently. She relieves herself on the nearest patch of grass.

"Hold on," I tell her, once she is finished. "Sit." Seeing the dog obey, I quickly run to the garage to get the mangled old football.

I open the door just enough to crawl inside. It's dark in there, so I feel around for the light switch. The neon-strip bulbs sleepily come to life.

Looking up, I spot the scratched fiberglass underside of our old canoe. Which makes me suddenly curious.

I get the ladder and stand it up against a solid beam. Then I climb up and have a look inside the canoe. There, I find a life jacket half dangling over the side. This is probably the one I was wearing when they pulled me from the river, I'm guessing, which Dad then tossed back up rather than getting out the ladder. I pull it loose. It lands with a thud on the concrete floor.

Feeling around the cold inside of the canoe, I retrieve an old yellow children's life jacket and then another one just like it. I drop them to the floor as well.

I then find something unexpected. Lodged under the paddles are two more life jackets. I pull them out. Two more orange ones.

I drop them and climb back down the ladder.

I stand there, looking at them in disbelief. There are five life jackets on the floor. Two small, yellow children's jackets and three regular orange ones.

Three orange. All identical.

I know for sure we never had three. Why would we? It's a two-person canoe—there was never any point. But now we have an extra one.

I remember once having to bring the orange life jackets to someone's cottage and how my mother wrote our names inside them in marker so they wouldn't get lost. I open one. *Cole*, it says on the inside breast. I open another: *Cal*.

Okay.

I open the last one—the first one I chucked down from the canoe, the one that had been hanging from the side.

Callum, it says inside.

I fall off my feet, landing in a sitting position. *Cal. Callum*. How many of me *are* there in this family?

I hear a bark. With a jolt I remember that I've left Jess outside alone. With the busy road out front, it's a dangerous thing to do, especially for this long. Abandoning the life jacket, I quickly grab the football and duck out from under the garage door. I scrape my back in the process and swear.

Jess barks again and comes hurtling over to me. "Good girl," I tell her, relieved as she runs circles around me. I kiss her on her forehead. "Good girl."

Thank God she stayed put, I think as we make our way down the drive. It was a stupid mistake; I couldn't have lived with myself if she'd been hit by a car. Turning at the bottom of the path, I continue puzzling over the life jackets. There must be plenty of reasonable explanations. Maybe my life jacket was misplaced for a while, and they bought me another. Maybe my mother wrote Cal in the first one and then Callum in the new one.

Except I don't remember that. Except I get a chill every time I think about the extra jacket. Because there's something wrong. But what I keep thinking makes no sense.

It's only when I see the fork in the road leading up to the campground that I start paying attention to where we're going. We've gone the wrong way, back toward the campground.

I can't be bothered turning around now. And why

should I care? It's a public road—Guise himself agreed. Besides, I'm through being afraid of people. It's time to crack some more heads.

We head up the dirt road, Jess keeping pace right alongside me. She seems so different. I remember her always straining at the leash as soon as we were out, loving life and in a hurry to get on with it. But now she seems cautious, like a working dog that fears being beaten.

Well, we're going to fix that, right this minute.

The field still isn't mowed, so we'll have to stick to the road. But with the campground pretty much deserted, I don't expect much, if any, traffic coming along.

"Come on, girl," I say, taking Jess off her leash. "Let's play fetch!"

Confidence hums like an electric current through my whole body as I wind up. With a snap, I throw the ball. It's the best spiral of my life, soaring high and straight above the road.

Jess can't resist it: the sight of the brown bomb arcing across the clear, blue sky. She's off, barking with joy at the chase.

"Go on, Jess! Go get it!"

The ball bounces only twice before the dog brings it down. Pleased with herself, she trots proudly in a circle before ravaging the kill. I laugh. Hearing me, she comes running back down the road and drops the slobbery thing at my feet.

"Good dog!" I praise her, scratching her behind both ears. "Good dog!"

It's enough. I can see she loves me again, her friend, her master.

I snatch the ball from her. "What? Who's got the ball? Who's got the ball?" I ask in the baby talk I use whenever we are out of earshot of anyone else. I wind up but don't throw a few times, teasing Jess, who begins barking in happy frustration before I finally let it rip. Again the ball sails through the air like a bullet. It feels easy now. Is that all I needed? Confidence?

Again, Jess is after it.

We keep this up for a while, having a blast together. Jess becomes more reluctant to hand the ball over, and I have to run after her, heading farther and farther down the road toward the park. But I don't care. Other than the fact that my arm is beginning to ache, I don't care about anything anymore.

"One more, girl, okay? Then we gotta head back."

None of this is in Jess's vocabulary, of course, especially when she is having fun. But despite my exhaustion, this last throw is among my most impressive, overshooting the mark I was aiming for. It bounces several times before Jess can catch up to it, ending up out of sight, over a ridge.

This I feel nervous about. Even though the road seems dead, I can't see what's coming, and the idea of Jess running headlong into an oncoming vehicle gives me the shivers. I shout for her to stop, call for her to come back. But she either doesn't hear or doesn't care. She disappears from view as she goes after the ball.

Telling myself not to panic, I begin jogging after her. I call her name a few times, hoping she'll appear, ball in her mouth. But she doesn't. I start running.

Reaching the top of the ridge, I see the football lying in the center of the road. Where's Jess? But then I see her about twenty feet ahead, standing by the side of the road like a statue.

"What's up, girl?" I call, slowing down. I'm winded and getting a stitch in my side. Bending over to pick up the ball, I feel like someone's stabbing me with a spear.

When I stand up again, Jess still hasn't moved. She just stays put, staring at something in the distance.

I look ahead, guessing it's a cat. There are always a few of them around here that have been abandoned by their owners when they left in their RVs and trailers. I always wondered how those poor house cats must have felt, coming back late from their explorations to find themselves left behind. They probably didn't feel bad for long, because soon their instincts would take over, and they'd be murdering field mice wholesale. Or eventually end up at someone's back door, meowing for mercy.

I'm wrong. There's no cat—it's a person leaning against the old trailer. But it's not Mr. Guise. It's him: the guy in the Crocodiles jacket.

He doesn't move except to stop leaning. And then he just stands there, watching us from a distance.

Jess has her nose in the air and is huffing and puffing. Something is disturbing her. Hindquarters low, she suddenly dashes back toward me, scampering behind my legs. But then she decides to keep going, running back over the top of the ridge.

I turn to look back at the figure in the hood, who is still standing there motionless. He seems to want a face-off. And I want to storm down toward him.

That's when I hear something behind me: an engine and the sound of tires braking on dirt. And then—omigod—the crack of a bumper hitting something.

"Jess!" Cold with fear, I run back up the ridge. "Jess!"

There I see a vehicle—a pickup. But it's skidded off the road and smashed into a tree.

Jess is fine, just running scared in the grassy field.

"What the hell!" Mr. Guise is already out of the truck, heading around to inspect the damage. "Damn mutt! I shoulda run you over!"

He looks up and notices me.

My bravado pours out so fast, it almost makes a puddle. The man might not look as drunk this time, but I'm sure he's ten times as mad. And probably not helping his mood is the fact that someone appears to have recently punched him out. His left eye is black, and his lip is fat and split red down its center.

This is a bad situation. It's so bad that, for a second, I consider joining Jess in the grass. But the stitch in my side is still killing me, and I'm no longer sure I can outrun this guy now that he's sober. My only hope is that Jess will come rushing to my aid and maul him. But I'm not banking on it.

To my surprise, Guise suddenly raises his hands in the air, like I have an invisible gun on him.

"I didn't hit your dog!" he protests. "Fact is, I damn near killed myself avoiding it!" He squints at the damaged truck, then turns back, raising his hands again.

"Relax," I say. But I must admit, it feels good to see him like this. Maybe a beating taught him some manners, or at least not to mess with people he doesn't know. I walk down the slope toward him. He starts backing away in fear. And I can't help it—just like after putting the hurt on that kid in the hallway, I feel incredibly good, incredibly powerful.

"Whoa, whoa!" he says. "You're all hooked up now. Go see for yourself. Electric, septic—you're good to go. Best unit on the lot, I swear! Just take it easy—I don't want no trouble!"

I have no idea what he's talking about. But as I draw up, the man is pressing himself against the vehicle to get away from me. I can't get enough of his fear—it's like popcorn, and I want big handfuls.

I insert my thumb and forefinger into my mouth. It's

my only sure talent: blowing an earsplitting whistle that no one can equal. Not even Cole.

Mr. Guise looks about to wet himself.

Jess comes bounding out of the grass to my side. Tucking the chewed football under my arm, I walk away with her, back toward the campground.

I'm going to have that face-off, with the guy in the Crocodiles jacket. Now.

CHAPTER 14

The campground is deserted. There's no sign of the croc, as I'm beginning to think of him. But like a croc, he's probably got his beady little eyes poking up somewhere. I just have to spot them.

The trailers are filthy looking, black with dirt and plastered with wet leaves. I can't imagine what sort of deranged vacationers would ever want to stay in any of them. I peer through a few windows with slightly parted curtains and see dark, grimy interiors full of ugly furniture and cracked cabinets.

I begin trying doors. The first few are locked, but it doesn't matter. I'll try every single one before I'm done. I'll listen at each door for the sound of a shuffling, skulking croc.

I approach a group of trailers that look slightly less seedy, as if someone has at least bothered to hose them down in the past year. I notice one of them has a light on inside.

That's more like it. The den.

"Come here, Jess," I whisper, taking her leash out of

my jacket pocket. I secure her to a young birch nearby. "Good girl. I'll be back in a few minutes."

I sneak up, hoping to catch the croc off guard. Thankfully the muddy path is free of leaves, and my progress is silent. I reach the door and grasp the handle. I breathe in deeply. It's time.

I climb the stairs and fling open the door. I'm expecting an instant assault, like something Cole might do, jumping from the dark in the basement to pummel me. This time, though, my fists are at the ready, clenched hard, aching to be thrown.

But there's no one inside. I see the source of the light: a lamp in the lounge area, its shade missing and the bulb bare. It's illuminating a pretty scummy scene, with potato-chip bags and candy-bar wrappers all over the place, half-empty plastic pop bottles on the floor, and cigarette butts stubbed out straight on the kitchen counter. Worse still, it reeks of body odor in here—but it's a familiar odor, my nose tells me. Like Cole's. Or like my own, after running laps in the gym for Keller.

The only other thing of interest is a camera, sitting on the table in the dining area. I walk over and pick it up. Pressing the On button, I wait as the camera whirs to life in my hands.

After a few seconds, a photo is displayed on the screen on the back. It's of Ross, I'm stunned to see. And Mrs. Holden. Both naked.

That's when my head fills with pain so electric, it's only an instant before the world disappears around me.

···

My chin is on my chest when I awake. The back of my head is throbbing, and my brain feels like it's bruised. I smell the body odor again, this time even more intensely. Everything is blurry when I open my eyes. But I am still in the trailer, I realize. I am in the trailer, sitting on the dirty, garbage-strewn floor with my hands tied tightly behind my back.

I'm scared now. Really scared.

Suddenly a lampshade appears in front of my face. A lampshade with eyeholes. If I weren't so scared, it would almost be funny. But it's not funny—especially as I'm yanked to my feet and thrown down the length of the trailer, to land on the U-shaped sofa.

"Take it easy!" I yell, lucky my arms aren't broken. "Take it easy!"

But the lampshade isn't taking it easy. The lampshade is furious, seizing a half-empty bottle of pop off the floor and whipping it at me. It turns end over end before cracking off my skull. There is more pain as the plastic breaks and I'm showered with lukewarm cola.

That's when the gun makes its appearance, drawn from the back of the lampshade's waistband. The hole of the barrel end looks jet-black, like a tiny abyss, and I feel like my face is being sucked right off the bone into it. I'm going to get shot now, I know for certain, straight through the Harris nose—and then my head is going to explode, and I'm going to die, on this greasy sofa in this dirty trailer.

And I can't even make a noise in protest.

But then the lampshade suddenly lowers the gun. He swears, making a strangled sound of frustration, and begins bashing the butt of the pistol against one of the kitchen cabinets until the door smashes into pieces.

That's when I finally notice the lampshade's Crocodiles jacket. Well, you've finally caught up to him, I think. And whoever he is, he's a total psycho. I flinch as he continues to lay waste to anything that splinters under the punishing steel.

I can hear Jess outside madly barking. I can imagine her straining at her leash, trying to free herself. But the frantic dog only seems to be unhinging the lampshade further. Glancing at the shaking gun, he looks like he has made up his mind to storm out of the trailer and put a bullet in her head. Again I want to shriek in protest, but again I'm unable to make a sound, I'm so struck dumb with fear.

"Shut up, bitch!" the lampshade screams through the closed window. And thankfully it's enough to silence Jess. Instantly. He then stands there, holding the window frame, panting with rage.

I wait and wonder. Maybe I should say something. Something reasonable. But that's a bad idea. I have to pretend that I'm not here, that I don't even exist, and just hope he calms down.

My plan proves to be a good one. I can see his breathing gradually slowing, and his muscles relaxing, until he finally stuffs the gun down the back of his pants again. A warm feeling of relief flows through me. But it's a stupid and pointless feeling. Because everything is not okay, not even close, as I'm reminded the second those two eyeholes turn my way, hate still blazing from them.

"What did I do?" I find myself asking, against my better judgment. There is a flash of renewed fury, but it subsides fairly quickly, and instead he begins sifting through the trash on the kitchen counter until he produces a yellowed old notepad. He snatches up a pen and begins writing. When he's finished, he tears off the sheet and shoves it in my face.

WHO ARE YOU?

"Huh?" I'm not expecting this. "My name is Callum Harris," I tell him. "I go to Crystal Falls High. . . ."

This answer does not please the lampshade. Not at all. Because he winds up and punches me one, again in the head. And from the pain, I feel like I can't take another—one more blow, and my skull is going to crack open. I'm sure of it.

"What do you want from me?" I blubber. "What do you want?"

The lampshade does not answer. He rushes over to the kitchen counter, writes some more, then storms back to thrust another message at me.

DID THEY FIND NEIL?

"Neil?" I reply, uncertain. I flinch as the lampshade winds up to hit me again. But he stops himself. "You mean Neil Parson?" I ask. "No, they didn't find him."

He stands back, nodding repeatedly to himself as if this is a desirable answer. He wanders back to the counter and stands there for a while. Then he scrawls out another message and tears it off. He approaches slowly and holds it up to me.

SCREW IVY AND YOU'RE DEAD!

The words are right there in front of me, but I can't believe I'm reading them. "What? Ivy? No, listen . . ."

But the lampshade is not listening. The lampshade is drawing the gun again. The overwhelming terror is back—I have just made a fatal mistake by not having the right answer at the crucial moment. . . .

He doesn't shoot me though. He does pound me one with the butt of the gun. And if my skull doesn't actually crack open, it sure feels like it. For a moment anyway, before I feel nothing and am out cold.

I wake up to a wet nose snuffling in my ear. It's Jess. Her leash is still tied to the birch tree, and she's whining. She wants to know if I'm okay. From what I can tell, lying here in the leaves and the mud, we are alone.

I struggle into a seated position. My hands are free. Blood is caked in my eyebrows, though, and drying uncomfortably in my eyelashes. My headache is the worst I can ever remember experiencing in my life. But this is no time to feel sorry for myself—I have to get out of here.

I stagger to my feet and manage to untie Jess. Letting the dog lead the way, I stumble toward the campground exit, past Mr. Guise's darkened trailer and his empty parking spot, and then along the hilly road, where I puke several times. And finally it's out onto the highway, where I realize I must look like a mess, because cars are slowing down, their drivers staring at me before making the decision to speed away.

Thanks for the help, citizens.

And after what feels like an eternity, I get home. Opening the front door, I let Jess off the leash and then crawl upstairs, thankful that my mother is busy in the laundry room. I go straight to the bathroom to investigate my wounds.

Looking in the mirror, I confirm that the worst of my injuries are above my hairline, making them easier to hide, at least. But still I'm a mess. Combing through my crusty hair, I find ugly cuts. I wonder if they need stitches. I don't know. But they have stopped bleeding, mostly. So I say no.

They do need to be seriously disinfected though. And that is going to really, really suck.

I flick the switch for the fan, hoping its hum will cover up the worst of whatever grunts and groans are coming. Then I rake through the medicine cabinet until I find something that will do the trick.

Peroxide. This is the stuff I need, and I'm in luck, because there's plenty of it.

Uncapping the bottle, I kneel on the fuzzy bath mat and lean over the tub. To prepare myself, I take a deep breath—and then begin pouring the contents onto my scalp.

For a moment it just feels cold, like I've dunked my head in ice water. But as the foaming, hissing liquid seeps into every nick and every gash, the real pain comes, lighting up my head like I'm a human torch.

It's awful. But there's no going back now. So I keep pouring.

The pain increases, making it almost impossible to keep from screaming. But I have to keep quiet, I tell myself. I have to.

There's a knock on the door. Oh, come on . . .

"Cal?" my mother calls above the noisy fan. "Is that you in there?"

"Yeah, Mom," I call back, my eyes now also searing as

the peroxide seeps into their corners. "Just a minute . . ."

"You didn't take off your shoes!" she complains.

"Sorry," I reply, my strained voice echoing from inside the tub. The pain now flares to impossible levels, and I shudder and grit my teeth as it overwhelms me. "I really, really had to go," I tell her.

My mother says something else, but I can't make it out—her words are swallowed up by the fan and my agony. Thankfully she leaves.

By the time I drop the empty plastic bottle, the bottom of the bath is streaked with blood. After wiping it down the drain with my palm, I turn on the hot water and put in the plug. As I strip off my clothes, I watch the bottle fill up again and sink to the bottom.

I climb in after it and lie down. The gashes are still burning underwater, but it is better. I lie there, not even bothering with soap, until the bath goes cold.

....

Lying semiconscious on my bed, I try to make sense of things. The extra life jacket and the maniac wearing the lampshade. Their connection.

I finally become aware that I'm being called down for dinner. I look at the clock; it's past seven already. Getting up, I check myself out in the mirror on my closet door. From what I can tell, the peroxide didn't turn my hair blond, luckily. I quickly realize that my scabbing wounds are pretty obvious. Which will not only likely ruin the family meal but make for a conversation I don't want to have right now. So I find a baseball cap in the closet and try to put it on as delicately as possible.

"Cal!" my mother calls again. "Didn't you hear me? It's dinnertime."

"I'm coming!" I yell back.

When I get downstairs, my mother and father are at the table, already eating. "We started," Dad says reproachfully. "The food was going cold."

"That's all right."

"What's with the hat?" he demands as I sit down.

"Sorry. My hair is really dirty and gross."

"But I thought you had a shower when you came home," my mother points out. "Didn't you wash your hair?"

"I had a bath. I guess I forgot."

I forgot—the words are my pocket Aces for any explanation. They drop the subject.

"Any plans for tonight?" Dad asks me, obviously trying to lighten the mood. But as one of the seams of my hat starts digging into my aching scalp, the questions are starting to make me cranky.

"Plans?" I repeat. "No."

"Really? It's Friday."

"So?"

"Since when don't you have plans on a Friday night?"

"I don't know. Since nobody's asked me to do anything."

"I'm just asking," my father says.

"And I'm just telling you. No."

A silence falls over the table. I turn my attention to my dinner, which has gone cold. I try to eat it, but with my hat killing me and the flashes of the terrible scene in the trailer, I have little appetite.

Afterward I help my mother clean up the dishes. She seems surprised but on edge as I put the plates in the dishwasher and wipe off the table. Once done, I excuse myself and head back up to my room.

Plans. Who would make plans with me now? Normally I would drag myself up to Bryce's for some gaming or to make fun of a movie. And recently I've been passing on that and instead meeting up with Willow.

Well, neither is on offer, tonight or ever. Without even looking at the title, I pull one of the few remaining novels from the shelf. I open it and find an inscription scrawled inside, in my own handwriting:

Mr. Potts likes eating snots.

There's a scratch at the door. It's Jess. I open the door, and she trots in, jumping up on my bed. I join her. It's nice to feel her warm side against my leg. I've missed it.

A couple of hours later, I hear a car roar up the drive. I jump up. From my window I can't see who it is, but I have a good guess, based on the engine sound and the skid with which it comes to a stop.

A minute later the doorbell rings.

Oh, come on. No. Not now.

"Cal, it's for you!" my mother calls.

Crap, I think, looking at myself in the mirror. I look awful. But there's nothing I can do about it now. I head downstairs.

"Hi, Ivy," I say to the girl standing in the entranceway. My mother gives us some privacy, even turning up the TV in the living room. "What are you doing here?"

"Making sure you go to Becca's party," she tells me. "Omigod, you look like hell! What happened?"

"I had a bad afternoon."

"No kidding." But her sympathy stops there. "Well, nothing fixes a bad afternoon like a kick-ass evening," she assures me breezily. "So get yourself together, and let's go."

"Look, I really don't know if I'm up for a party," I say. "I have a headache." I decide not to mention the dizziness and the ringing in my ears.

"Cal! You're such a whiner lately. Seriously. Take a pill and get in the car. . . ."

I think about it. It is tempting. Ivy is looking particularly amazing tonight, wearing very short shorts with sheer gray tights and heels. And if anyone could take somebody's mind off crippling pain, it would be her, I suppose.

"What about Hunter?" I ask, hoping to finally get the story about what's going on there.

Ivy rolls her eyes. "Hunter's mother is having some fancy birthday party, a big catered family thing. I was invited, but I passed. But he's stuck there, at the house, all night. . . ."

Ivy leans in close, and I can smell her perfume again. Her resemblance to the girl in the poster I ripped down from my bedroom and locker is suddenly incredible. Except she's not faking anything. My body is in charge now, and it wants to head off with her, into the night.

"Okay," I reply.

"Just get rid of that goofy hat," she says. "Oh, and don't forget the stuff," she whispers. "Where is it, by the way?"

"Where is what?"

"The box of booze," she says, sounding frustrated.

"Oh, it's up in my closet. My parents would never look there. It's a mess."

Ivy sighs. "Are you out of your mind? What a stupid place to stash it." She flashes a glance at the living room, where both my parents sit. "How are you going to get it outside without getting caught?"

Get it outside? "I don't know," I admit. Because, until now, I hadn't ever considered moving it at all.

"Seriously, Cal," Ivy says, her voice angry but still low. "Just go get it—I'll distract your parents. Okay?"

I nod like a dumb animal before heading back upstairs

to my room. There, I change shirts, putting on something I hate but think Ivy might like. I look in the mirror and remember the comment about my baseball cap. But how can I go out without it? When I check the hooks on the back of the closet door, I find a knitted hat. Wincing, I peel off the baseball cap and then roll the patterned hat over my head. I look like I'm wearing a tea cozy. But whatever. It feels a lot less painful than the stiff cap.

I uncover the box of whiskey and hoist it to my chest. It feels unbelievably heavy this time. I'm nervous about this. But it will be a relief once the stuff is finally out of the house.

As I reach the top of the stairs, Ivy holds up a hand. She marches straight into the living room.

"Hello, Mr. and Mrs. Harris!" she says, as if they're eighty years old and deaf. "How are things with you both?"

This is my cue. I hurry down the stairs, fingers barely gripping the box. Squeezing into the entranceway, I get a knee under it to help and manage to exit the front door. Seeing Ivy chatting up a storm through the living-room window, I quickly hide the box behind her car.

Back inside, I can hear Ivy telling my parents about all the activities and sports she is involved with at school. The question hits me again: Why is she even interested in me? My sex appeal? Come on.

But that does seem to be the central attraction as Ivy

tongues my ear on the way to her car after saying good-bye to my parents. It's exciting but also sort of gross, especially afterward, when I have to use a finger to clear out my ear canal in order to hear what she's saying.

"Forget about the trunk, just stick the box in the back-seat," she's telling me. Like usual, I do exactly as she says and then get in the passenger seat. We drive off, leaving the blue, flickering light from my house behind.

CHAPTER 15

If Ivy's driving seemed scary during the day, it's downright terrifying at night. Constantly drifting across the line, burning around blind corners, and flooring it through red lights, she is so reckless, I'm actually amazed to arrive at Becca's house in one piece.

There are already a lot of cars here, so we have to park down the street. Which means carrying the box of booze far. Ivy misreads the pained look on my face as we get out. "Oh, sorry, did you want to drive? You should have said something. But you have to get over yourself, Cal. It's really sexist of you to keep saying that I can't drive."

"Sorry," I say.

"Well, you're the designated driver then." Ivy throws me her keys. "Don't forget the alcohol, Cal!" she shouts.

"Sorry."

I open the back door and get out the heavy box. I realize I'm doing an awful lot of apologizing around Ivy—for slamming the door too hard, for a wet sneeze in her car, for turning down the volume on her sound system. I think it's getting on her nerves. Catching up with her, I almost start apologizing for my apologizing. *Shut up, Callum.* I just have to relax, but she's stressing me out. I never felt this way with Willow, I realize. I always felt relaxed with her.

I follow Ivy up to the house, where we let ourselves in. The music is blaring. People are everywhere, mostly seniors, but a number of juniors I'm not expecting to see.

Everyone cheers when they see me. And then they swarm me. Next thing I know, they're sticking money in my face.

"How much for one bottle? Can we get a deal if we get two bottles?"

I really don't want to sell the whiskey. But at least it will get rid of the evidence, not to mention the heavy box I'm stuck with. "Uh, six dollars a bottle," I tell them, picking a number off the top of my head. "Two for ten."

"Cal!" Ivy yells. "What the hell?"

"What's wrong?"

"Why are you giving it away like that?"

"What do you mean?"

"It's twenty-five bucks a bottle!" Ivy corrects. "Like usual."

The buyers are pretty unhappy to hear this, with a lot of voices chiming in that I should honor my original offer. Ivy is firm, though, and tells them to take it or leave it. Still, things are getting ugly. But then the low supply and high demand becomes apparent, and people start bidding against one another. First ten a bottle, then twenty, then the twenty-five . . . And they don't stop there. By the end twelve buyers are left standing, each walking off with a bottle for a cool fifty dollars apiece.

Which means that not only am I finally free of that stupid box, but I have six hundred bucks in my hands. Six hundred bucks! I'm still counting it in disbelief, grinning like a nutcase as people walk off in a huff.

I know this is wrong, but I just can't stop smiling.

"Who are you?" Ivy suddenly wants to know.

"What?" I answer, feeling uneasy. "What do you mean?"

"Are you Cal's evil twin or something? Because that was a piece of genius you just pulled off."

"What can I say?" I reply smugly. "I guess I'm just a natural-born businessman."

"More like a master manipulator."

"It's the same thing."

Ivy laughs and kisses me on the mouth. It feels incredible, her soft lips combined with the thick fold of bills in my hand. And this time I don't feel sorry about anything at all—until she suddenly stops.

"Hey!" she says, punching me in the shoulder with surprising force. "You didn't save a bottle for us!"

"Oh, yeah," I answer, not that I wanted any. I remember the tasting session my father once gave us of his product and how I ended up with my face in the toilet bowl. "Sorry."

"Who can blame you at those prices?" Ivy admits. "Anyway, don't worry. We should be able to score enough swigs to keep us going."

I shove the money deep into the front pocket of my jeans. We start making our way around the party, which is in full swing. I notice that some kids have beer and look happy enough, despite missing out on the whiskey. We pass a hefty senior showing off by crushing a beer can on his face. Some other dude tries and really hurts himself, putting a bleeding dent in his forehead. Everyone laughs, including me.

I keep close to Ivy, who helps herself to every bottle of whiskey she comes across. She chugs it straight, winces, and then passes it back to me. I put the bottle to my lips and pretend to take a drink. Even a splash is too much, making my eyes water and my stomach clench. I guess I just really hate alcohol.

Ivy clearly doesn't share my distaste though. Before long she's totally losing control: stumbling around, dancing terribly, and laughing at everything anyone says. Meanwhile I'm ignored, feeling like her chaperone. When she does remember I'm here, she yanks me over for a kiss, but our teeth clang or her tongue pokes me in the eye. It's both disgusting and annoying. Each blast of her hot whiskey breath makes me gag—I feel like I'm on a date with Mr. Guise.

I finally leave to go look for a bathroom. Not finding

one on this level, I head up to the second floor.

It's dark up here, and much quieter, which is a nice break from the chaos and pounding music downstairs. I find the bathroom, but it's occupied. Rather than hang out at the door, I wander off to have a look around the house. I come across a TV room, where a girl sits, looking bored.

"Willow?" I can't believe it—what's she doing at a party like this? She looks amazing wearing a cute black dress and some makeup. More amazing than ever, in fact.

Willow seems happy to be recognized. But seeing me, she makes a face—the same disgusted expression she made after I slammed that kid's head into the locker.

"Listen, I know you don't like me now," I say. "And who can blame you? But I just wish you would give me a chance. Because I really need to tell you something."

"What?" she demands, I'm guessing more because she's a prisoner in the room than because she's curious.

"I'm not the guy you think I am. Well, not exactly the same. To be honest I don't really know who I am anymore. . . ."

Willow runs out of patience immediately. "I don't even know you, Cal, other than how you run around school, acting like a jerk. Okay?"

My head drops—this is not going well. "Look, I know it looked bad, but I'm not like that. Please. I don't want you to think that about me. I'm not a jerk. I'm really not."

"Why do you care all of a sudden what I think about

you, anyway?" she exclaims. "You never even knew my name until a week ago. Now you're acting like my opinion is the most important thing in the world to you. . . ."

"Because it *is* the most important thing in the world!" I insist. Hearing my own embarrassing admission, I feel myself flush. Yeah, real smooth, Harris. But Willow just looks terrified of the red-faced psycho blocking her escape. "Wait," I say quickly. "I'm sorry for yelling. I know I'm not helping. I'm just trying to tell you that I don't remember things being like this between us. I've always known your name, Willow, since the first day I met you. Honest."

Either she doesn't believe me or she doesn't care. And I'm definitely making her even more nervous. She stiffens as I sit down on the sofa opposite her. I see her glance at the open door. I'm scared she'll run away, but I'm willing to take the chance in the hope that she'll feel more comfortable.

"Willow, listen to me," I continue. "Something happened. I don't know if it was to me, or to everyone. Before my accident, everything here was different. The whole town. It was cleaner, nicer. There were more stores on Main Street. And tourists—there were tons, coming to see the falls.

"And we were friends, you and I. We met last year in biology, in Mr. Schroeder's class. Do you remember that? We were lab partners."

"Yeah, I remember Mr. Schroeder's class. But we

weren't partners—and you were always thrown out of class for goofing around."

"No," I say. I rub my face in frustration. "Another thing—my best friend was Bryce."

"Bryce?" she repeats with a snort. "Nerdy Bryce?"

"Don't call him that," I reply. "He's cool." Which means I'm defending the guy who tried to murder me. But that can't be the same Bryce either. Whatever happened to me, and whatever happened to Willow, has happened to him too.

"Anyway, then I went over the falls and went into a coma," I tell her. "And when I woke up, all these strange things started happening. First, Bryce tried to kill me in the hospital, tried to smother me to death," I explain. "And then Ivy started . . . started liking me, I guess. And everyone started acting like I'm some kind of badass and a football star." I shake my head, wondering how I ever believed any of this, even for a second. "Except I'm not. I'm not! I swear to you, I'm just a regular kid, like anyone else!"

"Okay," Willow replies, still fearful. "Whatever you say. Just calm down, Cal."

I do need to calm down; I feel light-headed, like I'm running out of air. "And that's another thing!" I blurt out. "No one in Crystal Falls *ever* called me Cal before! Everybody called me Callum, except for my brother." The room starts to spin. "My brother!" I shout. "Who I'm now supposed to believe is completely paralyzed? Well, he isn't paralyzed! I know, Willow, because I saw him, right before the accident!"

Then something weird happens: Willow begins dissolving in front of me. Everything goes white. I feel myself slumping over, my head hitting the sofa cushion.

And then, like a bubble coming up from dark depths, another memory rises to the surface.

It's recent, I know, from the same day that I clung to the railing of the bridge. I've just come home, and I'm frightened for some reason, walking around, shouting hello into the eerie quiet.

There's no answer.

I notice that the attic stairs are down. The attic stairs are never down. Feeling more and more uneasy, I climb up, poking my head into the dim world above.

"Hello?"

My brother is there, at the other end of the attic, lit by a utility light. He's kneeling on the dusty floor, eyes clenched shut, a gun in his hand.

"Cole!" I shout. "What are you doing?"

Everything goes white again. Through the fog, I slowly become aware of Willow propping me up. "Are you okay?" I hear her asking. "Callum, are you okay?"

I'm crying, I realize, big fat tears slapping onto my pant legs. Embarrassed, I try to stop, but I can't. I sit there for a moment, sobbing, gulping air, trying to control myself.

Willow reaches around me uncertainly before putting a hand on my back.

"You never see your dad," I tell her, turning, my eyes still streaming. "He calls you, though, on your birthday, and on Christmas morning, and each summer when you finish school. Every year he says he's going to fly you out to the Bahamas, where he lives with his rich new wife, and their twins, Samantha and Phillip. Except he never sends a ticket. You've met your stepmother two or three times, including at the wedding, but your half brother and half sister—your flesh and blood, you called them—you've never even seen them other than in pictures."

I can see immediately from her face that these things haven't changed, at least. And that no one at school—no one in Crystal Falls, for that matter—has ever heard this story. I know, because I was the first person she ever told, and that was only a few weeks ago.

I hear a toilet flush, and the bathroom door open. "Willow, girl! I know you're up here. Stop being so shy and get down to the party!" a voice calls.

A girl appears in the doorway—it's a friend of Willow's named Lizzie. They used to hang out a lot, but lately Willow has been with me instead, feeling guilty as she ignores her calls.

Lizzie notices me still crying. "Oh, sorry, am I interrupting something?"

Without a word, Willow gets up and races out the door.

I collect myself in the bathroom and head downstairs a few minutes later. My eyes are still red, but big deal, so are a lot of people's. I jostle my way from room to room, looking for Willow. I can't find her. I'm starting to think she left. I become sure of it when I see her friend Lizzie glaring at me accusingly.

I want to get out of here too. I want to find Ivy and return her car keys and then walk home. It will probably take an hour, but I don't care.

The music stops. It goes unnoticed at first, because everyone is still yelling. But finally someone detects the missing bass and backbeat.

"Tunes!" he shouts. "Who's in charge of the tunes?"

No one seems to know. People start shouting for Becca, a person I'm still kind of curious to identify, if only to see the face of the girl who would throw this kind of party at her parents' house.

I don't get the chance. A murmur rises among the crowd, and everything feels suddenly tense. Have the cops shown up for a noise complaint? Or did Becca's parents come home?

But it's worse—for me, at least. I see Hunter, flanked by Ricky and some other meathead from the Crocodiles.

The party falls silent. Everyone moves out of their way, opening an alley that stretches across the living room straight to me. That's when I become aware of Ivy—who is hanging from me, chewing on my neck and grinding up against me.

"You!" Hunter shouts. "Get off my girlfriend!"

I want to comply, but since she's technically the one on me, it's easier said than done. Completely hammered now, Ivy doesn't even register the sound of her boyfriend's voice—she just carries on, making me look even worse. Boiling with fury, Hunter storms across the room toward us.

No, no, no . . . I really don't want to get hit again today—especially in the head. But that's exactly what's coming—and then some—unless I get out of here right now. Which is also easier said than done.

Within a second, Hunter is on us. Hoping that even he draws the line at punching girls, I spin Ivy around as a shield. She giggles like a ballroom dancer getting an unexpected twirl.

Hunter is stunned, looking more wounded than angry for a moment. "Ivy!" he yells miserably. "What are you doing?"

That's when the girl finally clues in—sort of. "Oh, hi, baby!" she slurs, letting go of me immediately and wrapping herself around the huge football player. "Wha' joo doin' here?"

This is my chance—my only chance. I leap over the coffee table, sending a stack of empty beer cans flying, then dive through a gap in the wide-eyed onlookers. Hunter shouts after me. But I don't look back. Like a rat with a broom at its ass, I flee toward the kitchen, scurrying under and over anyone in my way.

From there I make it through the half-open door leading outside. I run down the back porch and across the lawn. Unfortunately I discover it's a dead end, fenced in high on all sides. And now I'm really scared, because I'm wasting time trying to find a way out. The gate that leads to the front yard is padlocked shut. Swearing, I shake it in frustration.

"Cal went out the back!" I hear someone say. "Like a second ago!"

Well, I'm done. I put my forehead against the gate. The scrawled words from the trailer are written in fire on my brain:

SCREW IVY AND YOU'RE DEAD!

So that's it—it was Hunter with the lampshade on his head. But no, that guy was smaller, I'm certain. I remember how I first chased the hooded figure, running across the field and vaulting over the fence after him.

Wait . . .

Go over, go over, go over!

But in the dark backyard, it's not quite that easy. My sneakers squeak as they slip on the planks of the fence. Come on, come on!

"Yo, there he is!" a voice shouts.

I can hear my sprinting pursuers just as I find a foot-hold. My adrenaline spikes—I propel myself upward and clear the top. But I land hard, falling on my side. There's a bang as someone runs straight into the gate, the crack of splitting wood.

The lock holds though.

I scramble to my feet and take off, as fast as I've ever run in my life. No burning lungs, no heavy legs. Run or die, my body knows.

I bolt straight out into the road, nearly getting hit by a pickup. Was it Mr. Guise's? I think so—I saw a dented bumper. It was moving so slowly, I thought it was parked.

I don't confirm. I keep running. Because the last thing I need is another enemy on my tail.

I see Ivy's car ahead, gleaming like a jewel under a streetlight. I have her keys, I remember.

And I am the designated driver. . . .

I'm forced to slow down in order to get the keys out of my pocket, which are luckily on the left and not stuffed under the roll of bills. I glance quickly over my shoulder as the automatic locks open. No one on my heels. I jump into the car.

Despite what Ivy believes, the only actual driving experience I remember having is lumbering my dad's van around a parking lot four or five times. But that's not a big concern right now. More pressing is locking the doors and getting this heap into Drive.

Looking in the mirror, I suddenly see Hunter and his friends. But they are surrounding that pickup for some reason, shouting and slamming their palms against the side panels. I hear the sharp sound of breaking glass.

Whatever, I think, and start the engine. Before they realize their mistake, I'll be out of here. I floor it.

Dad's van does not accelerate with anything near the power that Ivy's little sports car unleashes. Barely missing the bumper of a parked car in front of me, I'm thrown back against the seat as I struggle to keep the car pointed straight down the road.

Once in some sort of control, I breath out in relief. It occurs to me that Ivy is going to be pretty unhappy at finding her brand-new car missing. I know I would be. Remembering how drunk she was, I wonder if I'm actually doing her a favor.

But about a mile away, when I take a corner too fast and crash the car into a pole, I wonder no longer.

CHAPTER 16

An air bag is not something you want exploding in your face, it turns out. This time, it's the Harris nose that takes the brunt of it. Still, I guess it beats being dead.

And now I have to get out of here. For all I know, Hunter and company are already chasing me down in another vehicle.

I manage to get the door open and pull myself out. After tossing the keys inside, I ditch the hissing wreck, clawing my way through some woods until I arrive on another street. I then start hoofing it back, sticking to the shadows and the backstreets as much as I can.

It's a long journey on foot. By the time I arrive home, my parents are in bed, and the house is dark. I fall into bed, exhausted.

The next day, I don't even turn on the computer, much less log in and check my messages. My face is a real mess, particularly my nose. I just sit in my room, refusing to come out, expecting the sheriff and Ivy's parents to pull up in the drive at any moment.

They never do.

Later I pretend I'm sick with a cold so I don't have to go down for dinner. My mother brings me soup and toast and doesn't say much, other than to comment on my swollen nose. By the evening, my big, red schnoz looks like I've been blowing it for the past two days. I've even filled my garbage can with balled-up tissues to complete the effect.

Saturday goes. And then most of Sunday. I'm now wondering if I'm actually going to get away with this—destroying a car and walking off like nothing happened. It seems incredible. But I still have to go to school. What's in store for me there, I have no idea. Something is.

The phone rings for the first time this whole weekend. I jump out of bed and rush to the door. I can hear my mother answer downstairs.

"Cal!" she shouts, making me jump. "Phone for you!"

I look at the phone. I'm scared to pick up.

"Cal!" my mother calls again.

I lift the receiver and clamp a hand over the mouthpiece. "Got it!" I shout back. I can hear the downstairs phone disconnect as I put the receiver to my ear.

"Hello?" I say.

There's nothing on the other end—no breathing, nothing.

"Callum?" a familiar voice finally asks.

"Yeah," I say, overjoyed to hear my full name. "It's me."

"Hi," the voice says. "It's Willow."

....

Monday morning comes. I stand by my bedroom window with a towel around my waist. Rain pounds through the leaves. I'm exhausted, having hardly slept at all.

The conversation with Willow felt like it went by fast, but we must have been on for a while. Because the story I ended up telling her was long.

Willow sounded more like herself, if not as friendly, at the beginning of the call. She'd found my family's number in the phone book, she explained. She'd been thinking about all the things I'd said about her father's new family. How could I know all that? she wanted to know. Because, just as I thought, she had never told anyone, not even her best friend, Lizzie.

I did most of the talking after that, trying to explain. The whole story just poured out of me, all of the things I'd recently experienced, from the terrifying moment of my fall to the increasingly dangerous present. I told her every-thing—about the town's transformation and the sheriff's interview; about the figure in the hood and the attack in the trailer. I even told her about the gun I found in my desk, about stealing the whiskey, and crashing Ivy's car. And finally I told her how sorry I was for hurting that kid in the hallway, that I had never done anything like that in my life before, and how much her horrified face had haunted me afterward.

From time to time, it became so silent on the other end that I'd panic and ask if she was still there. But each time she'd respond, her voice soft but uncertain.

When the story was finally finished, I began talking about her, about all the things I knew about her past and her present. Again, she stayed on the line, mostly in silence, giving me no idea of whether any of the things I said were still true. And then I talked about the friendship that we'd shared.

Finally I sputtered to a stop.

"Okay," she said. "So what now?"

"What do you mean?"

"Well, what are you going to do now?"

It was a good question—one I had no answer for.

"I don't know," I admitted. "I really don't know."

The conversation ended soon after, when Willow's mother came home. I put down the phone. It struck me that she'd never once said that she believed any of it. But she did, didn't she? Otherwise why stay on the phone? Why ask me what I was going to do next?

A jolt of fear went through me as I considered that it might have been some sort of a setup, by the police or someone, to get me to admit to my crimes. If so, I was in a lot of trouble. Willow now knew everything. But I couldn't believe that. She would never do such a thing.

Still, I was no further ahead. Willow had only listened to me, not magically become one of my best friends again. And she hadn't given me a shred of advice on what I should do next.

Which means I really don't want to go to school. But I have no choice, and it's getting late. I take off the towel and dry my hair some more, careful not to press too hard on my scabs. Then I go through my drawers, pulling out clothes. I pick out a long-sleeved T-shirt and some jeans.

I head down for a quick breakfast—a bowl of cereal and a piece of toast. I drain a cup of coffee and notice my hands shaking as I jam my lunch into my schoolbag. But it's not the caffeine, I know.

It's the fear—it's worse than ever. But it feels like something is pushing me out the door.

Mom insists on driving me because of the rain. "You're still recovering, Cal. You could get pneumonia in this weather." So much for my latest plan: to ditch and hide in a park or something. But by the time we get to the car, we're both already soaked. I couldn't spend the day out in this; there's no way.

We set off in the hatchback, wipers squelching across the windshield. It's really coming down now. I can't even see the falls as we cross the bridge. I think about Mr. Schroeder fishing for something in the river and the blue thing I saw bobbing up just before. Was that what he was trying to snag? If so, he wasn't even close to succeeding.

Ten minutes later we pull up in front of school. In this weather, nobody is lingering outside, not even the tough kids who usually steal smokes behind the trees out front.

"Thanks for the lift," I say to my mother.

My mother smiles thinly. "Be good, Cal."

"Okay," I answer. If she only knew the things I've done, I think, pulling up the hood on my rain jacket. What I've had to do. From the look on her face, it's like she already does.

I enter the lobby dripping wet. I keep my hood up and head to my locker. There I find my timid little neighbor blocking my lock. "Excuse me," I say. He jumps like I poked him with a stick.

I check the schedule taped on the inside of the door. I don't want to hang around the halls for long, especially at my locker. But who knows where my books are under all this crap?

Just as I start gently pulling, hoping to avoid a landslide, I spot Ivy heading down the hall. Okay, here we go. Because I've decided Ivy is a person I should not avoid, but rather face immediately. And I've already figured out how. I'll say I gave her back her keys, but that she was drunk and waving them around on a pinkie. She must have dropped them, and someone must have gone for a joy ride.

Then, before she gets a chance to argue, I'm going straight on the attack, accusing her of nearly getting me killed. Why are you messing around if you have a boyfriend? As Cole taught me so many times, the best defense is always a strong offense.

As she draws near, I stand up and square my shoulders.

"Did you *crash* my car?" Ivy yells, eyes blazing.

"Ivy," I say. I feel my shoulders roll forward; my offense has already unraveled. "Listen, I'm really sorry. . . ."

"You crashed my car!" she shouts. "And nearly killed Hunter!"

A crowd is gathering. "What?" I reply, honestly shocked. "I didn't nearly kill Hunter!"

"Yes, you did!" she insists. "They're all in the hospital, Cal—Hunter, Ricky, and Dwayne! You beat them up!"

Dwayne? Who the hell is Dwayne? Wait, the name is familiar—he must have been the third goon chasing me. But beat him up? How? The guy is easily two hundred and twenty pounds. And taking out Hunter and Ricky on top of that? Be serious.

Ivy is raging, poking a sharp nail into my chest and screaming abuse at me. I don't know what she is more upset about, her car or Hunter. Her car, I'm getting a definite sense. But I want to know what happened to the football players, who I last saw swarming that pickup truck.

Unfortunately I don't get the chance to find out, as I'm clapped by a heavy hand.

"Mr. Harris," a voice says behind me. "Come to my office, please."

It's Principal Fernwood. This can't be good. Ivy strides off, acting like she wasn't even talking to me.

"Mr. *Harris*," the principal says again, with more force. "The *office*."

"Uh, sure. Okay."

Ushered along by the elbow, I don't resist or ask any questions—because, as any fool knows, the principal hates that. Along the way I start noticing looks from students: curious, horrified, gleeful. There is a big story going around about me—I'm just not sure what it is yet. As I'm directed into the principal's office, even his secretary looks at me like I'm going up in front of a firing squad.

"Sit down," the principal orders.

It's only the second time I've sat on one of the two chairs positioned along the wall by the principal's desk, although I wouldn't be surprised if a full pack's worth of Cole's chewing gum was stuck underneath. Made from steel and hard plastic, the seats have painful ridges that dig into the undersides of your legs. It's almost like they were purposely designed by some sadistic maniac. A cushioned pair faces the desk, exclusively for the use of adult visitors. That's where my parents sat the other time I was in here, after my beat down by Hunter and Ricky.

It's funny—even that time I remember feeling like I'd done something wrong. Why did I allow myself to be used as a punching bag on school property? The rules are clear. . . .

Fernwood closes the door. Grunting, he takes a seat behind the desk but doesn't say anything more. Instead he sits there staring at me with his evil dragon eyes. I squirm in his gaze for a few seconds before deciding that an innocent person would pipe up and say something by now.

"Did I do anything wrong, Mr. Fernwood?"

He doesn't answer. So I start shifting around in my seat, hoping to get blood flowing down to my feet. Someone knocks on the door.

"Come in," Fernwood calls.

It's the sheriff. I swallow what feels like a handful of nails as he saunters in.

"Morning, Tom," the sheriff says, once the earsplitting bell finally stops. "How's Wendy?"

"Fine, Marlon, thanks for asking. Hey, how is Roscoe doing? I looked out the living room window yesterday and saw him limping around your yard."

"Yup. Infection in the paw, the vet says."

"Poor guy."

"His own fault. And if he keeps licking it, he's gonna

find himself with one of those plastic cones on his head. . . ."

"Ha! He'll look like the life of the party!"

I'm getting agitated.

"What's wrong, young man?" the sheriff says, turning his entire chair to face me. "Can't sit still for a few minutes?"

"Not really," I answer. "I don't want to miss class."

"Uh-huh," he replies. "How was the weekend?"

"Not great. I was sick."

"Sick?"

"Yeah."

"A hangover?"

"No," I say. "I have a cold," I lie, putting on a stuffy-sounding voice. Fortunately my nose is still red and swollen this morning from the exploding air bag. But that makes me nervous. If the sheriff is investigating the car crash, surely he'll be looking for just such an injury.

"And Saturday? Did you do anything? Day or night?"

"No," I answer. "That's when I started getting sick."

"Gotcha." This is apparently interesting enough to get noted in a little book the sheriff produces. "And how about Friday night? What did you get up to then?"

Now things are getting trickier. I want to play it safe and stay on the Nothing theme, but I remember that my parents actually saw me leave the house with Ivy. One phone call and I'm done. Plus there were too many witnesses who saw me at the party, some of whom might be looking to get back at me for cutting them out on the whiskey. Selling stolen liquor—another thing I might be in trouble for.

The thought makes me look down at the front pocket of my jeans. To my horror, I see it's bulging with the fat roll of bills inside. Oh no—the six hundred bucks! I'd forgotten about it. If I'm searched, I'm done.

I need to play it smart. I rewind back to Ivy walking off in the hallway. Angry or not, she obviously doesn't want to get involved in this. Who knows what story she told to cover up being drunk and lending me her keys?

But what did happen at the party after I left? There was some sort of scuffle around the pickup truck—that much I saw myself. The neighbors would have heard the commotion and called the cops, no doubt. So I'm sure the police already know about the party. I can just imagine the scene, all the drunk and stoned kids scrambling to get away. It's almost funny.

The cops would have caught a few of them, at least. Still, my gut tells me no one said anything about me. Everyone would be too busy worrying about themselves and how mad their parents would be. Not only that, if they gave me up, they'd only lose their supply of liquor, not to mention making a dangerous enemy, which is how people apparently see me.

Yeah, no one told the police anything, I'm sure.

Which means I just need a decent enough story. But I'm certain the sheriff must know about the demolished sports car, which would have been peeled off the pole by now. So there's no use pretending I didn't get into the car earlier.

"I went out," I tell the sheriff, "with Ivy Johansen."

"What time?"

"She picked me up around ten, I guess. I don't know— I don't wear a watch."

The sheriff looks disgusted—he obviously can't stand people who don't wear watches. So would I, if I were a cop interviewing a suspect. "So you left around ten. In her car?"

"Yeah," I say. "What a beauty. Smells brand-new."

The sheriff doesn't acknowledge this. "Where did you go with her?"

"She said there was a party at some girl's house, but I didn't end up going."

I hate lying—it feels like I'm tying knots in the rope I'm later going to hang from.

"You didn't go?" the sheriff asks. "Since when does a guy like Cal Harris not like a party?"

"Since I got in a fight with Ivy."

"A fight? Over what?"

"Over her driving," I say. "She's terrible. You should really give her a ticket so she learns her lesson. Otherwise she's going to kill someone one of these days."

But the sheriff doesn't bite. "So you had a fight. Then what?"

"Then she threw me out of her car. Which was just as well, as far as I was concerned, because I wasn't sure we'd make it across town anyway."

The sheriff stares at me for a moment. "So what did you do then?"

"I don't know. Walked around and stuff."

"You walked around in the cold by yourself all night."

That does sound ridiculous. "Well, no. I ran into someone."

Uh-oh. This is a mistake. Because now I'm involving someone else. And I can't just make up a person, saying I met some drifter and had a midnight picnic or something. The sheriff is going to want a name.

The obvious question comes fast: "Who did you meet?"

"A girl," I tell him, hoping it's enough. Of course it isn't.

"What's her name?"

"Willow," I say. I feel strangely proud about the possibility, even though it's a total fiction.

"Last name?"

"Hathaway."

Hold it. That was stupid, stupid, stupid—I've got to be the worst juvenile delinquent in the history of mankind. I deflate as the sheriff confers with Fernwood and confirms that she's a student here. He writes down her name.

But wait. Maybe it isn't the worst idea. She did leave the party, after all, so she definitely wasn't picked up by the cops. And after last night's phone call, she's probably the closest thing to a friend I have at this point. Still, I don't want to ruin things already by putting her in a position where she has to lie.

Or maybe she won't lie. Maybe she'll tell them the truth: that I was there at the party, crying and acting crazy, and then pass along every wacko thing I told her over the phone. In which case I'm either going to jail or a mental institution.

"Right. So you say you ran into this girl. And then what did you do? Just the where and when is good enough—save the X-rated version for your buddies."

"Hey," I object. "It's not like that—she's just a friend!"

"Easy, Romeo. I'll ask again. Where did you get all friendly? And for how long?"

"I don't know. Like I said, I didn't have a watch. We walked around, sat in the park, talked for a while. I don't know. For a couple hours after Ivy dropped me off, I suppose. Then I walked her home, and that was it."

"Why didn't you go to the party with this Willow girl?"

"Because Becca—the girl having the party—lives too far away to walk. And plus Ivy would be there, mad at me."

The sheriff nods. I'm doing a good job of this, I think.

"Did you meet up with any of your football buddies afterward?" he asks.

"Football buddies?" I repeat. "I don't have any friends on the football team."

"I reckon you don't," the sheriff agrees with a laugh. "Not anymore anyway."

This sounds a little too sinister, like he's trying to scare me. But it's working. "What does that mean?" I want to know.

"Cal, you need to cooperate," Fernwood interrupts. "We need to hear your side of the story. Those boys got hurt pretty bad. Maybe nobody's talking yet, but believe me, they will. . . ."

"Tom!" the sheriff shouts, slapping his forehead in frustration. He glares at the loose-lipped principal, who obviously hasn't watched enough TV to know how to interview a suspect. Rule number one: Never give away how little you know.

The principal turns red. "Sorry, Marlon, sorry. Please continue."

But it's game over. Thanks to Fernwood, I know enough. They think I beat up those three guys, as does Ivy. Which is insane. They're football players! Meanwhile, I'm barely a hundred and forty pounds. The team's daily allowance of Gatorade weighs more than I do.

Which means there's no real evidence against me. Otherwise the sheriff wouldn't have waited all weekend to interview me. This is all just a hunch he's working. Play it cool and I'll be fine.

"Did you meet up with your friend Ivy again?"

"No," I answer, scoffing. "She was still mad at me when I saw her in the hall just now. Right, Mr. Fernwood?"

"Did you borrow her car?"

"Her car?" I answer, sounding surprised but not too surprised. "Of course not."

I feel like I'm really getting a handle on this whole delinquency thing. Maybe I could give a master class to all the stupid kids and make another six hundred bucks.

But even the master is rattled by the next question: "Son, do you have access to a gun?"

I get a chill thinking about the .45 missing from my shoe box. This is the part on TV where suspects ask for their lawyers—I even have the cash on hand to pay for one. But this also makes people look instantly guilty, something I want to avoid.

"A gun? No," I answer. And it's true, because I don't have access to it anymore. But my face still feels twitchy. "Why, did somebody get shot or something?"

"Not that I know of," the sheriff says. "But I do know the marks a pistol leaves when you beat someone with one. And I've got three boys with faces full of them."

Even the principal looks horrified. My hand, meanwhile, shoots up to the scabs under my hair. I put my hand down just as fast.

Fortunately the sheriff doesn't notice it. "And I also know that a gun would sure even the odds in a three-on-one with a bunch of burly guys," he adds. "Wouldn't even need to fire a shot to take the fight out of them. Just point it and get them on their knees. And then start bashing away while they piss their pants."

"Well, I don't have a gun," I tell him. "And I definitely didn't bash anybody."

"Of course you didn't," the sheriff says. "A choirboy like you? But just so we're good, do you mind showing me your hands?"

I shrug and hold them out. The sheriff leans over and examines my knuckles and then my palms, both of which show no sign that I was involved in a scuffle. Nevertheless I can feel myself trembling in his grip.

"All right," the sheriff says, releasing me. "While you're here, let's talk about Neil Parson again," he says. "Anything you want to get off your chest about that?"

"I told you before," I answer. "I don't know Neil."

"You still sure about that?" the sheriff asks.

"Yeah."

"Okay. Then explain this."

Principal Fernwood looks as surprised as I am when the sheriff produces a color printout, which he hands over to me. It's a photo—a video still. It's overexposed, with the sidewalk looking like a snowbank, but yeah, it's me, all right.

And walking beside me is Neil Parson—there's no mistaking him. Slouched forward, he walks on his tiptoes, his skinny legs sticking out from that puffy blue jacket of his. Everybody made fun of it. Baby-Blue. That's what people called him, I remember. That's what I called him.

"It was pulled from the security camera outside the bank on Main Street," the sheriff informs me. "Anything coming back to you?"

"No," I say with a shrug. As I hand back the image, I notice the paper is shaking. "When was it taken?"

"That's the really interesting thing—it was the afternoon Neil went missing. And the same day you took your little dip."

I'm floored to hear it. I wish I could remember something—anything—about those missing hours and the day everything changed. But it's all still a blank. Everything except the cold, wet night and the swaying footbridge. Then the shadowy figure running toward me and the terrible, lurching feeling as my fingers slipped . . .

"Look, Neil isn't my friend!"

"Who said anything about friends?" the sheriff replies, his eyes narrowing. "I just want to know why you were walking around town with this boy."

"I wasn't!"

"Listen, son," the sheriff says, "sooner or later, young Neil is going to surface," he continues. "And when I say *surface*, do you know what I mean?"

The vision of Dutch popping up in front of the couple replays in my mind. And then I think about the blue thing I saw, in the water by the falls. Baby blue. I want to puke right into the principal's metal garbage can.

The sheriff presses on. "And when that happens, you'll be in a whole world of trouble," he assures me. "So wouldn't it be better to come clean now? Just explain your side of things. You're a minor, and that should help. Stay clammed up, and the state might try you as an adult. Then you'll be sorry you didn't take my help when I offered it."

My stomach folds inside out. I've heard enough. "I told you everything!" I shout, jumping out of my seat. The principal flinches as if I'm going to hit him, but the sheriff doesn't budge. "I'm telling you, I don't know anything about Neil!"

"Take it easy, Cal," Fernwood says. "Sit down."

I ignore him. "What are you saying, Sheriff? That I killed Neil and threw him over the falls?"

The sheriff doesn't respond, but instead he gives me a look like he's taking me apart and putting me back together. A thin smile stretches across his yellow teeth.

I stop myself from saying any more. I have to get a grip; otherwise, I'm going to do or say something I'll regret. Then I will get dragged out of here in handcuffs. Which is just what the sheriff wants.

I think about the image outside the bank. It's only random video, I tell myself—not serious evidence. We weren't even looking at each other; we could have passed in the street. And I haven't done anything, I'm sure of it. I hardly know Neil and have no reason to ever hurt him.

Other than calling him Baby-Blue.

"Last chance," the sheriff says.

I'm scared, but there's nothing to say. I turn to the other man, who is sitting there, stunned. "Principal Fernwood, can I please go to class? I'm really behind in my schoolwork after everything that's happened. And being late isn't helping me."

The principal looks at the sheriff. The lawman chews his pen for a moment, then nods. He looks disappointed, like a fisherman having to return a big out-of-season catch to the lake.

"All right, Mr. Harris," Fernwood tells me. "You can go."

I throw open the door and leave it that way. And I don't look back. I head down the deserted hallway to my locker, then down again to my first class. It's science, a subject I am actually close to bombing out in, falls or no falls.

The door is already closed. The whole room turns to stare as I enter. I don't have a note, I realize, but the teacher doesn't even ask for one. He just waits for me to sit down.

Everyone looks away as I take my seat. I spot Willow

sitting in the front row. I wonder what she's thinking this morning about what I told her last night. I can't even begin to imagine. Does she think I'm insane, some kind of delusional maniac?

I don't know. She doesn't look back.

I put my head on my desk and wait for the bell.

CHAPTER 17

I escape school without being arrested or beaten to death by the remaining Crocodiles, who glare at me whenever I pass. Once, I run straight into Holt the Buffalo, bouncing off him like a tennis ball, but fortunately I'm able to slip away into the crowd.

The day can't end soon enough.

After the bell I pull another Cole maneuver and quickly jam everything into my locker before exiting with an empty schoolbag. I then head outside and wait.

Luckily it's stopped raining, and there's actually an occasional ray of sun lighting up the leafy puddles. I'm standing by a tree, hood up, feeling a lot like Mr. Lampshade himself. I watch as the students start pouring out, some in a hurry to get home and others boarding buses or goofing around and talking in small groups.

Twenty minutes later, when Willow does not emerge, I start getting nervous. Could she have left out the back? Or maybe I just missed her. I realize I may not recognize her clothes now, just like I didn't know the black dress she wore to the party. Is she getting tutored or did she stay late for some team or a club? Somehow, I don't believe any of these explanations.

The library—the old one. It's worth a shot.

I jog back to the school, relieved that the doors aren't locked. I hurry upstairs. It's a risk, I know, because Willow might be leaving her locker at this moment.

The library is a graveyard. There's no one at any of the tables or in the comfortable seats set up around an old rug somebody must have donated. I'm wasting time—I have to hurry back outside. But first I check the stacks.

That's where I find her. She's already got a few books piled up beside her on the floor and is busy looking through what's on the shelves. She doesn't know I'm here.

"Ahem," I say, in the staged way Willow used to find funny. But now she just gasps, frightened out of her wits.

"Sorry! It's just me, Callum." It strikes me that this may be the very reason she's so terrified—because the maniac has her cornered again. "Look, I didn't mean to scare you. I don't know. Maybe trying to find you after school was a bad idea. I'll just go."

I turn and start heading toward the exit.

"Wait!" she says a moment later, and follows me out of the stacks. "It's okay. You just startled me. Come look at these."

I sit down at a table, staring at the beautiful girl with the dark hair and blue-green eyes.

"Are you listening, Callum? I need help going through this stuff."

I'm brought back to earth. "What am I looking for?"

"I don't know. Anything that might explain what's going on with you, I guess."

It's then I see what Willow has collected. There are books on the brain and on psychology, not surprisingly, but also on the paranormal, space, religion, philosophy, and even physics. All together there must be four thousand pages to go through.

"Are you sure this is going to help?" I ask.

But Willow just holds up a hand and silences me.

I know that gesture. She uses it when she's getting serious.

I grab a book at random. It's about physics. I'm wishing I'd picked up the one with the werewolf on the front, which I remember rejecting as useless for my Bigfoot project. I open the physics book anyway. On the inside cover, I see somebody's drawn a pretty decent cartoon version of Mr. Schroeder, all wild-eyed and waving the pointer he loved to use. The speech bubble is mean, though: *I've gone bonkers!*

It's just so typical of Crystal Falls High. Even the nicest, most fun teacher in the whole school can't escape the abuse. If I hated it here before, I hate it even more now.

"Hey, wait," I say. Willow looks up. "Last night, did I tell you about Mr. Schroeder?"

"No. What about him?"

I tell Willow the whole story about running into our teacher on the bridge and the "message" he threw off it. I mention how he accused me of being a terrible student, something Willow confirms, even though I insist I paid complete attention and got good grades.

"Actually, wait," Willow says, cutting off my attempt to repair my reputation. "Didn't Mr. Schroeder teach physics to the seniors? Wasn't that his specialty?"

"Yeah, why?"

"Well, there are all sorts of advanced theories in physics. Quantum leap. Multiverses. The subject goes into space and time even, into black holes and stuff. Here, give me that. . . ."

Willow helps herself to the book in front of me. Is a library book really going to solve the question of who or where I am? Not likely.

"Callum, can you look something up on the internet for me?"

"Hey, kids, sorry but I'm closing up," the librarian comes over to tell us.

"Why? It's not even four," Willow protests.

"The carpets are getting cleaned. It happens twice a year. Be glad. Be very glad."

"Okay, well, can we take these out?" Willow asks.

The librarian comes over and examines the stack of books. "Sorry, they're all reference only, except this one."

She holds up the one with the werewolf on it. "I can keep the rest for you behind the counter, if you'd like."

"Oh, forget it," Willow says. "Thanks."

I walk Willow down to her locker. She wants to continue our research on the internet, but she isn't sure her mother will like coming home to find a boy she doesn't know in the house. I'm not surprised; I remember how nervous her mom was about leaving us alone at first.

"There's my place, but it's across the bridge," I tell her. "And my computer sucks."

"Well, maybe we should both go home, and we can compare notes over the phone later," she says. I agree, noticing that she's looking me in the eyes a lot more and how the little creases at the corners of her mouth have returned.

It's good to have Willow back, if only in small ways.

We walk together until we reach the end of her block. I remember the sheriff and the false alibi about hanging out with Willow.

"It just came flying out of my mouth," I say, after running down exactly what I said to him. "I don't know what I was thinking."

Willow doesn't look happy to hear this.

"Listen, I know you didn't mean to do anything wrong, Callum. But did you have to involve me? It's the police . . ."

I feel like the little boy with the matches again, sitting in front of the burning garage. "I know. I'm sorry."

"Well, you're lucky you told me before the sheriff asked. I was actually supposed to stay at Lizzie's but came home after you said that stuff about my father. I told my mother we were at a party but that it got out of hand, so I left. So now she thinks I'm really responsible." Willow laughs at this, but I don't know why, because I always thought she *was* really responsible. "Anyway, if anybody asks, I'll say I met you in the park on the way and that you walked me home. How does that sound?"

"Great. Thanks."

"Just don't let it happen again. I mean it."

"Never. I promise."

"Good."

I shuffle around uncomfortably as we say good-bye, something else that hasn't changed. We agree to talk later that night.

I continue on through the town, feeling amazing. Other than getting my dog to like me again, it's the first time I've felt hopeful since waking up in the hospital. And even if everything does stay the same—and never goes back to the way I remember it—at least there's one person in town who hasn't changed that much. We can build a new friendship, I hope, once I get all this stuff behind me. Then I can go back to being the old Callum, the boring one.

But is that what I want? I think about the money in my pocket and the way girls now look at me. I'm not sure I want to give up either.

Passing the diner, I notice I'm hungry; I was too tense to eat lunch. With the long walk ahead, I probably should eat. I look at the menu in the window and decide that a deluxe cheeseburger would hit the spot. It's expensive, but I do have a fat pocketful of bills, after all. I just need to peel one off. I'll even get change back.

Anyway, it's probably best to spend this money as quickly as possible. But on nothing too flashy. Movies. Food. Treating Willow, maybe.

Just then Bryce passes me in the street. He doesn't notice me, too busy unwrapping himself a chocolate bar as he walks. He's got a bad addiction to candy, that guy, and it's getting him into trouble. Last year he had seven fillings. Seven! He has to kick that stuff.

He's carrying a plastic bag full of groceries his mother must have sent him to get. Despite my hunger, I decide to follow him. He has some answers I'd like to hear. And unless he has a bottle of chloroform and a pillow in that bag, I'm not really not too worried about my safety.

It's not long, though, before Bryce looks back and becomes aware that I'm following him. I'm worried he might run for it, but instead he just quickens his pace a bit, wrapping up the chocolate bar and putting it in his pocket.

But I'm on to his game, because I know where he lives.

As soon as he reaches the top of his block, he cuts hard and starts running for it. Oh no, you don't. Half a bar of chocolate isn't enough fuel for Bryce to outrun me, even when I'm on an empty tank.

The full plastic bag taking him out at the knees doesn't help. I tackle him onto a lawn, splitting the bag and sending a carton of milk and assorted fruits and vegetables flying.

"Help!" Bryce screams. "Get away from me! Get away from me!" he shrieks hysterically.

I drag Bryce behind a hedge by his jacket. Then I sit on him, pinning his arms under my knees like I used to do in our play fights.

Except instead of laughing, Bryce is crying now. I feel awful. What if Willow saw this? She would never speak to me again. But she's at home. And I want answers.

"Why did you do it?" I demand to know. "I heard you, Bryce, in the hospital room. Your voice. Why did you try to kill me?"

Bryce keeps on whimpering, tears streaming. This is useless, I think. He's too scared to talk, and I can't just sit on him until it gets dark. But all of a sudden, he looks up at me, his face red and contorted with rage.

"Because you killed Neil!" he spits out. "Because you killed my best friend in the whole world!"

I stand up. "Why do you think that, Bryce?" I ask as he scrambles into a defensive position. "I mean, seriously:

Why would I ever do something to Neil?"

He doesn't need much coaxing. "Because he wouldn't cheat for you anymore!"

"Cheat?" I repeat. "Why would I get Neil to cheat for me?"

"Oh, shut up. I know everything, Cal. What classes, how much you were paying, everything. And I know how, when he told you he couldn't do it anymore, you got mad and threatened him. But then he said he knew about the booze you sell, and if you didn't leave him alone, he'd tell. Because I was there, in the bushes, when you flashed a gun and made him take a walk with you."

I know Bryce pretty well, and he doesn't seem to be lying. But still, would I really carry a gun around town and threaten people with it? I wouldn't even consider the possibility had I not seen one in my own drawer.

But paying someone to cheat—I'm too cheap, I would have thought. I'd rather fail—and I'm saying this with six hundred bucks in my pocket.

At this point, anything seems possible. I have to hear him out.

"Then what happened?"

"I followed you guys. You were going to the falls. But when I saw you again, you were running back toward town. Alone. And Neil hasn't been seen since then!"

"Come on, Bryce," I say. "Why didn't you tell the police? Why didn't you just tell them what you saw?"

"Because I want you dead!" he shouts at me. "So does half the school! And I don't want you just thrown in some detention center to get sent back here three or four years later so you can come after me. I want it finished—I want you dead. And as soon as Hunter Holden gets out of the hospital, oh man, is it going to happen. You're dead, asshole! Dead!"

It's horrible, to see my former best friend's face so twisted with hate, to hear him wishing me dead and smiling at the prospect. But he's probably scared, too, about what he did. He's thinking that if he goes to the cops now, I'll just tell them what he tried to do while I was in a coma. There are plenty of cameras at the hospital—he must know. He must have been hoping to make it look like I died from my injuries.

But who cares? I need to fix this somehow. "Listen, Bryce, I understand why you did what you did at the hospital. And don't worry, I promise to never tell the police or anyone. But I don't know what happened to Neil, I swear. I don't remember the cheating or taking him on a walk, any of it. You see, after my accident, the whole town changed. . . ."

I'm ready to give Bryce the same story I gave Willow, before telling him secret things I know about his life, when he suddenly makes a noise, choking on tears and snot. Then he reaches out and grabs something from the grass. It's a potato that fell out when his shopping bag busted—a big, brown baker.

I'm just about to continue when Bryce hurls the thing at me. Thrown from point-blank range, it beans me square in the forehead. I feel incredible pain and see stars. Next thing I know, I'm on the ground clutching my face and yelling.

"Bryce!" I shout, trying to control the anger in my voice. "Wait, stop, Bryce!"

But he's gone. As I writhe on the ground, I can hear him thundering up his porch steps. His door slams. I'm sure he's triple-locking it, just like his mother always tells him to do.

A few minutes later, I get to my feet. Staggering around the yard, I pick up the fallen groceries, including the bricklike baking potato, and carry them with difficulty to Bryce's porch. There, I lay them all out.

But I'm finally overcome with pain and frustration. "Goddamn it!" I shout at the front door. Then I roof the potato.

I head home. I'm no longer hungry but nauseated. Cars honk at me as I stumble like a drunk into the street. I'm scared too—scared that Ross might run me over or that the sheriff will pick me up or that I'll run into any of the seemingly endless number of people in town who wish me harm these days.

I make it home alive. But this time there is no hiding the injury from my mother, who greets me at the door.

"Cal, omigod, your forehead! What happened?"

"I got hit by a potato," I say. It sounds almost funny. "A big, raw one."

"What? How did that happen?"

"Someone threw it at me," I admit, beyond lying anymore.

"Why on earth would they do that?"

"The same reason anyone would," I reply. "Because he hates me."

"Oh, Cal. Sit down on the couch. I'll get something for the swelling."

My mother returns a minute later with a dish towel full of ice cubes. She sits down and presses it against my forehead. I grit my teeth, grunting at how sore my head feels. "Who was the idiot who threw it?" she asks.

"It doesn't matter. And he isn't an idiot. He was just scared."

"Scared of what?"

"Of me."

"Why?" my mother asks, the sympathy draining from her voice. "What did you do to him?"

"I don't remember doing anything. But he thinks I did, and that's enough. And I only made things worse. Besides, it doesn't matter what I do—it's what people think that counts."

I decide to shut up. We sit there for a while. My forehead is stinging from the cold. I take the ice pack from my mother and try holding it up myself, removing it every so often to reduce the freeze. It's better. I'm just feeling numb.

"Tell me what happened to Cole," I say.

My mother looks at me, shocked. "What do you mean?"

"I mean, tell me what happened. Exactly. Why Cole is the way he is."

"You know what happened," she says. "You were there."

"No," I tell her. "I mean, I don't remember anymore. Ever since the falls, I don't remember much of anything. So I need to hear it again. I want you to tell me every-thing—tell me like I wasn't there. Do you understand? When it happened. Where it happened. Everything."

"You really don't remember? Cal, there *is* something wrong! You need a doctor!"

"No. I don't want to talk about that. Just tell me. Now."

My mother's face looks like a question: *Why are you doing this?* But when I don't budge, and sit staring from under the ice pack, she finally gives in.

"It was summer," she says, "just before we came to Crystal Falls. You and your brother were upset about mov-ing, about having to leave all your friends. So your father and I decided to take you out for a treat, to a fancy, new water park that had just opened up about an hour away."

"I know," I tell her. "I remember that day perfectly."

"Then why do you want to hear it again?"

"Because," I say, wincing as I press the ice pack too

hard. I don't know where this is leading. It was one of the last nice days we had together as a family, as far as I remember.

But my mother looks confused and upset, like I'm torturing her on purpose. She carries on. "Your father and I went on a few rides with you guys, but soon we had enough. So we found a picnic table in the shade and just sat and read while you and Cole went off."

"Yeah," I say. "Go on."

"Well, you were gone for about an hour or so when—" She breaks off. Her eyes fill with tears.

"Mom," I say. "When what?"

"When we heard people shouting for help. And saw lifeguards running by. We looked up and saw people crowding around the bottom of the big slide."

This part I don't remember. My mother looks away, toward the window. She swallows hard and sniffs. I give her a moment instead of pushing her.

"I decided to go see what was going on," she finally says. "Your father stayed behind, telling me not to be another gawker. But I had a terrible feeling. So I ran up—there was a hill—and heard someone say they'd just taken somebody out of the pool at the bottom of the big slide. I couldn't see much, because of the people in front of me, except that it was a teenager who wasn't moving." My mother fights back a sob. "And then I saw the red-and-yellow bathing suit. . . ."

Cole's surfer trunks.

"No," I stop her. "That's wrong. Nothing happened to Cole on that slide. I went down just after him."

"No, Cal," my mother tells me. "Don't you remember? You were too scared to go up, so Cole went by himself. But he started showing off, like he used to, and he went down headfirst. And somehow he fractured his spine."

"No!" I shout. "That didn't happen. He didn't go down headfirst. Because I went up with him and told him off, saying I would tell on him if he didn't follow the rules. He went down normally, Mom, I saw him. He was fine, waiting at the bottom for me. I remember. He told me I got nice air!"

"Cal, please stop," my mother begs me. "It wasn't your fault. You know what your brother was like back then. He was difficult, a daredevil, and he never listened to anybody. Just like you are now, I suppose, which is why we worry so much about you. But it was just an accident. Even if you had gone up, you could never have stopped him. . . ."

"But Mom, I did go up!" I yell at her. "I did stop him! And it never happened! That never happened!"

Bursting into tears, my mother gets up and races out of the room. I hear her go upstairs, into her room. The door closes.

I feel bad. But what she said isn't true, I know it. Not unless I've gone crazy.

But maybe it's that simple. I'm crazy—or more like damaged. I sank to the bottom of a raging river; I would have drowned, but the cold kept me alive, and now this is my brain fizzling and popping, making me believe in some imaginary other life.

It makes perfect sense; I just have to prove it.

I go upstairs and turn on the computer. And wait. And wait. I want to punch the screen.

Finally I type in a search. It's not for "quantum leap" or whatever other nonsense Willow was talking about. But I don't look up head trauma either or multiple-personality disorder or *Dr. Jekyll and Mr. Hyde*. I search for something else, something simpler, in order to get my diagnosis:

"Cole Harris water slide accident."

The number one result is a news article dated four years ago. I click it and read.

So it's settled. I have gone crazy.

CHAPTER 18

Willow phones that evening, but I don't take the call. My father unhappily passes along a message that I'm asleep. Mom still hasn't come out of her room, nor have I, and Dad has come home to nothing to eat. He comes into my room at one point and tries to get me to tell him what happened, but I answer that I've just lost my mind, that's all.

He closes the door and tries speaking to Mom again. But that doesn't sound like it goes much better.

By the time the phone rings again for me, Dad has had enough. "Cal, would you pick up the damn phone? Some girl really wants to talk to you, and I'm not your answering service. If you don't feel like chatting right now, you can tell her yourself."

I sigh and pick up. "Hello?"

"Callum? Sorry, it's Willow. You were asleep?"

"No," I admit. "I'm just not in the mood to talk right now. Can it wait until I see you at school tomorrow?" This is assuming I even make it to school. I could be in a rubber room talking gibberish to myself by then.

"Well, I guess it can wait," she answers, sounding

miffed. "I just thought you'd like to hear this as soon as possible, since it concerns your life and everything. . . ."

"Look, I didn't mean to be rude," I reply. "I got into a scuffle on the way home, and I'm feeling pretty sore."

"A scuffle? You mean a fight? With who?"

"With Bryce," I reply. "But it wasn't exactly a fight. I was trying to explain everything that's been going on, but he wasn't buying it, and he hit me with something." I decide to spare her the embarrassing detail about being laid low by a vegetable. "Listen, I really think my memory is just screwed up from the accident. Maybe I should stop screwing around and see a doctor."

"Oh really?" she says, sounding completely annoyed now. "And how did you screw up your own memory but then suddenly know everything about my personal life? Did you ask yourself that?"

She's right—that piece still doesn't fit. "Okay, so what did you find out? Anything?"

"Not really. I tried looking up cases like yours on the internet, but there wasn't much, and it was all pretty stupid and useless. I even tried looking up quantum mechanics, but I didn't understand much, to be honest. There was a lot about some cat in a box that gets poisoned by gas when an atom does something, and how it can be both dead and alive at the same time, creating two branches of reality.

"The important thing is that it got me thinking. And

it made me remember something weird that happened a while back."

"What?" I ask, feeling lost.

"Well, you know how my half brother and half sister are twins, right?"

"Uh-huh," I answer impatiently, this being one of the details I used to convince Willow of my story.

"And do you remember studying human reproduction in biology with Mr. Schroeder?"

"Sort of. I was sick that week," I tell her. "That was the one test I flunked." It was a big disappointment, because I thought my biology average might have put me closer to making my parents happy and into new-computer territory.

"What do you mean you were sick? You were making dirty jokes the whole class until the teacher threw you out." Willow pauses. "But that's the point! Maybe that wasn't you!"

"What do you mean?"

"Hear me out. As I was saying, we were talking about human reproduction. After class I hung around to ask Mr. Schroeder what the difference between fraternal and identical twins were. I still didn't understand how my father could have a boy and a girl but that they could still be twins."

"Well, that's easy. It's because they came from two separate eggs," I tell her. Heck, even I knew that, and I failed the test.

"Yeah, yeah. Anyway, when we were talking, Mr. Schroeder mentioned that he actually had an identical twin brother."

"I know that too," I say. "I met him in the supermarket. I told you that ages ago."

"No, you didn't," she answers, sounding like this is somehow exciting news to hear. "You never even spoke a word to me until recently, as far as I'm concerned, remember? But anyway, you couldn't have met him! Not here, at least."

"Why not?"

"Because his brother died when they were kids!"

"So Mr. Schroeder really is crazy if he's going around pretending to be his dead twin brother."

"Let me finish," Willow says. "I remember feeling bad to hear it and saying how sorry I was. But he said it was all right; it had happened a long time ago. And at least he knew his brother was alive and well in another universe. A nearby universe, in fact."

"He said that?"

"Yeah. I made a joke, saying wouldn't it be nice to go visit him. But then he got really serious and said that he planned to do exactly that."

"Come on, Willow. He *is* crazy, then. Totally nuts."

"Hey, you saw him throwing a message off the bridge. What was that about? Who was it for?"

"Like I said, he was just being wacko."

"Okay, then explain this," Willow says. "How come Mr. Schroeder agrees with me and thinks you were a jerk in his class?"

The accusation is really getting on my nerves. Biology was my best subject. I paid complete attention and tried really hard, at least until we got a new teacher.

"No," I reply. "I never acted up in class. And I did well in biology."

"Which means it must have been a different class— and a different Mr. Schroeder. One whose twin brother is still alive! Do you get it?"

Willow is talking so fast, I'm having a hard time processing everything. What is she getting at?

The answer hits me like a potato in the forehead.

"Wait, are you saying you think I come from another universe?" I can't believe that I've just said it out loud. "The universe Mr. Schroeder was talking about?"

But instead of laughing at me, Willow yells: "Yes! A universe where your parents did split up but where your brother isn't paralyzed and where everyone calls you Callum!"

Listening to this, I feel a strange tingling sensation race across my body. It reminds me of the time Mr. Schroeder explained how we are each assembled from the bits of exploded stars. Though it sounds amazingly plausible, I can't really believe it. Because I don't feel that special. Exploded stars? Coming from another universe? I'm a kid, that's all. A kid who goes to Crystal Falls High. There's nothing extraordinary about me.

"If that's true, then how did I get here?" I ask. But this time, I'm not lagging behind for long—I don't even need to hear Willow's answer, which she yells into my ear.

The falls.

I must have come through when I went over. When I went under.

"But if I'm not from here—if I really came from somewhere else—doesn't that mean—"

I stop talking, putting the phone against my chest. Willow is saying something, but I can't hear her. I can't hear anything over the rush of blood in my ears, knowing that the proof is very possibly only a short jog away from here.

"Willow, I have to go," I say.

"No, Cal, wait!"

I hang up the phone.

I go to the closet and start riffling through the mess. The phone starts ringing again, but I ignore it, and so does my father. I'm throwing out shoes, balls, gear, all stuff I've never seen before. When I find what I'm looking for, I don't even recognize it, other than noticing that it's made of wood and has the word *Slugger* burned into it.

Not that it matters. Wood or aluminum, a bat is a bat.

And a bat is a decent weapon.

I don't answer my father when he demands to know where I'm going or why I won't answer the phone, which is once again ringing as I put on my sneakers.

Instead I throw on a jacket and go out into the night.

I want to get there in a hurry, but I decide against jogging. With my stomach empty and growling, I'll need all the energy I have. I'm hoping my body has been working overtime to replace all the adrenaline I've used up this week. Is it possible to run out?

I take the turn up to the campground, thankful for the moonlight, since I wasn't smart enough to bring a flashlight. Looking like a cool, blue river, the road is easy to follow, bordered by the tall grassy field. Still, it's dangerous going, as a few times I step in unseen potholes and nearly sprain my ankle.

I reach Guise's seedy trailer, but there's no dented pickup parked outside. Blue light flickers behind the drawn curtains as I pass. Peeking between a gap, I see that Guise is inside. He's drinking whiskey and watching TV, his head lolling around like he is seriously out of it. As I move off, I'm startled by the sound of him violently clearing his throat before spitting vilely. I hope it's into a nearby garbage can.

The disgusting image this creates drives a spike through my stomach. But it seems that the cupboard is not yet bare of adrenaline, because it's leaching into my system, making my heart pound and my pace quicken. Still, I need to be careful—to slow down and keep quiet. The last thing I need is for Guise to hear something and come looking.

Then again, he's wasted. He's not going anywhere. It's odd, though, that his pickup is gone.

Shaded from the moonlight, the trailer park itself is much darker and harder to navigate. Several times I walk straight into obstacles—trees, poles, sometimes entire trailers—and constantly clatter the baseball bat off unseen objects. Once I even go sprawling over a plastic bench and end up on my hands and knees in the cold dirt. A ninja I am not. But slowly my eyes are adjusting, and I'm walking into things less often, making progress in the direction I remember.

A lit window appears. I see it now, the same trailer where I was beaten up. There's a truck parked out front this time, a newer model. It's only when I get up close that I recognize the bumper sticker.

KEEP HONKING, I'M RELOADING!

Oh no, it's Ross. Are you kidding me?

But wait. It's not like I need to say hi. I just need to see his face, the hooded figure's, with my own eyes. Then I will know for sure if it's true. Then I can start doing something about it.

And what exactly will that be? I ask myself. Tell my

parents? If it's all true, they're strangers anyway. Go to the police? I can imagine their reaction, considering they already think I killed a kid.

Another worry occurs to me. If I'm not from here, not supposed to be here, who will miss me if I vanish? As much as I should know this guy, I'm pretty sure he's psychotic. And he has a gun, and he probably killed Neil. Who can say what he will do?

Suddenly the baseball bat feels a lot less comforting.

I peer through the open curtains for a while. There's no movement—no flickering, no shadows—and there are no sounds. I think back to hearing Mr. Guise hack up a lung in his trailer—it was like he was standing outside with me. Which means there's probably no one in there. Either that, or they're fast asleep. With the lights on.

But what about Ross's truck? It doesn't add up. Still, I need to take a look. I have to peek, see if there are any signs of recent occupation. That's what I came here to do. And that's what I'm going to do.

I try the door. It's unlocked again. I hesitate, remembering what that bit of luck got me last time—a terrible beating. But then I open it. And climb the stairs inside.

This time I'm really not fooling around though—I'm going to crack the skull of anyone who comes near me. I can assemble the shards and ask questions later.

But in my sweaty grip, the bat feels like it's been greased. One swing, and I'm probably losing hold of it.

And in these cramped quarters, that swing is going to be pretty unspectacular.

That's when I see the lampshade, the two eyeholes staring straight at me. They are burning full of hateful flames. I recoil in terror, clutching the bat with about the same menace as I'd hug a teddy bear.

It's only the lamp, I see, with the shade back on. With a stifled laugh, I relax. But then I look at the floor and see Ross.

At least I'm guessing it's Ross, based on his length and bulk. And the name embroidered on his work clothes.

His face, however, offers no confirmation. It looks like a caved-in pumpkin that's been sprayed with red paint.

I stand there, rigid with horror, a scream lodged in my throat.

At that moment a vehicle pulls up, its headlights blinding me through the window. It skids to a stop outside the door. I hear a door slam and footsteps. Unable to move, I just stand there helplessly. When I finally turn, I see myself standing in the doorway shaking my head. It's like I'm looking in a mirror, except in my reflection I have greasy hair and am wearing a Crocodiles jacket.

"Think fast." The baseball bat clatters onto the floor as I catch a roll of plastic sheeting. "Since you're here, you might as well help clean this up."

"What?" I answer. I'm talking to myself now. This feels like a dream. A really horrible dream I can't wake up from.

"Help me clean this up," the other me answers irritably, face hard as he pushes by. "This is just as much your problem as it is mine."

"Huh?"

"The bastard tried to kill me," I say—he says—walking over to the body. The other me toes an arm, which flops onto the floor holding a large-caliber pistol. "Must have followed me when I took Guise's truck to get supplies at the gas station. We have an arrangement, the old bastard and me. Or at least we had one. But with Ross out of the picture, I don't know how the hell I'm going to keep up my end of the bargain. Any ideas? Do you have any money?"

I stand there, mouth open. The smell of sweat in the trailer is now unbearable. I can't remember ever reeking like that.

"Whatever. We'll think of something. Anyway, we're lucky Ross didn't make his move at the house—otherwise he might have shot Mom as well. He was waiting for this chance, and he had a good one, all right, with Guise too drunk and deaf to hear a shot. He had the drop on me too—rolled up to the door real quiet, lights off and everything."

I watch the other me remove the cap from a pop bottle and take a swig. It hisses as he slams it back on the counter.

"But you had to lip off first, didn't you, big boy?" the

other me shouts at the dead body. "Too bad you're not as fast with a gun as you are with your mouth. Oh, and by the way, about your bumper sticker? Honk, honk! Honk, honk!"

I watch the other me cackle at the joke. He's insane. That's when I'm hit with the full horror of the corpse with the blown-off face. Retching, I drop the sheeting and bust through the door to the toilet.

I barely make it in time.

"All right, all right. I know it's gross," I hear my own voice calling, when I'm done heaving. "Look, I've thrown a towel over him, so it doesn't look so bad. You can come out now."

But I don't move. I stay in the bathroom, dripping with sweat. Every thought, every little motion, makes me queasy beyond belief. I don't want to leave this room. Maybe I don't have to. Maybe I can just lock the door.

But I'm too late. The door is thrown open, and I'm yanked to my feet. "I said you can come out now. Stop screwing around. We're wasting time."

I'm hauled by the collar back into the living area, where a glance confirms there's now a towel lying over Ross's head. A red stain is quickly spreading across the center.

"Yeah, so anyway, you want to know how this is your problem too? Well, imagine if he had shot me and buried me in a hole or something. Then he goes out for a drive and passes you prancing down Main Street. What do you think he'd do next? He'd come after you, at home maybe, which would mean Mom and maybe Dad would get it—maybe even Cole too, to make it look like some real maniac did it. So you should be thanking me. I saved your life, buddy. And probably saved our family's life.

"But I was thinking, to hell with chopping him up into pieces. I personally don't think I can handle that, and listening to you in the john, you're even worse.

"So I say we just wrap him up in the plastic and chuck him over the falls with the gun. There's a chance they'll find the body, but there's no way they're finding the gun." I watch the other me pry the weapon from the dead man's hand and admire it. "Anyway, we've got a new one that holds more bullets. So we're good."

I look on in disbelief as the other me flicks on the safety and jams the gun down the back of his pants. The butt of the .45, meanwhile, hangs out of the Crocodiles jacket pocket.

The other me takes another mouthful of soda and belches.

"It shouldn't be too hard moving him," the other me assures me. "I saw a dolly in the back of his truck, a heavy one with straps. We'll take him up, dump him, then come back here and wipe down this place properly. I bought rags and bleach, which were cheap. By then everybody should be asleep, and we can park Ross's truck back in his driveway. Then we're done."

I still feel like I'm in a dream, like none of this is real.

"Who are you?" I ask.

The other me laughs. "Wasn't I asking you the same question? As far as I can tell, I'm a better version of you. Or you're a really shitty version of me. Either way, go figure."

I notice that my voice is a little different from this other version of myself, who sounds more like a recording of me. I suppose that makes sense—you never hear your own voice as it actually sounds.

"What happened to Neil Parson?" I ask next. "Did you kill him?"

The other me turns with a glare. "I didn't kill Neil," he replies through gritted teeth. "But yeah, he's dead, it's probably safe to assume."

"What did you do to him?"

"Nothing!" He sighs, frustrated. "I just wanted to scare him, is all, keep his mouth shut. So I took him up to the falls, where I thought I'd threaten him a little. But then he ran off on me, back across the bridge. Everything was slick with rain, and he slipped. Man, I still don't know how he did it, going under the rails like that. I mean, Neil, what the hell—just grab on, dude! But he was a skinny kid and uncoordinated. So that's what happened. Didn't even hear him scream or anything. Whoops. Sploosh. Gone."

The other me rubs his face, then breathes out heavily.

"So I panicked, worried somebody saw us together.

And with good reason, because someone did, right—Bryce? I thought I saw the little pecker when I was heading back. Anyway, I decided to lay low for the night, in case I had to make a run for it. I broke into the trailer and slept in there until Guise caught me in the morning. So I ran off and kept to the woods the next day, all the time watching the river. Then, sure enough, the cops and the paramedics came. But instead of snagging Neil, they pull out some other guy. You.

"I got up pretty close and watched the paramedics putting you in the ambulance. I couldn't believe my eyes. I thought maybe I'd lost my mind. But later, there you were, in the hospital, unconscious. Another me. I saw you through the window.

"That's when Bryce came into the room. Who'd have thought the little stain had it in him? Oh, and you're welcome again, because it was me who scared him off. Yeah, I was mad. You wanna play rough, pecker? I'll show you rough. But he must have gone out a side door at the hospital, because I lost him. And later, well, I guess I didn't think I could actually kill someone. On purpose.

"But whatever. Bryce is scared and keeping his mouth shut, which is good. And we don't need any more bodies. Plus we got lucky with Neil—the falls have him, and I don't think anyone's ever finding the guy. Which hopefully will be the case with Ross here as well."

Listening to this, it's getting easier and easier to accept

that this person is not me. His face, full of psychotic pride, is becoming more alien than familiar. I can see this guy as the Crocodiles star running back, completing passes and faking out teenaged monsters, all the while wearing the same smug smile he's got on now. Even standing over the body unfolding the plastic sheeting, he looks like he's somehow happy—and in control.

"So I was thinking," he says, "you and I could really make this work, really make an enterprise out of what we've got. Now we'll have to figure out the accommodations, because there's no way I'm living in a trailer for the rest of my life, but maybe we can get some sort of schedule going. You know, swap around: One week at home, one week here, or wherever we decide. We'll have to be careful, though, because we don't want to get spotted in two places at once, which is pretty easy to do in a pissant town like this one.

"But if we play our cards right, we can start pulling off some serious stuff. Rake in the cash. With two of us, there are so many possibilities! And when we need an alibi? We lock one down and make sure there are plenty of witnesses. Meanwhile the other guys puts on a mask and knocks over a bank or a jewelry store or whatever.

"We keep going like that until we're eighteen and can get out of here, and then we'll get a place together. Because I don't know about you, but I want out. And when you think about it, it's really in the city that we'll start seeing the benefits of one of us not really existing.

"In the meantime, as far as our social life goes, we'll split that up too. You know what? Screw Ivy if you want. What do I care? So long as she thinks it's me, no hard feelings. But it's only fair—you gotta let me tap whatever action you're getting in return. Like what do you have going on with the little dark-haired chick from concert band? Anything good?"

Now I'm the angry one. I snap up the baseball bat lying at my feet. "You keep away from Willow!" I shout, ready to bash his head in. "I mean it! I'm not going along with any of this crap! Do you understand?"

The other me makes a disappointed face and then in one fluid motion draws Ross's gun. The barrel stops level with my forehead, already marked with a bruised bull's-eye. "I thought you'd be smarter, Cal. You're me, after all. But think. If you don't go for my plan—which is a great one, by the way—then you're useless to me. You go back to being the guy who is screwing up my life even worse than I already did myself—and, trust me, I've done a pretty good job.

"So if you're useless, then what? I want my life back, Cal. I want my house, my room, my stuff, and most of all my shower and washing machine, believe it or not. I want it all enough to kill for. Do you understand me?"

I do understand him. Perfectly. "I said stay away from Willow!" I shout.

The other me doesn't even flinch, just looks ready to pull the trigger and put a round in my head if I take another step forward. Which I don't.

"If that's your big issue, fine," he finally says, lowering the gun. "I don't really go for the mousy types anyway. But that means Ivy is off the table—I mean it. Anyway, enough about that for now—let's get this cleaned up. Do I have to point out that your fingerprints are probably all over the place? Something tells me they're just like mine."

I take another look at Ross, whose blood has completely soaked through the towel. It crosses my mind how the women of Crystal Falls are safe now from his unwanted advances at least. But then I start retching, so uncontrollably that I double over and drop the bat.

"Omigod," the other me says. "Listen, pussy—go out to the truck and get the dolly already. I'll wrap him up myself. We have to get moving!"

Panting, I rest my sweaty forehead against the wall.

"Are you listening to me?"

I nod.

"Then go!"

Head spinning, I stumble out the door.

CHAPTER 19

The air outside helps a bit, but nausea is still overwhelming me.
I climb unsteadily up onto the truck's bumper and jump
in, scraping my leg on something jagged. Even with the
light spilling out from the trailer, it's dark and I can't see
anything. Every object I find seems to be a tool with some
sort of blade I hurt myself on.

What am I doing? I have to wonder. I'm out of the
trailer now. I'm free. I can just run off.

But I'm too scared. I'm too scared of this person who
looks like me and talks like me. He would destroy me, I
know it.

I could hide. But then I think about how he would still
take my place. With a hot shower and a change of clothes,
no one would know the difference. Because here in this
world, there would be no difference. This is the Cal everyone knows. This is the Cal everyone fears.

And fear is the only reason I'm feeling around the
dark truck bed trying to unearth the dolly from the pile of
other crap in here. When I manage to find it, the thing is
surprisingly heavy and hard for me to lift over the edge.

But I manage. The steel frame hits the ground with a clank. I jump down after it.

On its wheels the dolly is easy to move, and I manage to pull it up after me into the trailer, one stair at a time. By now the other me has already finished wrapping up the body and is securing the plastic with duct tape.

"Doesn't it feel like Christmas Eve in here?" he asks, grinning at me. "I wonder what a kid would say if he found this present under the tree in the morning. . . ."

The black humor that Bryce and I once would have found so funny now seems totally demented. I watch, sickened, as the other me finishes up by tearing the tape off with his teeth.

He orders me to bring the dolly over. I do as he says. Now he wants help lifting the body up.

I finally understand the term *dead weight* as we strain to lift Ross off the ground. We try propping him up on the dolly, but it tips and crashes to the floor, taking us with it.

It's a grotesque moment, but it more or less gets the body into position.

"Help me pull him up!" the other me barks. "His feet, his feet! Get them on the plate. There, that's good. Now let's strap him on, good and tight."

Somehow I get my part of the job done, all the while telling myself none of this is real, that there isn't really a person under all that plastic, just a big side of beef that needs to be moved to a refrigerated location before it spoils. But with my stomach lurching again, I don't know if this image doesn't only make things worse.

Once the body is secure, we lift the dolly up to a sixty-degree angle.

"Okay, get out of the way!" the other me shouts, taking the handles. I leave him in charge of maneuvering toward the door. "Actually, go outside and grab the bottom. It'll be easier to carry him out like he's on a stretcher than bounce him down these steep stairs."

While this might be easier, it's in no way easy. Combined with the heavy dolly, the load must be two hundred and fifty pounds, and it feels like I'm taking most of it. There's no way I can do this. The stairs crack audibly when I finally drop my end, and I'm lucky not to be crushed as the rolling corpse comes bouncing toward me.

Thanks to gravity, it's done though—the grisly load is now out of the trailer and on the ground.

"Dumbass!" the other me shouts from the stairs. "Why did you let go?"

"I didn't let go. It was too heavy."

"Well, you're a weakling *and* a dumbass then. Anyway, let's get a move on. Lead the way."

"To where?"

"To the falls, moron. Didn't I already tell you?"

The other me is smart enough to have brought a flashlight, which he promptly hands over. I turn it on and look for the path. I find one made of hard-packed dirt. I don't know which direction to go though.

"It's left, genius," the other me says. "Haven't you ever walked up to the falls this way before?"

I suppose I haven't. I always felt shy, walking past the paying campers to the south end of the falls, where the footbridge connects up to the north side of town. A few times I tried taking a shortcut home from the other side, but that was enough. I never liked that bridge. I only go on it when other people make me, when I'm forced to swallow my fear. I never thought it was safe.

Which it isn't, apparently, as demonstrated by Neil. I even said the gap under the lower rail was too wide, but Cole just laughed at me. "If you're trying that hard to fall off, you deserve what you get," he answered. But poor Neil didn't deserve anything that horrible. It was an accident.

The other me sounds like he's having a hard time rolling Ross along the now bumpy, overgrown path to the falls. Grunting and swearing, he never asks for help though. He just keeps shouting at me to hold the flashlight so he can see where he's going. It's weird, hearing my own voice, grim and terrifying, like a whip at my back.

I'm feeling pretty worn-out by the time we arrive at the falls. Turning around, I see that the other me looks even more exhausted. Soaked with sweat, he is also now stinking like a skunk. How can he stand his own smell?

He probably has the exact same nose as me, after all.

"Get the light out of my face!" he shouts at me. "Man, that was hard. Give me a minute."

I switch off the flashlight and wait. Standing by the stairs to the footbridge, I try to tune out the terrifying roar of the falls. But I can't. There's no sound I've heard that matches its power. Nothing in this world can silence it, outside of an earthquake or an ice age.

"Okay, I'm almost out of gas. You're going to have to really help me get him up the stairs."

Shoulder to shoulder, I stand by whatever he is—my twin, my alternate, my doppelgänger—and pull the dolly onto the bridge stair by stair. "Keep going," the other me says upon reaching the top. "Keep going till the center." We keep pulling, the heavy load making the bridge's sway feel all the more pronounced and unbearable. "Okay, stop here."

We stand the dolly upright against the railing. The plastic-wrapped body looks like a mummy in the autumn moonlight, which once again shines down brightly on us. I can see the headlights of vehicles crossing the bridge not far away. Can they see us at this distance? I have no idea.

The other me removes the .45 from his jacket and without a word chucks it into the falls.

"Okay, if we release the straps, I'm betting he goes forward and over," the other me says. "But be ready in case he needs a push. Whatever happens, don't let him hit the ground; we don't want to have to hoist him over. I don't know about you, but I don't think I have the strength anymore."

I don't want any part of this. Still, I feel helpless to ignore the commands of my crazed opposite. So I start unclipping the bottom straps while he works on the top. And before long the plastic cocoon holding Ross's lifeless body begins pitching forward.

"Now!" the other me shouts. "Push! Push! Push!"

This time I do nothing. I just stand back and watch as he does all the work. It doesn't take much. The body lands on the railing and stays there for a moment in what looks like perfect balance, which is almost comedic. But then the body slides forward and falls. There's a pause and then a huge splash—bigger than I've seen from even the largest dropped rock.

"Holy crap!" the other me squeals with what sounds like delight. "Did you see that?"

But I didn't see it. Because I was too busy. Too busy reaching for the gun that barely remained stuffed down the back of the other me's pants. He turns around as I flick off the safety and aim the business end at his head.

"Oh come on, Cal, you can't be serious."

"It's *Callum*, ass-wipe."

"Really?" he asks with a laugh. "Well, I don't care if it's Dave or Donny or Dixie, for that matter, because I know you aren't going to shoot me."

"Oh yeah?" I ask. His face looks so sure, I really do feel like putting a bullet in it. His face—my face. The gun wavers.

"That's right," he says, grinning at the sight of me. "It's hard to shoot someone when he looks just like you, isn't it, Callum? I know. Otherwise I would've splattered your brains all over the trailer the other day. So what's it going to be? Are you going to hand over the gun and play nice, or am I going to have to take it off you, which won't be nice?"

I don't know—I haven't thought any further than this. I always thought that when you had the gun, it was game over. But my next move isn't obvious. If I shoot him, I'll be the only Callum Harris walking around, which sounds like a good start. But then what? I'll be a murderer—with two bodies on my hands.

But if I don't shoot this psycho, something even worse is going to happen.

"Why are you like this?" I ask.

"Huh?" he replies, obviously not expecting this question.

"Why are you like this? You just killed a guy and made jokes about it, and then you dumped his body like it was trash. You bullied a harmless kid, and now he's dead. You're beating people up, cheating in school, stealing booze, nailing some guy's girlfriend. So I want to know:

Why are you like this?"

The other me stares back, eyes narrowed. "Why am I like this?" he asks. "Why not? The world is an unfair shit hole, and I'm at war with it. Is that a good enough answer, old buddy? Look at you: You're supposed to be identical to me. So I think the real question is, why *aren't* you like this?"

"Because I like my life!" I shout. "Because I have good friends, and we have fun together. Because I love my parents and my dog. And because I love my brother, Cole, even though he's a pain in the ass who's always getting into trouble, like you."

The other me frowns. Now he is furious. "What do you mean he's always getting into trouble? He's paralyzed!"

"No," I correct him. "You're the one with the paralyzed brother. Mine is totally fine. He never had an accident at the water park, because I went up and stopped him from doing something stupid. That's all I do actually—try to stop him from hurting himself. And it's a full-time job!"

Speechless, Cal stares back at me. He's shaking from head to foot. Even in the moonlight I can see his eyes shining with tears. He doesn't look like the badass anymore. He just looks like a broken boy.

And here I am, holding a gun on the guy. So who is the monster now?

I haven't lowered the weapon more than a few inches

before he punches me one, right in the jaw. I'm knocked clean off my feet and land on my back on the wet bridge. There's a *clonk* as something hits the metal deck.

The gun. I've dropped it. But where?

The other me has already got it. I know that, because he's dragged me onto my knees and is cramming the barrel into my mouth.

"What do you mean you went up with Cole?" he's shouting above both the wind and the falls. "What do you mean you stopped him? We didn't go up. We didn't stop him!" But I'm no longer listening or thinking about the water park. Instead I'm back in the attic, where my brother is also on his knees, with a gun in his mouth.

....

"What are you doing?" I demand to know.

"Me? Nothing," Cole answers, removing the gun and waving it around like it's just the TV remote or something.

"Where did you get that gun?"

"Oh, this?" Now he's acting like he's surprised to find it in his hand. "It's Granddad's."

"Where did you find it?"

"In a trunk. I found it when we were moving, when I carried up all the stuff to be stored in the attic. I was looking through his things: his old uniform, his medals, his letters. And then I found the gun, wrapped up in cloth in a secret compartment."

"You found a gun, and you didn't tell Mom and Dad? Why?"

"Why do you think? Because they'd take it away, dimwit."

"So you just hid it."

"No. I just put it back where I found it, where I could get at it if I needed it someday."

"Needed it for what?"

"Who knows? Serial killers. Zombies. Whatever."

"Look around. Do you see any serial killers or zombies?"

"Can't say that I do, Cal."

"Then why do you have a gun, and why are you sticking it in your mouth?"

Cole sighs. "Little brother, you're asking a lot of questions. And I don't really feel like answering them right now. So I suggest you just go back downstairs and leave me alone before I lose my temper."

"Why?" I ask. "Are you going to shoot me if I don't?"

"Stop with the questions!" Cole shouts. Standing up, he cracks his head on a beam. "Ow! Look what you made me do!"

"Give me the gun, Cole!"

"No way. You'll shoot yourself in the foot or something. And then I'll be in trouble." He smiles. He thinks this is funny.

"Give it to me!"

"And then what?"

"Then I'm taking it up to the falls and throwing it in!"

"Don't be stupid," Cole says. "This is our grandfather's sidearm from the war! He wore it in the jungle, defended himself with it. For all we know, this gun is the only reason Dad and us got to be here. It's a family heirloom!"

"If it's such an heirloom, why are you hiding it from everybody?"

"Like I said, I'm not hiding it. It's in exactly the same place I found it. I'm just making sure it *stays* in the family, is the thing. And I know that might have looked bad, but I was only fooling around."

"Cole, give it to me or else."

"Or else what, *Callum*?"

"Or else I'll tell Mom and Dad!" I yell.

"Tell them!" Cole bellows at me. "By the time they get here, I'll be dead anyway. So what does it matter? *Go tell them!*"

I burst out crying. It's the same noise I would make when I was seven and my brother was determined to destroy something I loved. And just like then, Cole doesn't appear to care. He kneels back down and cups the gun in two hands.

"You really wanna watch?" he finally says. "I wouldn't. But that's your choice. Don't say I didn't warn you." He raises the gun, and this time he points it at his temple.

"Cole!" I shout. "You wanna do something stupid?

Okay, well, so do I! So fuck you!"

I thunder down the attic stairs and leave him to it. But he won't pull the trigger. Not until he knows what I'm up to. I know him too well.

"Cal!" I hear, just before I slam the front door behind me.

My brother finally finds me in the garage, busy putting the ladder up against a beam. At a glance he looks like he no longer has the gun, at least.

"Cal, what are you doing?"

"Getting a life jacket."

"Why?"

"Because I need a life jacket, jackass," I tell him, climbing up to the top of the ladder. "Why else?"

"What for?"

This time I don't answer. I grab the first orange life jacket I find and toss it down, purposely aiming for my brother.

"You missed."

"Whoops."

I climb down, pick up the jacket, and head out the garage door without a word.

"Cal, what are you doing?" my brother calls after me. "If Dad drops by, he'll be pissed you left the ladder up like that, you know."

"So?"

"So you'll get in trouble."

"Then move it if you care so much. I'm busy."

"Busy doing what?"

"I told you," I say over my shoulder. "I'm doing something stupid."

I march down the drive to the road, putting on the jacket so I don't have to carry it. It must look funny, because I'm getting amused looks from drivers. But they can go to hell. Everyone can go to hell.

My brother is tailing me, staying about fifty feet back. From time to time he calls my name, but eventually he gives up and just keeps walking after me. It starts raining, but I don't care. I don't stop. So neither does Cole.

We head along the road where I take Jess for walks, along the mowed field where we play fetch. We then make our way through the campground, which is empty except for a few hardcore outdoor types who look up curiously as we pass. We must make a strange spectacle: the quietly crying boy wearing a life jacket followed by his older brother into the darkening evening.

At the end of the campground, I reach the marked path that leads up to the falls. It's well trodden, almost like a gully winding its way through the forest. I'm getting tired now, keeping up this pace. But slowing down will make me look less determined. So I take it up a notch instead. My brother sighs and does too.

"All right, Cal. Come on," he says when I finally reach the stairs leading up to the bridge. "Enough is enough.

What are you trying to prove?"

"I'm not trying to prove anything, Cole," I answer. "I'm doing something."

"What are you doing?"

"I've told you like five times already!" I shout at him. "Something stupid!"

It's at this point that I start fastening all the belts on the life jacket, which, from a glimpse of the name written inside, proves to be mine. Having grown a bit since last using it, I can't get the clips to snap. But when I suck in my gut, I somehow manage it and continue walking out onto the bridge.

My brother follows.

"Okay, now I'm really curious," he says, having to pitch his voice above the sound of the falls. "What stupid thing are you going to do? Besides this whole ridiculous walk, I mean."

"I'm going over the falls, Cole."

My brother laughs at me. "Oh, really?"

"Yes, really."

"You're going to kill yourself."

"I didn't say that," I correct him. "I just said I was going to do something stupid."

"Oh. So that's why you're wearing a life jacket?"

"That's why, Einstein."

"And you think a life jacket will save you after going over a waterfall?"

"It's better than no life jacket, that's for sure."

"Well, think again. Because you'll die, dickweed."

"I'm not so sure," I reply. "I think my chances are better doing this than shooting a gun at my head."

"Statistically speaking, I wouldn't bet on that, Cal."

"Well, I guess we'll find out."

I never liked playing chicken with my brother. I never won. I think mostly because he probably made up his mind to ram into me if I didn't get out of his way. It didn't matter if he was on a skateboard and I was on a bike—he wouldn't swerve. So I'm feeling pretty nervous as I vault over the wet railing and land on my toes on the other side. But immediately I know I've got the upper hand. I can hear it in Cole's voice.

"Cal!" he yells. "That's not funny! Stop screwing around!"

"It's not meant to be funny," I say as calmly as possible, despite my fluttering stomach and pounding heart. "It's meant to be stupid. Now don't come any closer, or I'll let go."

"Cal, stop! Seriously!"

"No."

"Please," he begs. "You've made your point."

"Really?" I ask, leaning back. The railing is so cold, it's making my fingers ache. "Because the point I'm trying to make is that when I go over, you're going to be very sorry. And then you're going to wish you'd done things differently so this never happened." I lean back some more. "But for me, whichever way it goes, it'll be over quick. Maybe I'll make it and be the coolest kid at school. You can be my witness! But if I don't, well, that's just your tough sh—"

That's the moment my sneakers slip.

....

The punch in the face probably didn't happen quite as fast, but I didn't expect it either. And having the cold gun barrel jammed up against my gums is not only just as terrifying, it's extremely painful.

"Where did you come from?" Cal wants to know, yanking my head back by the hair and pushing the gun harder into my face. "Where is my brother okay?"

"I don't know," I confess, struggling to speak. "I was trying to teach him a lesson, and I fell from the bridge. That's when I woke up here. That's when all of this started."

But Cal isn't satisfied, not one bit. "Don't hold out on me, man, or I swear I will blow your head off right here, right now. Something is getting figured out on this bridge tonight. Do you understand me? Something is getting figured out!"

"All I know is Mr. Schroeder, the old physics teacher, thinks there's some sort of other universe nearby, one where his dead brother is alive. He told Willow he was going to visit him. I saw him here the day I chased you through the forest. He threw some sort of device—a message, he called it—into the falls. It was a metal tube with a blinking red light on it. He said the message said he was on his way. . . ."

Cal thinks for a moment, then nods excitedly. "Yes! Yes! *Yes!*" He pulls me to my feet. "The flashlight," he shouts, "where is it?"

"It's in my pocket. Why?"

"Give it to me!"

Cal trains the gun on my chest as I hand over the flashlight. Still aiming at me, he shines the beam on the railing. "Aha! Here it is! Look!"

"What is it?"

"I thought I saw the old bastard looking for something, some sort of marking. He found it just as I jogged up, before he recognized me, I think. Anyway, this must be the spot!"

I look at the section of railing illuminated by the flashlight. Carefully scratched into the paintwork is an arrow pointing toward the thundering drop-off. *This way down,* it practically says.

"It could be anything," I suggest. "Some kids fooling around with a nail, anything." The truth is, there are all sorts of initials, not to mention swearwords and crude pictures, gouged into the paint. And I'm guessing this other version of me has probably made more than a few himself. So he can't be taking this seriously.

"But I saw him!" Cal shouts, looking elated. "He was definitely looking for exactly this! Which means this must be the spot!"

"The spot for what?"

"To go over!" Cal yells, eyes shining with moonlight. "To get to the other universe you're talking about!"

"Hold on a second. We don't know that," I warn him. Actually I'm starting to think the whole idea is crazy, partially because this nut job is buying into it so fast. "And there's no way we can know for sure."

"Maybe not. But there's a pretty good test we could do," Cal says.

"A test? What test?"

Cal raises his arm. The black handgun is now pointed straight at my forehead. "Jump over," he tells me.

"What? No."

"Jump over at the arrow, Callum," he orders again. "Jump over at the arrow, or I will put a bullet in your brain."

My knees buckle. I want to puke. This is not a choice I'm being given. But I have to make one. Or he will make it for me.

"Wait!" I beg him. "This is ridiculous. Even if I do jump, you'll never know for sure what happened to me."

"That's true," he agrees. "But it will prove one thing."

"What?"

"That you believe the story enough that you're willing

to take your chances with the goddamn waterfall. Now, on the count of three, you'd better jump. Because on four I'm shooting you in the face!"

"Wait. Stop!"

"One."

"Cal, listen."

"Two."

"Cal!"

"*Three!*"

"No! No! No!'"

EPILOGUE

Okay, let's get this over with.

A solid material formed by a repeating, three-dimensional pattern of atoms, ions, or molecules, each with a fixed distance between them, is known as:

    a) A crystal.

    b) A mineral.

    c) A dead cat.

I'm going with *c*. If you're gonna be wrong, you might as well be funny, as I always say.

The totality of all known matter and energy—including our planet, other planets, other galaxies, and the vast emptiness known as space—is called:

    a) The crystal.

    b) The universe.

    c) The same cat, except this time it's alive and well.

I'm putting down *c* again. Screw this test. Screw this class!

The chances of going over a waterfall not once but twice and surviving is:

a) Slim.
b) Zero.
c) Pretty good, if both times you jump from exactly the right spot.

I guess I'll have to go with *c* again. But only because I really hope that's the right answer.

....

Cole and I got pretty sunburned by the end of that day. Mom wasn't happy about it, not one bit. She'd told us a bunch of times to reapply some lotion, saying that it was getting washed off in the water, but we didn't have any time to waste. There were too many slides to ride. So we just ran off on her, saying we'd stay in the shade.

By the time we got back to the car, it was four forty-five, and I was already feeling pretty miserable. My face felt as tight as a drum skin, and my T-shirt was practically melting into my shoulders. Mom gave us some sort of cream that we rubbed all over ourselves until Dad started complaining that we were getting it on the seats.

Still, it was a happy sort of miserable, coconut-scented. It turned out to be a great day, after all, I had to admit to myself. Soon I settled into playing my favorite road game: focusing on a speck of dirt on the window and making it jump over passing obstacles—trees, fences, houses, barns—using small movements of my head. Tunnels and telephone poles didn't count, however, nor anything else impossible to make it over.

Though the slides and the wave pool were all great, I kept thinking about this one other ride at the park. Well, I don't know if you could even call it a ride—it was more like a giant suspended bathtub that was supposed to look like a huge mushroom or something cartoonish like that. Every five minutes or so, it would completely fill up and then tip over, dumping a flood of water on anyone standing underneath. Then the tub would turn upright and start filling again.

The concept was pretty simple—a ton of water fell on you—but the experience was surprisingly intense. Because it was amazing just how much anticipation would build up in the crowd waiting below, who couldn't help but look at their neighbor; scared but laughing, happy that at least others were suffering it too. Everyone, it felt like, held out some faint hope that this time the thing wouldn't tip over and that somehow we'd be spared from the upcoming disaster.

But of course no one was spared, because the tub

always tipped. The water would fall in one big downpour, with so much power that it was hard to even remain on your feet. Most people didn't, in fact, probably making the tub the most dangerous attraction in the whole park, at least for bumps and bruises.

Of course Cole thought it was stupid.

"You've waited around for five minutes to get water dumped on you," he said. "Three times now," he added, thrusting the same number of fingers in my face. "Which is fifteen whole minutes. Fifteen wasted minutes of life that you are never getting back."

"Fifteen of the *best* minutes of my life," I replied. "Jackass."

Cole didn't understand a lot of the things I liked, the speck game among them. If he ever caught me moving my head around in the backseat, he was liable to pound me in the shoulder over it. "It's annoying to sit back here with a life-size bobble-head. Knock it off."

But that day Cole was too wiped out to notice. I peeked behind his sunglasses to be sure he was asleep, a state in which he'd remain until we pulled up to the house and Dad shook the living shit out of him. I always loved seeing the expression on his face the moment he woke up, confused and vulnerable, not knowing where he was.

I guess that day was it—the moment before the big bathtub tipped over and doused our whole family. I know, because I felt the exact same fear in my stomach the next morning as we started packing up our things. The feeling that something big was about to drop on us—and that there was no way we could stop it. Except this time I didn't like it. It wasn't fun. Not at all.

My father found me sitting on the floor of my room. I was looking miserable among all my things and the empty boxes I was supposed to fill with them.

"Cheer up, Callum," he said. When I didn't answer, Dad came and sat on my bed. "You know, it's good to shake things up sometimes," he told me.

"Why?"

"Well, if everything stays the same forever, you stop enjoying what you've got. And stop appreciating people. I'm telling you, buddy, this move is going to change your life in ways you can't possibly imagine. Just you wait and see."

Oh, he was right.

....

There are three men here now, wading into the freezing river. Three men pulling me out. I really know only one of them, but I met the other two, and I feel like I know them all now.

"Hello, Mr. Schroeder," I say, through chattering teeth, to the first man. "Hello, Mr. Schroeder," I then say, to the second.

"Do you know this boy?" says the third—the grumpy

one from the supermarket, I'm certain.

"Hello, Mr. Schroeder," I say. "What was the big deal with that orange juice anyway?" I laugh, because I've made it back. I've made it home.

I've gone over Crystal Falls and survived. Twice.